"You must b

His voice was as thick ~~as~~ love to her. He clearly was not, but Zach's low, I've-waited-for-you-all-my-life tone had seduced her when they'd met the first time.

She'd been unable to forget him. He obviously hadn't bothered to remember.

Seeking composure, she crossed to his desk and offered her hand. "Call me Olivia." For their son's sake she had to feel out the situation and wait for the right moment to remind Zach of their past.

When he closed his fingers around hers, memories flooded back, images of his hand on her waist, at her breast, the scent of him as he lowered his head to kiss her. She gritted her teeth, recognizing the texture of his palm as if she were touching her own skin.

Why had this man remained such a part of her? As if what she wanted to feel didn't matter. She backed up a step. He had to release her. Curiosity flickered in his gaze, but not recognition.

Her first love had forgotten her.

Dear Reader,

Welcome to Bardill's Ridge, Tennessee, and to the Calvert family. You're about to meet three cousins who find love in their own Smoky Mountain backyards.

Put yourself in Olivia Kendall's shoes. You thought your son's father, a Navy pilot, died five years ago during a training mission. Then you see him on the news, a small-town sheriff, foiling a bank robbery in Tennessee. You've gotten over him—or have you? You've made a life that doesn't include him. You could even choose not to tell him about his son, but a man has a right to know he has a child.

And besides, where's he been?

Now think about Zach. He lost one of his best friends and his memory in the crash that ended his Navy career. He lost his ability to believe he had a right to life or happiness. When Olivia comes to town he discovers he has a five-year-old son and a lover he doesn't remember. Together, Olivia and Zach find love that heals the wounds of their past and forges the family that is their future.

I'd love to hear what you think. You can reach me at anna@annaadams.net. Come back to Bardill's Ridge in November when Zach's cousin Dr. Sophie Calvert abandons her bodyguard groom, Ian, at the altar.

Best wishes,

Anna Adams

The Secret Father
Anna Adams

HARLEQUIN®

TORONTO • NEW YORK • LONDON
AMSTERDAM • PARIS • SYDNEY • HAMBURG
STOCKHOLM • ATHENS • TOKYO • MILAN • MADRID
PRAGUE • WARSAW • BUDAPEST • AUCKLAND

ISBN 0-373-71154-9

THE SECRET FATHER

Visit us at www.eHarlequin.com

Printed in U.S.A.

To Debbie, my cousin, but much more—my sister

PROLOGUE

Six Years Ago

OLIVIA KENDALL HAD three problems. She was pregnant, she couldn't find her baby's father, and the moment her own father—James Kendall of Kendall Press—found out, he was bound to fire her to avoid the shame of her unwed motherhood.

Six months out of Columbia's School of Journalism, she'd spent the summer and fall learning Kendall Press from the mail room up. She couldn't afford to get fired. Even if she found Lieutenant Zach Calvert, she'd need a salary to support her unborn child.

Behind her the door opened, and every head in the room bent toward the monitors in front of them. After his daily management meeting, her dad always hunted her down to remind her she was wasting her time and his with her learn-it-all attitude. He crossed the quiet, equipment-filled room. "Any news today?"

Her job this week was her favorite—scanning the wires for good stories. "Plenty." She clipped the word, tugging down the hem of her blouse. She couldn't be more than seven weeks along, but James Kendall hadn't reached the top of the media heap by ignoring other people's secrets.

He stopped beside her desk and pulled up a chair.

"You're always defensive at work because I'm right." Lowering his voice so that it was covered by the computer's hum, he flicked the screen she was reading. "You shouldn't distract yourself from your true job with these menial tasks."

"Learning how Kendall Press runs *is* my job, Dad."

"I'll teach you. My father taught me."

"The same father who suggested you park me with him and Grandma while you sowed more wild oats?" Her mother had died in childbirth. Her dad had never remarried.

"Father may have appreciated the value of a good nanny, but he left me a strong company and I'm passing you an empire. Who else can show you how to nourish it?"

He was in his CEO frame of mind. Olivia inched away from him, too stressed to deal with her dad or her curious co-workers. "I'm busy." And their same old argument meant nothing compared to the fact that her child's father had disappeared. A Naval pilot, Zach had embarked on a two-week training mission over a month ago.

The weeks had passed. He hadn't called. He hadn't shown up. She'd left countless messages on his cell phone. He'd never given her a number for his apartment or his office. She couldn't even say where he worked for sure. They'd always arranged to meet somewhere neutral. He'd been in Chicago since the end of summer to train on some sort of equipment he'd avoided discussing. She'd seen his apartment once, and only because they'd been desperate for each other and her father had been home that night.

Zach had been more than reserved about his life. He'd been secretive.

Working on very little sleep and even less food, she felt queasy, frightened and idiotic for getting herself in this fix. She refused to leave one more message begging Zach to call her.

Suddenly her father took her arm and turned her to face him. "What's really wrong with you, Olivia?"

"I don't want to argue about work." She avoided his dark brown eyes. "I understand how you feel about Kendall Press. I love knowing what's going on in the world before anyone else. It's a rush of power, but I have to learn the job my way."

"Why don't you trust my judgment anymore?"

She took refuge in the glowing screen in front of her. She'd changed because she was going to have Zach Calvert's baby, and when her father knew he might force her out of her livelihood and her home.

Home. A place Zach had described with a softness so unlike him. He'd longed for the farmhouse and the relations he loved in Tennessee. His hunger for family felt foreign to the only child of an only child.

"Olivia, tell me what's got you on edge." Losing patience, her father spun her chair.

She stared at him, but her head was with Zach. What if he'd gone home? To Bardill's Ridge and all those Calverts. The possibility tempted her to confess everything. If anyone could find a guy in a small Tennesseean town, her dad could.

"Good God." Realization lit his eyes. "That pilot dumped you." He'd always said Zach, at twenty-six, was too old for her, his job too dangerous. What he'd meant was he didn't want her to love someone whose work could take her away from the family business. "Olivia?"

"Yeah." She'd told James about the training mission. "Zach was supposed to come back weeks ago. If he's home, he's avoiding me."

"Have you called? Did you go to his apartment building?"

"I only have a cell phone number he doesn't answer and I've leaned on the buzzer at his building so many times I think his doorman's about to set the police on me."

Her father's head went back as if she'd struck him. "How serious are you about this guy?"

She barely kept from touching her belly where their baby grew, but the truth—that she loved Zach—wouldn't come out of her mouth either. Not even she trusted true love at twenty-one. She blinked back tears that seemed to stun her dad.

"Exactly where was he training? The address."

"He couldn't tell me." Maybe he just wouldn't.

"What do you know about his family?"

"I saw pictures at his apartment and I asked about everyone in them." His grandparents, hugging each other in photos on his mantel and his cousins, Sophie and Molly, who'd been his surrogate sisters. His mom, Beth, he'd seemed anxious about. She'd also never remarried after his father's death, and he thought she was lonely.

If his mother's loneliness mattered to him, wouldn't his lover's?

"You believe he had the training assignment?"

She nodded. Except for the moments when he'd made love to her, his mission had occupied him as if he was already gone. She took a deep breath and applied some logic. "Maybe he took leave and went to Tennessee. He was homesick."

"That's where he's from? I'd give you time off to go see him if you'd get over this guy and concentrate on work."

"He didn't invite me." He'd made her want to know his "people." He'd made her love the place. He'd *needed* the blue-and-green misty mountains that backed every photo on his wall and each memory in his love of home. The air and the soil and the Smoky Mountains that formed Bardill's Ridge, Tennessee, ran in his blood like the blood of his family.

It wasn't her way or her father's. They cared for their North Shore entry in the National Historic Register, but it was entrusted to them. It owned no part of her soul. Zach was rooted in those Tennesseean hills.

She turned back to the monitor on her desk. A headline, something about a pilot caught her eye. She clicked to read it.

A photo took shape. Even though she was thinking of Zach, she never expected to see his face.

But there he was. The full headline burned itself in her mind. "Pilot Lost On Mission—U.S. Navy Refuses Comment."

Loss slammed into her. Her muscles clenched. Olivia splayed her fingers across the picture. She squeezed her eyes shut and tried to breathe, praying she'd imagined his face. She made herself look again.

Zach. Dear God, Zach. "No." Shaking her head, she sucked a breath out of dwindling oxygen.

"Hey." Her dad caught her just in time to keep her head from slamming into the monitor.

In that second life changed. Forever.

She straightened, though her body felt ten times its normal weight. Tugging free of her father's helping hands, she crossed both arms across her flat stomach. Her baby took precedence over a freefall into grief.

Zach was gone. She'd be their baby's only parent, and she'd never know whether Zach had loved her even a little bit—enough to want their child.

"Dad." His name broke in pieces in her mouth as she stared at her dead lover's face. "I'm pregnant."

CHAPTER ONE

A BLUNT FINGERNAIL PRODDED Sheriff Zach Calvert's shoulder from behind. "You're the law," said a woman's voice. "Can't you order those tellers to speed up?"

Zach turned, and Tammy Henderson, who co-owned Henderson Seed and Feed with her husband, tucked a brown deposit envelope beneath her elbow.

"How many times have I asked you and Mike to call me before you bring that?"

She elbowed the zippered bag closer to her body. "We took your advice and started making three deposits a week."

That was about the best he could hope for in a town where the citizens believed crime happened everywhere except here. He checked the clock above the gray granite counter. "Is that right?" It was two minutes slower than his watch. "This is my weekend to have Lily."

Tammy twisted her own watch and then nodded at the clock. "Tennessee Standard Bank and I match. What time do you have to be at Helene's?"

"Six o'clock." Or his ex-wife would make a stink in front of their four-year-old daughter. Helene liked to punish him for imagined transgressions and she had

an advantage. He'd do anything to keep from hurting
his child.

"I've heard how Helene tries to keep Lil…"

Zach lifted his brows. Tammy stopped, her mouth
open, her weathered face reddening. When she looked
away, Zach felt like a bully, but gossip bred like
kudzu in Bardill's Ridge. Being the number-one topic
over the Formica tables at the Train Depot Café didn't
sit well with him.

And how would Lily feel if she heard the talk?

Zach tapped his holstered gun as the long black
arm on the clock swept each second away, and the
guy in front of him, a hunter in camouflage, twitched
from foot to foot.

Time to give up and eat the late fee on his car loan
payment. But as he turned, the town librarian marched
to the counter, her back ramrod straight with annoyance. The hunter took her place at the front of the
line, yanking his jacket as if he couldn't make it fit
right over his shoulders. Three and a half minutes ran
by before he crossed to the next teller.

Another time check. Helene would explode in exactly twenty-two minutes. Unless he made it. Which
he just might do if another patron walked away right
now.

The camo guy turned. Zach almost breathed a
thanks heavenward, but the other man opened his
field jacket and revealed the reason he was uncomfortable. A silver cannon—or a gun the size of one—
rested on his hip.

"Nobody move, or I'll kill you all." Something—
fear?—sent his voice into an unnaturally high pitch
as he pulled the gun out.

Not good. If he was scared, he might shoot anyway.

"Damn." The word slipped out of Zach's mouth as he eased in front of Tammy Henderson and her deposit bag. Any chance of reaching Lily in less than twenty minutes had just gone down the barrel of that gun. At least he'd caught the armed thief's wild gaze.

"I said no talking, and especially not you, Sheriff." He used the back of his hand to wipe spit off the top of his lip. "I'm in charge here." He swung the weapon, his finger tightening on the trigger. The gesture told Zach that pulling the trigger took pressure. A good thing or else half the customers would be dead now.

The guy turned to the nearest teller, his gun veering in a silver arc that made Zach clench his hands in two fists. What kind of a coward did this to innocent people?

"Don't even breathe near the alarm. I can see all four sides of this building from the windows."

He nudged the nearest young woman with the gun barrel, shaking so hard the metal bumped her chin. Her eyes sparkled with tears, and Zach actually pictured himself snapping the other guy's spine.

"If a police car comes, you die. Anyone makes a move, you die." The thief swept the other patrons with a scornful gaze and stamped his booted foot. "Put your damn faces on the floor!"

Zach took his time, sparing a glance for Tammy, who was obviously trying to hide a third of a week's profits. Zach grabbed the bag and slid it over to the thief's feet.

"Hey," Tammy protested.

"You want him to think you're stingy?"

"You got more, lady?" Camo guy scooped up the bag and then came over to kick the purse wrapped around Tammy's arm. "Dump it."

Zach focused on the weapon while the robber looked to see whether Tammy was hiding any more money. As if he were reviewing a schematic, Zach saw exactly how to part the man from his gun and put him on the floor unconscious and on his stomach—bonus points for ease of cuffing.

Noting that the citizens in his care had all reached the marble, Zach sank the rest of the way, calming his rage to prevent impairing his response. He angled his gaze to keep an eye on the gunman.

"What are you looking at?" the guy asked. "I'm happy to start killing now. With you."

People cried out around him, but Zach waited, forcing a few more seconds to go by. Keep it low, non-confrontational. No need to get anyone killed.

"How do you plan to escape? The second you leave, the law will pour in from all the nearby towns where everyone knows everyone else. You're going to stand out."

"Stand out?" This time he jabbed the gun in the direction of Zach's head. "I didn't ask for advice, Andy Taylor. Why don't you keep your mouth shut?" He nodded at the tellers. "Faster with the money—I want it now."

Zach smiled as he willed his body into the air. A fraction of a second later his foot connected with Camo Guy's cheekbone. The thief rose off his feet, flew about a yard and landed on his face. Out like a light.

And no one died in Bardill's Ridge. But damned if

he didn't long to kick the punk lying at his feet for threatening his people.

Instead, he leaned over the gunman, grabbed the weapon and took it apart. He'd flown helicopters in the Navy until he'd been trained to kill with the nearest weapon—or with his bare hands. A crash and a head wound had stolen his memory of that time and the two years preceding it. He sometimes discovered secrets about himself. Skills he shouldn't have.

Though he shouldn't know squat about any gun except the one he'd fired to qualify on the range, he scattered the pieces of the cannon across the marble floor. Continuing on unnerving instincts, he picked up the gunman's wrist to check his pulse.

Still fluttering. "When you get out of the prison hospital, you should consider a different line of work." He glanced at the closest teller. "Hit the alarm. Then get me Leland Nash on the phone."

Nash's family owned Tennessee Standard Bank. He was also married to Zach's ex-wife, a connection that had never seemed useful until today. With one phone call, Zach could arrange for Nash to inspect his property and also beg Helene to *allow* him to pick up Lily tomorrow.

He glanced at the unconscious man, his own actions disturbing him almost as much as his town's close call.

Before now, he'd controlled the bursts of rage he'd felt toward lawbreaking idiots who occasionally came to Bardill's Ridge. Throwing that guy headfirst onto the marble floor could have killed him, and vigilantism wasn't part of Zach's job description.

He didn't want to be a killer.

AT THE CHICAGO HEADQUARTERS of *Relevance* magazine, Olivia Kendall's office door burst open. Her assistant, Brian Minsky, skidded across the sandcolored carpet. "Picture this." He waved a printout at her as he collapsed in the chair across from her desk.

They'd worked together from day one on *Relevance*. Since they never stood on boss-employee etiquette, she waited for him to continue, half her mind still on the competitor's article she'd been reading.

Brian remained silent. At last she noticed and looked up, plucking off her glasses with two fingers.

Brian looked satisfied. "You're with me now."

"What's up?"

"I want you to listen. This story has a twist."

She'd learned to give Brian the time he required. "Okay."

"You've been in line at the bank for thirty-eight minutes, waiting to pay your car loan."

"Not that big a twist."

He offered a sour grin, the equivalent of telling her to shut up. "The guy in front of you gets to the teller and opens his coat to show off his big gun. He orders you and everyone else in the bank to lie on the floor while the tellers collect the money. What do you do?"

"I lie down." Her first thought went to her five-year-old son, Evan. Face to the floor, she'd be praying like crazy that she got home to him. "And if I survive, I arrange a payroll deduction for that loan."

Brian cracked a real grin. "Funny. But I'm not finished. The guy sees you're the local sheriff. You tell him he can't go far. It's a small town, and everyone will notice him. Instead of thanking you he asks who you think you are—Andy Taylor?''

She laughed.

Brian didn't, and she erased her smile. This must be the good part.

"What do you do now?" he asked.

"I point my nose to the floor, and I curse myself for not taking advantage of that payroll deduction option my helpful loan officer suggested." She paused. "And I propose to change my name to Andy. What do you do?"

"I do what this Andy—his real name is Zach—I do what he did. I kick the gunman's ass all over that bank, and then I tell him to look for another line of work after he gets out of the jail hospital."

"You're kidding." She sat back, trying to hide her Pavlovian response to the name *Zach*.

Old memories fluttered at the back of her mind. She pushed them back. This might be a good story. "Didn't Andy-Zach realize his response put everyone else in danger?"

"He says not. Apparently, he took the guy out by acting purely on instinct. Instinct that told him how to overpower an armed man with one blow."

"One blow…" She leaned forward, jamming her stomach into the glass desk's blunt edge. "What are you talking about?"

"Now you're on board." Brian slid her a photograph. "You and I want to know what's behind Andy-Zach's story. So will our readers. They're going to see the facts in brief paragraphs about stupid criminals in their Kendall newspapers, but they'll want to know more, and we can give them a bigger picture in Kendall's premiere news magazine. Is the sheriff an android or a man? He says he just reacted. A guy doesn't react like that without training." Brian leaned back. "Or I would have had a better time in high school."

She put her glasses back on and turned the picture around. The man's face made her breath catch.

Not again.

Her heart boomeranged painfully. He was older, his blond hair longer than a military cut, his eyes more cynical and his body leaner.

But once again, the man in the picture, the kick-ass sheriff, was Lieutenant Zach Calvert, looking pretty damn healthy for a man who'd died six years ago.

She scanned the brief column beneath the picture. After she'd told her dad everything, he'd gone to the Navy. He was perfect for the job; he could get to the truth about the Loch Ness monster.

He'd spoken to a Commander Gould, who'd explained that Zach's crash had been bad luck in a routine training flight. Today's article didn't mention the flight or the Navy or the crash that had supposedly killed Zach.

Olivia stared at his face in the grainy photo. She wasn't wrong. This was Evan's father. "Your daddy's in heaven" had become her mantra. She'd hoped a daddy somewhere would make Evan feel like the children he'd envied for having fathers at home.

Numb with shock, she didn't know whether to be furious or relieved. At least this time she didn't seem to be falling apart at the sight of a lousy photo. She'd grieved and recovered. For six years, Lieutenant Zach Calvert had been dead.

Did that make being a sheriff in Bardill's Ridge, Tennessee heaven? Or hell?

TWO DAYS AFTER Brian showed her Zach's photo, Olivia's plane drifted out of the clouds on approach to McGhee-Tyson Airport in Knoxville.

Her shock had dissipated and been replaced by pragmatism. Whatever Zach was playing at, he had a son. And her son deserved a chance to know and be loved by his father. She had to believe he could be kinder to his son than he'd been to her.

He'd gone to a lot of trouble to leave her. How had he persuaded his commanding officer to lie to her father? She'd barely stopped her dad from getting to the bottom of *that* question.

With any luck, looking after Evan would keep him too busy to hunt down Captain Kerwin Gould and pry the truth out of him. She wanted a word with Zach first.

After she'd called his office three times without being able to force a word out of her mouth, she'd asked Brian to set up the interview. She needed to see Zach's face the first time he heard her voice. She'd believed him to be an honorable and loving man. She had to know who he really was before she invited him into her son's life.

And she wondered why he'd agreed to let her interview him if he'd been so desperate to get away from her six years ago? Maybe he'd forgotten her.

Fine. He only had to remember enough to believe he might be Evan's father.

As the plane drifted on descent, she opened Zach's dossier. After his accident, he'd spent three months in a hospital outside San Diego. Four months after that, he'd married one of his nurses. Within eight months of their marriage, their daughter, Lily, had been born.

Which explained his silence. Had he been sleeping with Helene and her at the same time? Even six years later she felt like an idiot for trusting him.

Zach had been her first love. Tall and tough, unstoppable in his pursuit, he'd made her think she was all that mattered to him in the whole world. Combine that with his status as her father's last choice, and she'd hardly known how to resist.

Looking back through newly opened eyes, she no longer believed in his passion or her own. She'd taken a stupid risk the night she'd forgotten her birth control. And after his supposed death, she'd made up a loving father for her son. The part where Zach had abandoned her never came into her stories.

Finally she'd tried not to remember Zach at all. But then a day would start when Evan woke with sleepy, is-it-morning eyes that reminded her of his father, or he startled her with the long capable fingers that looked too uncomfortably much like Zach's.

She closed the folder and peered through the small window at the deep green forest flowing beneath the airplane. Dark and verdant, as mysterious as Zach's true intentions. What had he wanted with her? Not that she'd expected forever, but a phone call to tell her she was no longer in the picture would have been nice.

Looking at mountains that seemed to have no border with flat land, she felt like an intruder. She'd once prayed Zach would ask her to meet his family. Now, possibly in front of them, she had to find out who he really was so she could decide whether to tell Evan he hadn't died.

Olivia slipped the folder back into her soft brief-case and then fished out another clean, almost untouched file Brian had put together for her. She hadn't told Evan or Brian the truth, so she had to go home with some kind of story.

The bank photo lay on top. Beneath were clippings from all the other stories Brian had gathered on the attempted robbery.

After the plane landed, Olivia collected her bags and packed them into her rental car. As soon as she left the airport, the road began to rise. The interstate, narrowing into two lanes, had been cut into red clay and granite hills spiked with evergreens, smoothed by icy-looking streams.

Like a bad omen, clouds covered the sun, dulling the red and gold leaves of the hardwoods. Rest stops and traffic came few and far between, and her ears began to pop at the higher elevation.

She fumbled in her purse and briefcase for gum, but Evan must have found her stash. Her boy was a fiend for gum. She gave up and yawned to clear the pressure.

As she passed the first mileage sign for Bardill's Ridge, she breathed a sigh of relief. She ought to be able to find Sheriff Calvert's office just in time for her appointment.

At her turnoff, she followed the long ramp away from the interstate. No sign of life stirred within the trees. Such a heavy dose of nature could make a city woman a little anxious.

At the end of the ramp a sign pointing to the left offered her the chance to turn back. To the right Bardill's Ridge waited. Olivia opened her window and breathed in pine-laden air.

She could go home, continue the life she'd made with Evan and tell Brian the story on Zach hadn't panned out. Her heart pounded in jackhammer fashion.

A right turn would change her life, but it might also bring her son a father who could love him. What choice did she have?

She turned right and the road inclined again. Soon a white church spire peeked out of the leaves. Just beyond the spire a redbrick cupola topped a black-shingled roof. Extremely Norman Rockwell. Olivia's heart rate returned to normal. She could handle a Norman Rockwell town.

In front of her, a tractor turned off a dirt road onto the shoulder. The driver lifted his ball cap as she slowed to pass him.

That never happened in Chicago.

On the outskirts of Bardill's Ridge, she passed a large blue clapboard feed store. The sign that clung to the roof of a wide veranda-cum-loading dock shouted Henderson's in capital letters. Sticks of straw blew into the road from the bales on the porch. The men hoisting feed onto their trucks and into the backs of their SUVs looked up from their chores as she slowed to the speed limit.

Zach had been right when he'd warned the bank robber that people here noticed strangers. She passed a library, two small churches and too many curious faces.

Farther down the street, a sign painted with cartoon bears and rabbits and a bouncing typeface proclaimed the building behind it the ABC Daycare. Olivia missed Evan with a keen ache as the boys and girls spilled across the play yard.

Closer to the center of town, there were more office buildings. As she passed them the women and men who strode the surprisingly busy sidewalks watched her. No matter what he decided to do about Evan, Zach would have to explain about her after she left town.

Olivia glanced at her watch. Five past two.

At the next stop sign she glanced right and found the big white church. She turned, but had to stop again on the edge of a small square encircled by wrought iron. On one side stood the church. Beside her, a curlicued, Victorian theater promised the latest releases. Opposite, a high school looked buttoned up and busy, with papers on the windows and a teacher holding class outside as his students inspected a maple's bright shedding leaves. The redbrick building across the square was the courthouse, Bardill's county seat, according to a tall, black sign posted out front.

Olivia glanced at her briefcase, containing both folders and a photo vital to her plan. Zach had told Brian she'd find him in his office in the jail at the back of the courthouse.

She parked and grabbed her things. Fighting wind, she slipped into the square, via an iron gate. Her heels slid on the cobblestone path that crisscrossed the grass. At the other side of the park she exited through another gate and crossed the wide street. Breathing hard, she climbed the courthouse steps and scoured the map at the front door.

The jail was a left off the long, tall lower hall. Just beyond, a glass door led to a closer parking lot. Olivia swore and tried to tame her wild hair as her shoes clicked loudly on the marble.

Reaching Zach's office door exactly on time, she twitched her skirt into place, tugged at her sweater's neckline and then watched her right hand tremble on the doorknob.

If she'd known she was pregnant before Zach left, she would have told him. She was simply doing what she would have done then. If Zach didn't want Evan, she could still say she'd done her best for her son.

She opened the door, anticipating a dispatcher. Instead, Zach looked up from paperwork spread on a wide, scarred oak desk.

His dark blue uniform emphasized lean muscles and the dark blond hair that nearly touched his collar. From ten feet away, a bleak shadow in his green eyes startled her. He was the same man, but he looked at the world from a different point of view. Something had drawn extra lines on his face and added more than six years of weariness to his eyes.

Olivia clung to the doorknob, rocking back on her high heels.

Zach stood and came around his desk. His gaze swept her, cataloging her head to toe. Not the way he had when they'd been lovers, but the way a stranger took stock of someone he might not entirely trust.

Olivia forgot how to breathe. How much had she

changed? It didn't seem to matter. Zach's smile held
no hint of recognition.

He held out his hand. "You must be Olivia Kendall."

CHAPTER TWO

His voice was as thick as if he were thinking of making love to her. He clearly was not, but Zach's low, husky, I've-waited-for-you-all-my-life tone had seduced her when they'd met the first time.

She'd been unable to forget him. He obviously hadn't bothered to remember.

Seeking composure, she crossed to his desk and offered her hand. "Call me Olivia." For Evan's sake she had to feel out the situation and wait for the right moment to remind Zach of their past.

The moment he closed his fingers around hers, the past flooded back, images of his hand on her waist, at her breast, the male scent of him as he'd lowered his head to kiss her. She gritted her teeth, recognizing the texture of his palm as if she were touching her own skin.

Why had this man remained such a part of her? As if what she *wanted* to feel didn't matter. She backed up a step. He had to release her. Curiosity flickered in his gaze, but not recognition. Her first love had forgotten her.

"Have a seat." Zach gestured to two leather armchairs that flanked a low table in front of his desk. "Coffee?"

"Thanks." A few moments' distraction might remind her why she'd come. Sitting, she unzipped her briefcase.

"Cream? Sugar?"

"Both, please."

With a pleasant, interested smile, he handed her a foam cup and then took the chair beside hers. He stretched his legs in front of him. "You've come a long way to talk about a bank robbery that didn't come off."

She busied herself with her briefcase zipper, covering her shock at his continued detachment. She'd made a child with this man, but she'd clearly had no idea who Zach Calvert was beneath his skin. She plucked a business card from her briefcase and passed it to him. "Let's talk about your suspect."

Without a glance at her card, he slid it inside his uniform pocket. "I'm not sure I can add to the stories you've already seen."

Such a weak attempt to stall woke her share of Kendall determination. "I'd like to talk to the guy."

Zach glanced toward the back where the cells probably were. "The FBI already picked him up."

Olivia pulled out the robbery folder. "I read that he belongs to a local militia group?"

"Not local, from a town over the Kentucky border."

Zach sounded defensive, protecting his town's reputation. He still loved his home. What were his current feelings on family?

Olivia studied his knife-sharp collar, his gleaming black shoes, their high shine a hint of the Navy officer from Chicago. Addicted to danger and flight, he'd still been drawn to this rural mountain town, but he'd never mentioned a need to settle here for good.

Whatever had happened to him had made him focus on home and hearth. He'd quickly had a daughter. How would he feel about their son?

She gave herself a mental shake. "Did the guy want funds for a specific action?"

"He requested an attorney when he regained consciousness. By the time we found a public defender, the FBI showed up and took him to their office in—" He stopped as if he hadn't meant to say so much. "The feds are investigating the robbery and the suspect's affiliations."

"So you disarmed him, but now you're out?"

He frowned, interest turning into irritation. "I did my job when I kept him from killing any citizen of this town."

She was searching for a sense of responsibility that belied the way he'd left her. "Weren't you afraid the guy might kill someone when you attacked him?"

"I recognized his gun." His matter-of-fact tone implied anyone would have, and anyone would have acted. "I just had to make sure he was unconscious before he applied enough pressure to the trigger to fire."

"Your Navy training helped you do that?"

He narrowed his eyes. "How did you know I was in the Navy?" His tone had dropped another disquieting octave.

"I investigated your background before I came."

His expression went protectively flat, but antagonism jerked a muscle tight in his jaw. "What do you want, Ms. Kendall? Why come all the way from Chicago to talk about a three-day-old story?''

He suspected ulterior motives. It was the moment she'd waited for, and she went blank. All she could think was how loudly the clock ticked on his desk.

Time to come clean. ''Why are you pretending you don't recognize me?''

His chiseled face hardened to stone. ''I'm pretending?''

She licked dry lips. ''Maybe not.'' Her father would be appalled. No one forgot a Kendall. She'd cared so much for Zach, his response humiliated her, but Evan's best interests made her go on. Finding out who Zach had become was worth some loss of face. ''You and I met each other six years ago in Chicago while you were in the Navy.''

''Chicago?'' He sounded as if he'd never heard of the city.

''This is ludicrous. Surely you remember Chicago even if you forgot me?''

''No.'' He stood, his posture guarded, danger in his eyes.

She was probably seeing the same gaze the bank robber had just before he'd found himself unconscious. She rose on shaking legs and wiped her clammy palms down the sides of her skirt.

She could describe every sinew beneath Zach's dark clothing. She could tell him he slept with one arm crooked beneath his head, the other flattened on his belly. She should have the advantage. Instead, she was trying desperately not to collapse at his feet.

He turned to his desk. ''I was stationed in California until an accident forced me to resign my commission.'' His mouth tightened. ''Why are you here?''

Now they both understood she had the advantage, and Zach didn't like it.

''I came to talk to you.'' His stare accused her of setting an ambush. Maybe she should let him cool down before she told him about Evan.

''I have no information you'd want to print, Ms. Kendall.''

''You know my name is Olivia.''

He turned toward the door, his dismissive attitude suggesting she use it. ''We're done.''

She groped inside her briefcase for the framed picture she'd packed that morning. Zach shifted his hand to his holstered pistol. It wasn't in the least funny, but Olivia wanted to smile. He didn't trust easily either.

''I'm sorry to do it this way.'' She hadn't come here to be unkind. ''But I don't think you'll believe me without proof.'' She held the photo against her chest. ''I met you in Chicago. You were taking some kind of a class. I believed we cared for each other.'' She broke off. ''I'm rambling because I'm nervous, but here's what happened. You left for a training mission—it was supposed to last two weeks—but I didn't hear from you for over a month, and then I saw a wire release that said you were dead.''

He stared. For a moment, time tunneled. She was trying to reach him, but he'd left her behind. ''Zach, look at this photo.'' She turned it, showing him his son's face.

At first his eyes widened. His nostrils flared with each deep breath. When he opened his mouth, a sigh eased between his lips. "No." Anguish added a syllable to the word.

Olivia held as still as she could, considering she was trembling. His "no" didn't mean he'd denied Evan was his child. He could have trouble believing he'd forgotten his son.

"I would have told you I was pregnant, but you left before I knew."

Without looking at her, Zach came back, his leather belt creaking in the thick silence. Sweat beaded on his forehead. He curled his fingers around the photo's frame and her hand. Unable to bear the heat of his touch, she let the picture go.

"I've seen his face all over my mother's house."

She didn't understand. "What?"

"In photos of me." He looked up, his gaze soft, yet wounded. "He's six?"

"Five." What the hell was going on? "What happened to you?"

"I honestly don't remember Chicago. I trained there for a mission in a place not many people know about. I was on a team no one talks about." He met her gaze—no, he held hers with his intensity. "I was supposed to fly in and pick up an officer who was stuck in a place she shouldn't have been. She was killed, and I suffered a head injury that destroyed part of my memory—the two years before the accident— and you were part of the time I lost." A mixture of anger and despair fired his glance. He nudged the robbery file she'd dropped on the floor when she'd stood. "I also learned about weapons then."

His story was hard to believe. "Why did the wires

say you died? Why did the Navy tell my father you were dead?''

''The Navy?''

''My dad asked Captain Kerwin Gould, your commanding officer, what happened and he spouted the story about a failed training mission off San Diego.''

''Your dad?'' Zach nodded in recognition. ''James Kendall, I get it. Did he mention you when he talked to Admiral Gould?''

''Admiral?''

Zach shook his head. ''That's his rank now. Did your father tell him you were pregnant?''

''No. I only wanted to find out what happened.''

''But he would've told your father the truth if he'd known. He gave you the story we discussed. It kept me out of the media. I didn't want the public mess any more than the Navy did.'' Failure filled his eyes with heartrending emptiness. He lifted his hand to the back of his neck, striking her dumb as he twisted his head, a grown-up version of Evan under stress. ''I came home—here—after I left the hospital.''

''What about your apartment in Chicago?'' Having a place suddenly made no sense. ''Why did you— Your things were all over those rooms, pictures of your family—were they even your family?''

''Yes.'' He rubbed his neck again. ''The apartment belonged to the government. We were advised to bring our own belongings and make ourselves look like full-time residents. They figured one Navy officer in uniform looked like any other.'' He sat on the corner of his desk. ''I'm not even sure who packed my stuff and sent it home. It was just waiting when I got here.''

"But what about your career? You were gung ho."

His faint smile softened the lines in his face. "I resigned because the surgeons decided my injury made me unfit to fly."

Six years he'd been gone, and he'd never remembered she existed. "How can I believe you?"

He shook his head. "I don't blame you. I've had to ask Admiral Gould or other pilots about what happened." Guilt thinned his features. "I've listened to the crash tapes."

She couldn't ask for those details. They were too personal to him, too horrible to her. "How big is this team?"

"I have two friends who also went through the training." He angled the photo so they could both see Evan's innocent, laughing face. "You came here because of him? Why didn't you just tell me the truth? Why pretend you wanted to interview me?"

She didn't sugarcoat her answer. "I couldn't trust you. You were dead until you showed up foiling a bank robbery."

"Why didn't you look for my family?"

"You talked about them, but reluctantly." Heat swept up her throat. "I thought you didn't want to tell them about me."

"Because of my job." She shared the desolation in his eyes. "I could skim over the facts, but I wouldn't have felt safe involving you in my life outside Chicago." He stared at Evan, not realizing he was telling her he hadn't shared the depth of her feelings. "They'd have loved my son."

"At the time I was—" The agony of losing him swept back for a moment, but he'd never really been hers to lose. She shouldn't have come here. She blinked, gripping reality. Her son still needed his father, and Zach deserved explanations as much as she. "My dad was disappointed in me and I was scared, and later the idea of telling your family became as difficult as telling you is now."

"What about a funeral?"

She glanced at the nearest window, where orange and red leaves brushed the glass and shielded the rest of Bardill's Ridge from her view. "My face was in the news because I'd graduated from college, and my father's important. I didn't think I could hide who I was in a town this small." And she hadn't been up to pretending indifference.

"The boy makes everything different."

"Different, how?"

"I want to see him."

Good. She'd been hoping for that. "His name is Evan. Evan Zachary Kendall."

He stared at his son's face, a smile curving his mouth slowly, as if smiling no longer came easy.

"I wanted him to have something of yours. Your name was the only thing I could give him."

"Thank you."

Zach's simple gratitude touched her, but she couldn't let down her guard yet. She lived in Chicago. Zach lived here. They both had rights to Evan if Zach wanted access.

She grimaced. *Access.* A sterile term for making a life with a child.

"You can have the picture." She latched her briefcase and lifted it, comforted by its familiar heft in her hand. A touch of the cynicism she'd learned after

Zach's disappearance came back to her. "I'm not a big fan of amnesia stories."

He didn't seem to care. "It's the only one I have, and it's true."

Subjects who lied usually put on a big defensive show. But sometimes not.

"What you do next is up to you. I read that you have a daughter with your ex-wife, so I know you're facing complications. If you really want to see Evan, you have to make a decision you can live with the rest of your life."

He nodded, but she reiterated to make sure he understood.

"I mean this is a lifetime commitment."

He reached for her arm, but then stopped short of touching her. "I won't let you take him away."

She shrugged, her heart pounding in the back of her throat. He'd been twenty-six when they were together. She'd been more mature than most of her peers, but the balance of power had clearly lain with him. She didn't intend to let that happen again.

"I won't leave him alone with you until I'm sure you're telling the truth. What if you aren't good for him?"

His chest expanded beneath his shirt. Anger glittered in his eyes, but he controlled it so quickly she might have imagined it.

"I understand," he said.

That seemed to be that. She headed for the door.

"Where are you going, Olivia?"

His use of her name stopped her. "To give you time to think."

He set the photo on his desk, staking an unambiguous claim. "I share custody of my daughter Lily, but my ex-wife thinks I'm bad for her."

Olivia's stomach tightened, but she tried to look calm. At least he wasn't going to hide anything from her. "You're bad for Lily?"

"I should have said not good enough." His bitter smile held no humor. "My bank account could use some more zeroes. Helene married up when she became Mrs. Leland Nash, and she thinks Lily would be better off without her ties to the common folk."

"Leland Nash?" She'd read that name in Brian's file. "She married the bank president?"

He nodded. "I love Lily, and I fight for time with her. I don't want another troubled relationship with a child of mine, so I'm telling you what you'll hear about me when you dig deeper."

Again, her tongue felt tied. Was this his side of the story or *a* side? "I don't understand about your ex-wife." Money and social standing were the last thing Olivia cared about, but then again, she'd always had too much of both. "My first concern is Evan, and I'm giving you a chance to be his father."

"I am his father."

"You're talking genetics. Evan needs baseball games, Band-Aids on his knees and to trust that you'll show up at his door when you say you will. Don't let an urge to do the right thing make this decision for you."

"You're talking shared custody?"

He was calm under fire, but the concept of sharing anything about Evan filled her with terror. "Maybe. Someday."

His tension eased, but as he crossed the room and

reached for the door, she moved out of his way. He simply held on to the doorknob, effectively keeping her in the room. "I'm sorry," he said. "If I'd even been aware…"

"We're way past apologies." But his gentleness boded well for her son. "You don't remember, and it all ended a long time ago for me. We've both made different lives. You just have to decide what you want to do about Evan before we talk again." She patted her pocket. "I'm staying at a bed-and-breakfast." She'd written the place's name on a slip of paper that morning, a bit fearful the only accommodations she might find would be her old Girl Scout tent on the side of the road. "I found it on the Internet."

"The Dogwood," he said. "My uncle and aunt own it. Did you park in front of the courthouse?"

She nodded. "Beside the church."

"Turn left when you leave the square. Go straight for about a block. It's not that far from the bank, and you'll see a sign in the yard."

"The bank that was nearly robbed?" she asked.

"Tennessee Standard, the only bank in Bardill's Ridge." He stopped her again, taking a step nearer. "You really came because you saw my picture?"

She nodded at the stranger she'd loved. His story— reality—took some getting used to. "Because I never knew my mother. She died when I was a baby. I don't want Evan to grow up without one of his parents if you're a good man."

"You have the resources and the skill to find out about me, so I'll tell you I have a dead career, a broken marriage." Wrath infused his tone with husky richness. "But I'm still Evan's father."

She'd loved his voice when it was thick with any flavor of passion, but being a Kendall, she restrained a shiver of awareness to ask a question. "No one's ever figured out the truth? No one else who knew you in Chicago?"

"You were apparently the one mistake I made there." A warning lit his eyes. "You're not looking for a story, Olivia? I don't think you'd want to write that kind of article about your son's father."

He was right.

STARING THROUGH the square panes of his kitchen window into the pitch-dark night, Zach reached for the phone. He had one thought, to tell Olivia he didn't need time.

But he remembered the rest of his family and let the phone go. He had to talk to his daughter, to his mother and to his ex-wife. For Evan's sake he needed to prepare Helene. He turned to the fridge, opening the cabinet on his right at the same time to take down a glass.

A bottle of Scotch on the top shelf tempted him, but he opted for a quart of milk and a brown plastic container of chocolate syrup from the fridge. Using the long spoon Lily favored, he mixed a big helping of her favorite elixir and wished she were here to share it with him. Ice-cold chocolate milk started their bedtime ritual on her weekends at his house.

What would she think of a brand-new older brother?

Zach sipped his chocolate. He could imagine Helene claiming he didn't need Lily now that he had a son. And she'd blame their lousy marriage on his "subconscious" feelings for Olivia.

Olivia had said she'd made a mistake with birth control. Helene had made a plan, which she'd later admitted had been the worst mistake of her life. She'd thought she was marrying a military superhero who'd use his contacts and the medal he'd never taken out of its box to build a life she'd dreamed of as she'd worked in a hospital.

Her plan made no sense. Trusting her tender loving care, he'd shared his shame at being alive after losing the woman—whose life he was supposed to save.

His mission had been to fly into a restricted zone on a chopper so stripped he couldn't even carry the weight of a copilot. He was to pick up Lieutenant Kimberly Salva, a dear friend from the Academy, and bring her out. He'd failed. He'd needed the penance of guilt. Since the crash, he'd dreamed with rage that he'd actually killed Salva, who'd died in his hands on the floor of his chopper.

As part of the therapy he'd soon quit, he'd listened to the tape of his radio calls. No matter who told him Salva's death hadn't been his fault, that he'd done his best to save her, he continued to relive the moments he'd listened to. His obvious despair, his refusal to give up on her, had never relieved the guilt or the nightmares that had painted pictures like memories in his mind.

Salva's daughter, eight years old now, was growing up without her mother. How could he believe he had the right to survive?

Inexplicably, Helene had imagined he'd ride an unworthy hero's welcome into fame and fortune. But Zach had made another plan.

Losing two years of his life, his identity as a pilot and, most of all, his faith in himself, he'd searched for respite in Bardill's Ridge. Walking the woods he'd run as a youth, mending the barn he'd jumped off pretending he could fly, he'd come home because he'd needed the Calvert clan's strength and the sustenance of the haze-covered, blue-and-green Smokies.

Maybe he and Helene had never loved each other. She'd thought he was someone he couldn't be. He'd been grateful for the physical contact he'd needed to remind himself he was still alive.

After she'd become pregnant, he'd married her, and they'd come to Bardill's Ridge where his new wife had quickly deemed her life pure hell. Zach had worked on his family's farm for the first year. That had been bad enough in Helene's eyes, but after he'd taken the sheriff's position, she'd railed that "Andy Taylor" wasn't good enough for her and their daughter.

He was starting to hate that TV show.

After his wife met Leland Nash and they'd fallen in love, Helene tried to convince Zach he had no right to his own child because he didn't share Helene's priorities for Lily's future. He was just lucky Helene had found Nash and not some wealthy out-of-state tourist. Leland Nash's money had made East Tennessee bearable for Helene. It had made short work of Zach's marriage.

And even shorter work of his ability to trust a woman who'd borne his child. Olivia seemed different, but his ex-wife had shown him honesty could be a moving target.

After Olivia left his office, he'd researched her in every database he could access. She ran *Relevance,* a magazine positioned somewhere between *U.S. News* and *People.*

She was too young to be managing editor except her father owned the show and acted as the magazine's editor in chief. To get a feel for her work, Zach had read stories from her earlier career, and then he'd scanned several recent issues. Olivia might have gone straight to the masthead because of her connections, but she was a good reporter.

What if she really was after a story? The possibility made him set his drink on the counter so hard the glass clanked. Could her job be the reason she'd come here?

Evan was his son. No doubt about that, but what if Olivia still believed he'd deserted her? What if her whole story was true—except that unlike Helene, she'd put two and two together?

Her flimsy rationale for not telling his family about Evan troubled him, and her father had built an empire breaking secrets wide-open. She might decide he made a good story—failed rescue mission, lost memory, secret son and all.

He dragged the back of his hand over his mouth. He was tired of dreams shot with light like tracer fire from a weapon, tired of waking sweat-covered and panicked as if he'd run through enemy battle lines in his bare feet and still managed to get his friend killed.

Staring at Evan's photo, aching to see the boy, to hear his voice, Zach ran his finger over the cowlick his son would never be able to tame unless he got himself a military haircut. For Evan's sake, he wanted to trust Olivia Kendall.

Closing his eyes, he saw her—tall, breezing into his office on the strength of her own self-confidence, her wavy black hair sliding over her shoulders, gray eyes splintered with ice that melted only a little beneath occasional warm concern. She wouldn't research or write any story that would hurt Evan.

It wasn't so hard to believe he'd loved her. Inconceivable that he'd forgotten her if he'd cared enough for her to make a child.

Zach glanced at his watch. Why waste any more time? He reached for the phone to call Olivia and tell her he knew exactly what he wanted.

Once she knew where he stood, he'd warn his family they were about to meet his son. He didn't want Helene or anyone else to find out about Evan from a newspaper or TV.

CHAPTER THREE

"AMNESIA?" James Kendall's mirthless laugh nearly deafened Olivia through her cell phone's receiver. "He was never good enough for you, and this lame amnesia excuse just proves my point."

"Why would he lie, Dad?" Despite her own doubts, she tried to soothe her father's. At the first sign of weakness in her, he'd try running Zach out of the country. She stayed calm for several reasons. One, she didn't want him all over Zach. Two, he'd stuck by her through a pregnancy that had shamed him. And three, he loved Evan.

"He dumped you and he doesn't have the guts to be a man. Why are you willing to let him think about it? Evan deserves a father who simply wants him for a son."

"I'm not holding a grudge." Not much of one, and she'd fight every step of the way to make things right for Evan. "He couldn't help what happened."

"Why let him jerk you around?"

"I insisted Zach think about the obligations I'm asking him to take on."

"Did he argue with you?"

"No, but he was stunned, and I don't want him to do the right thing out of some knee-jerk response. What good would Zach's sense of duty do my son?"

"I didn't have to decide whether I wanted to be his grandfather."

She could have argued. He'd conveniently forgotten the day he'd suggested he could help her "not have" the baby. He'd made up for it too many times to count since. She twitched the curtain away from her window. Dusk hovered over Bardill's Ridge. In the street below, Victorian lamps glowed orange-yellow.

"You had seven and a half months to get used to the idea of Evan. I'm willing to give Zach a few hours, and I'll stay with Evan and him when they're together at first."

"Thank God you've still got some sense. Calvert should have considered his actions back then. When a twenty-six-year-old man knows he can't even be honest about his job with a twenty-one-year-old woman, the honorable thing is to abstain."

"You like to forget I was there, too, and you're still annoyed I didn't hold out for a wedding ring. You and I aren't selfless."

"More so than the man who left you holding the diaper bag."

"If Zach decides to become part of this family, I expect you to be civil to him."

"If you hold a single doubt about this man, I say we start the paperwork to sue him for support."

"Great idea, Dad. Evan will never need a dime from Zach, but he's gone without a father's care for five years. A lawsuit should fix all his problems." She dropped the curtain and opened the nightstand drawer to find a laminated pizza menu. "I don't think Zach's going to duck out. Why can't you give him the benefit of the doubt?''

"You are, and that's more than he deserves." Her dad went quiet. She hoped he was trying to find some restraint. The family counselor they'd seen when Evan was a baby had taught him to give Olivia room to parent her own child, but her dad was always happiest when he'd worked up a full head of steam. "When are you supposed to see Calvert again?"

"His name is Zach, and I'll let you know when he calls."

"Are we supposed to twiddle our thumbs while he decides? I should be there with you. In fact, I'm on my way."

Olivia laughed to remind her father he was overreacting. Suddenly, the phone at her bedside jangled. She eyed it with foreboding. "I have to go, Dad. You stay put in Chicago. Is Evan all right?"

"Sound asleep, or I'd let you talk to him."

He'd already admitted to spoiling her son with dinner and the richest cheesecake in Chicago at Evan's favorite "grown-up" restaurant. From there, her father swore Evan had hauled him to a batting cage. He'd exhausted the little guy.

The other phone rang for the third time. "I'll call you," Olivia said again. "Kiss him for me."

"Get back here and kiss him yourself, or let me bring him to you."

"I love you, Dad."

"I'll arrange a healthy meal for Evan tomorrow night."

"I'm glad." Her father was a man who showed his

love through service rather than affectionate words. "Bye."

She switched off her cell phone and lifted the other receiver. "Olivia Kendall." Putting this conversation on business terms was like suiting up in her best armor.

"It's Zach Calvert. I want to come by in the morning."

"To talk?" Who cared if she sounded eager? "You can come now."

"I'll be ready to travel in the morning, but tonight I have to tell my own family."

Her pulse tripped over a few beats. He was saying yes. He wanted to know Evan.

"Yes" terrified her. For her son—a little for herself. She'd once loved this man, and he was coming back into her life. She remembered desire and trust that had turned on her like Cleopatra's asp. She couldn't afford to get confused about long-dead feelings.

"Maybe it would be better if you didn't mention Evan to your daughter until you meet him."

"What?" The one word suggested she'd overstepped.

"Until you make up your mind, why disrupt Evan's life or Lily's?"

"You have nothing to do with my daughter, Olivia. I take care of my family."

His harshness hurt her feelings. She tried not to snap back. His anger might come from problems he'd had with Helene over custody of Lily.

"Bottom line," she said, pretending to ignore his quick temper, "I don't want my son hurt." She threaded her voice with sharp steel, just in case he considered her soft. "If he ever thinks you're sorry…"

Silence met her half threat. Seeing his expression would have been nice.

"Is eight o'clock too early to leave tomorrow?" he asked.

"Fine." She probably wouldn't sleep. "I'll arrange our flight."

"Let me."

"Face it. I have more pull." Zach could be in charge next time.

SHARING A GLASS of iced tea with her mother-in-law, Greta, Beth Calvert recognized her son's car downshifting to start the climb up her hill. Over a pot of chili, the two women had begun planning a party to celebrate Greta and her husband Seth's fifty-fifth anniversary.

They'd planned very little party and talked more about Seth's single anniversary request—more time with his wife. He wanted her to retire from her job as director of The Mom's Place as she neared seventy-six years of age.

Beth smiled. Greta seemed to feel her husband asked too much. Already pregnant with Ned, Zach's father, when she was in premed, Greta had worked nearly all her life, and pretty much all the time she or Seth could remember. Seventy-six wasn't too young to retire by any means, but around here country doctors worked a lot longer than that.

"I've asked Sophie to join me," Greta said. "At least to discuss it while she's here for our anniversary, but she swears she's happy delivering babies for those rich women in D.C. They have more OB/GYNs than they can choose from. I need her. My clients need her if Seth's going to make me step down. We have plenty of time—you know my parents both lived until well into their nineties—but Seth refuses to discuss my work anymore.''

Watching for Zach's car, Beth nodded in sympathy. ''You started the clinic. You've helped a lot of young girls in these mountains.'' Greta's paying customers, women who craved some pampered time before their babies came, provided funding for young women who found themselves ''in trouble'' in Bardill's Ridge and the surrounding towns. ''You own the baby farm and you want to put it in hands you trust.''

Greta expressed disapproval with a tart look. ''I hate when y'all call it the baby farm.''

''Sorry.'' Beth knew that, but this late, unannounced visit from Zach had sidetracked her.

''I don't believe Sophie's happy. She and Molly and Zach were like siblings when they were kids, and she's a Calvert just like the rest of us. She'll be happier among family.''

''Maybe you should advertise for another physician just in case.'' Beth craned her neck, waiting for Zach's headlights to sweep the dusk-shadowed turn in her drive. Something had troubled him since that bank robbery. Who wouldn't be upset to discover such violence in himself? ''Sophie will come home when she's ready. You can't push children.'' At last bright light feathered through the shrubbery that lined the gravel driveway. ''Even when they're grown up.''

''I'd expect Sophie to remember her loyalty to this

side of her family as well as to that rogue mother of hers."

"I don't think she sees Nita too often." Beth pointed to the car nosing around the bend. "Look— there's Zach. Wonder what he's after so late?"

Greta looked concerned. "Something wrong? Seth will be calling any second if I don't start home, but I can stay and help you—"

"I'm sure Zach's fine." She wasn't sure at all, but Greta had enough on her mind. The family had all assumed she'd work at the baby farm till she couldn't work anymore. Seth must have been insistent if Greta was considering retirement. "Would you like more tea?"

"No." Her mother-in-law stood, flexing her back. "I left my glasses at the office. Better get moving. Seth's also nagging me to stop driving after dark." She leaned down and aimed a swift kiss Beth's way. "Now, if he asks, we talked about the party, not work, right?"

"He must be really upset this time." Seth had retired from his seat on the county circuit court over ten years ago, and he'd expected his wife to join him in taking leisure.

"He's serious." Greta patted her hair. "So I'm paying attention. Good night, honey. I'm just going to wait by my car to speak to Zach."

"'Night, Greta."

The older woman floated down the stairs, reaching her car as Zach parked his. They spoke between their doors for a moment, and then Greta waved goodbye and drove off.

Zach headed toward the house, but trouble climbed

the wooden porch steps with him. Beth stood, sniffing wood smoke on the crisp air.

"Smell that, son? Fall's got us in its grip."

"It's your favorite time of year, isn't it, Mom?" He turned at the top step and joined her in appreciation of the darkening ridge that rolled from beneath her house. Out here the rising moon provided scarce light. Beth's nearest neighbor lived a stiff hike down the road.

Zach lived on his father's farm now, in the house she'd loved during her marriage. But she'd hated the place after Ned died. A tree had fallen on him as he'd cleared a field during a storm's early gusts. She and Zach, only eight at the time, had taken refuge from their loss on this lonely, untamable patch of ground that had once belonged to her family. She'd wanted no more farms.

"Tell me what's wrong, son."

He grinned. "How'd you know?" A little tired, a lot cagey, still wearing the uniform he usually took off the second he left the sheriff's office behind, he pushed his hands into his pockets. "Never mind. You just know."

"Better come inside. Want some coffee?"

She always had a pot on the warmer. Mr. Coffee had become her best friend the first day he'd shown up at the hardware store in town.

Her son towered over her as he ducked to cross the threshold into the small living room. Her grandfather had built this house, and every room formed a perfect square. Zach used to say the squares made him feel claustrophobic. He worked at the knot in his tie as she patted his shoulder.

"Come into the kitchen. I'll bet you haven't eaten."

"Try not to mother me, Mom."

"It's still my job."

He never gave her credit for the times she tried to let him alone. But she was a Southern woman—when she sensed a heavy load of dread on her son's shoulders, she got the urge to throw something in a casserole. Feeding him was her only refuge when Zach turned as standoffish as the bushy gray cat that sprawled in front of her fireplace.

Spike and Zach shared the same views on comfort. They wanted to be in the room, but they preferred a minimum of human affection.

Zach followed her. "I have to tell you something."

"How bad is it?" Since that day Seth had come up from the field to tell her about Ned, she tended to expect the worst. She tried not to, but she had to pray nothing worse than losing Ned ever happened to her while she had a son and a family who depended on her to be sane.

"It's good in a way. In a lot of ways." Zach opened the refrigerator and popped the top on a pale blue plastic bowl. "Chili? Smells great."

Elbowing him aside, she took the bowl and dished a couple of Zach-sized servings into a saucepan. No microwaves in her house. She cooked the old-fashioned way. "I'm waiting."

"I'm trying to think of a way to say it." He opened the door to the back porch. "Let me bring in some wood for you. The weather forecast says we might have a freeze tonight."

"Okay." She plucked a sweet onion from the wire

basket that hung above her counter. If he had to belly up to telling her, it couldn't be that good.

While the screen door banged open and then shut each time Zach carried a load of wood from the pile out back, Beth peeled the onion.

Spike slinked in to investigate the racket. He hunkered down at her feet while she diced onion the way Zach liked, in small chunks. With the cat twining around her ankles, she cut a hunk of corn bread and set it on a bread plate at the table. She was stirring the steaming chili as Zach got his fill of loading the bin.

He came back in, sniffing the chili's aroma. Again, like Spike. "I didn't even know I was hungry." He slapped on the faucet to wash his hands at the sink. "Aren't you eating?"

"I ate with Gran, but I might have a bite of corn bread."

"I hate to eat alone."

He never admitted that to anyone else, but she knew. It pricked at her during the long two-week periods when Lily stayed at Helene's. Zach's discomfort with being alone had started after the accident, too.

He needed a family. Helene hadn't been a good wife for him, but someday a woman would arrive sporting sense enough to value a guy who *always* did the right thing—even when it came to letting his wife go. Beth often wondered how much of Zach's pain came from a suspicion that, as Helene alleged, he hadn't been good enough for her.

"Mom, do you remember I was in Chicago before I took that last flight?"

It was an odd beginning, but she went with him.

"How could I forget?" She could have bitten her tongue off.

With a look of forebearance, Zach went to the counter where she'd set out a bowl. He ladled chili from the saucepan and sprinkled onions over the top.

"I knew someone in Chicago—a woman named Olivia Kendall."

"Olivia Kendall? I've heard that name."

He lifted his head so sharply chili spilled over the edge of the ladle to splatter the stove. "How? Did she write me here?"

"Huh?" Beth circled the counter to the family room and plucked a magazine from the stack beside her favorite chair. "No one wrote to you here. I always wondered why. I thought you surely had friends." She showed him last month's issue of *Relevance*. "I know her from this. How did you meet a woman like her?" All he needed was another Helene type.

"I'm not sure." He shook his head and then lifted his spoon for a bite. Normally, chili was the next best thing to nectar for Zach. He savored it like those folks on the food channel swilled choice wine. This bite, he swallowed almost without chewing, but then cringed and ran for the sink where he splashed water into his burned mouth.

"I'm sorry, son." She got him a beer, twisted the top and put the bottle on the counter. "Now, tell me about Olivia Kendall. What does she want from you?"

His still-wary gaze reminded her of the little boy who'd once thought she knew everything. After all

these years, some of that child's vulnerability remained in Zach's eyes. He'd hate it if he knew.

"I knew her well. I—" He broke off, his face tight.
She couldn't tell if the chili burn hurt him or if he
was struggling with the words. "Apparently, I cared
for her." He looked almost ashamed. "We have a
son. Olivia and I."

While she stared, mouth literally agape, he took the
bottle top from her hand and tossed it into the garbage
beneath the sink. Then he maneuvered her into the
nearest chair. He might be giving her time to take it
in. More likely, he was embarrassed. He'd had Lily
too quickly with Helene, too.

"How does a man forget a child?"

"Or the boy's mother," Zach said. "She was
young. I know what kind of resources her family has,
but I hate to think of what she went through, being a
single mother because I disappeared." He patted his
pockets as if he were looking for something. "Olivia
brought a picture, but I left it at home." He pointed
to the mantel in her living room. "He looks just like
those."

She turned her head slowly. She'd all but papered
her house in photos of Ned and Zach. She hadn't
wanted her boy to forget his father. "He looks like
you? Or your daddy?"

"So much like me you wouldn't be able to tell our
pictures apart." He pointed toward the end of the table, at his kindergarten graduation photo above a
dried-flower arrangement. "He's that old."

She stared at the picture, taking time to let Zach's
news sink in. Ned, as tall as Zach was now, but already more gray about the head than blond, had

hoisted their son in miniature cap and gown to his shoulder. As proud as if their Zach had finished Harvard magna cum laude. Good thing, because he'd been gone twelve years by the time Zach finished college on the government's dime.

She shook her head. "How'd you even meet someone like her? That family hardly keeps our kind of company."

"After she told me about Evan I didn't think to ask for details." His haggard expression was painful to see, but he turned away, rejecting her concern for a swig of his beer. "I left on my last mission before she could tell me she was pregnant, and then she saw my picture in the news. Her father tried to get more information out of the Navy, but Kendall was the last person they wanted to see, and they didn't know about Olivia—any more than she knew what I was really doing. She never heard I survived until she saw a report on the bank robbery."

"My God."

He took his chair again, his moving body pushing the heavy oak table away. "Yeah."

"Is she looking for support?" A mother's protectiveness sharpened her voice. For once, Zach didn't seem to notice.

"Olivia Kendall," he repeated, as if her name said it all.

It did.

"Still, I owe my son support."

True. "What else does she want?"

"A father for Evan." He stood again, his meal forgotten as he strode the creaking wooden floor. "That's what she says."

After Helene, it was a hard concept to follow. "Do you believe her?"

"I think so." He lifted a troubled gaze. "I have to because I want to see him. I don't know if Evan needs me, but I'm shocked that I've had a son for five years. He's at an age where it must be obvious he's different from other boys and girls."

"Nonsense. We don't live in that world anymore. People divorce now. Unwed mothers keep their children. He won't have…"

"You see his life through an adult's eyes. I'm trying to look through his." He turned. "And I need to know if you can be his grandmother—if you can love him as much as you love Lily."

"You have to ask?" He'd lost his ability to trust, along with those memories that had disappeared in his injuries. She worshiped her granddaughter. "I value every second with Lily, just as you do, and I'll love your boy as much. Let's ask Olivia and—" She broke off. "You said his name is Evan?" He nodded. "Let's invite them to your gran and grandpa's anniversary celebration."

Seth and Greta Calvert had loved her like a daughter. They'd made her part of their family the day Ned had brought her to these mountains, and since then they'd all claimed countless other "marry-ins." They'd claim Olivia and Evan, too, and make them welcome.

"I just hope we don't overwhelm him." Beth assumed Zach agreed with her plan, without giving him time to differ. "Does his mother have family I might not have read about?"

"Only her father." Distraction distanced Zach's

voice. "She named Evan for me, Mom. His middle name is Zachary."

Red-rimmed eyes described the gratitude he obviously couldn't voice. He already knew how to love this child who'd appeared out of the past he couldn't explain or defeat.

She went to him. "He's in Chicago?"

Zach nodded.

"When do you go?" Since the day he'd come home to heal, she hated to see Zach leave the safety of Bardill's Ridge.

"Tomorrow morning." He looped his arm around her shoulders. "Warn the rest of the family to treat Evan and Olivia right? Remind them not to confuse her with Helene."

"We're all protective of you." She hugged him briefly. He hardly ever allowed more. "If she's good to you, we'll love her."

He let her go and scooped up Spike, who inexplicably began kneading his fellow loner's shoulder. "No," Zach said. "You'll love her because Evan will feel more accepted if you do." With a last pat for Spike as he set him on a padded kitchen chair, he headed for her door. "I'll call you from Chicago."

"Are you bringing him home?"

"Chicago is his home. I thought he'd have an easier time if we met where he's comfortable, but while I'm there, I'll arrange visitation with Olivia."

"Another visitation agreement?"

He nodded, a frown creasing his forehead. "Or something like it. Olivia seems to believe we should take decisions slowly. I have no intention of losing contact with my son, now that she's told me about him, but I figure we'll fight the battle of how often I get to see him when it comes.''

Hardly good news, but she stomped down hard on her opinions. Zach stopped at the door.

''Everything will be fine, Mom.''

He offered the same reassurance every time he left town. He expected no answer. He was only promising he wouldn't die when he left Bardill's Ridge. Obviously, she knew something could happen, but he was a good son to try to persuade her not to worry.

She added some comfort of her own to her ''I know'' smile. When he came back they'd all find a way to live with another custody arrangement. She waved him off, and he tried to smile back, but his hard-edged face lingered in her mind after the door slammed at his back.

She slumped against the table. Apart from the fact that he'd clearly been reckless six years ago, he didn't deserve all this. A past that wouldn't let him alone and a child who'd been a secret from him. When would Fate let up on her son?

She reached for the phone to circle the family wagons for support.

THE MOON BARELY LIT his way as he got out of his car in front of the Dogwood, his uncle Patrick and aunt Eliza's bed-and-breakfast. His cousin Molly erupted from the front door, flying as fast as one of her roguish kindergarten students. On seeing his truck she stopped short. As she waited for him to climb out her smile bent the other way into a frown.

''What's up, Zach? Something bugging you?''

''Sort of.'' He wrapped an arm around her waist,

at ease with being Molly's hero. No matter what he did, he'd maintained his status with her since Patrick and Eliza had made her their foster child. No small feat, considering the neglected life she'd endured until they rescued her. "Where are you headed in such a hurry?"

"Parent-teacher conferences at school tonight. I have to change clothes." She slapped her jeans. Molly, the hellion Aunt Eliza had saved from reform school liked to appear demure in front of her students' parents.

"You'd better go," he said, laughing, "if you plan to reach your classroom before midnight."

"Ha ha ha." She caught his arm as he tried to pull away. "That was homage to your lousy sense of humor. Now explain your problem."

"I have no problem." He had to talk to Olivia. His mom would cover the family bases for him.

Molly's smile faded again. "You're scaring me."

Calverts large and small had treated him as if he were on the verge of a breakdown since the accident. Maybe if he'd managed a happier marriage, maybe if he and Helene could be civil to each other... "I'm fine, but I have to talk to one of your mom's guests before she goes to bed."

"Ah." She glanced at a second-floor window bordered with Victorian gingerbread that their cousin Sophie's father had carved during Patrick and Eliza's restoration of the old building. "Olivia. I just took her fresh towels and bath oil." Molly slipped him a sidelong, sisterly glance. "Or was that for you, too?"

He looked away from her, as distracting, erotic pictures of Olivia formed in his head. "I hope the parents

and the other teachers don't know you talk like that."
He ruffled Molly's hair, but she surprised him with a
hug rather than the karate chop she usually dispensed
for such a gesture.

"If you don't explain, I'll only ask your mom."
She headed for her car, waving goodbye over her
head. "I'll bet she needs firewood."

"I already carried in enough for the whole winter."

"I'll paint her kitchen."

"If you can persuade her to give up that classic
wallpaper."

Molly tossed a condescending glance over her
shoulder, but he only grinned. Crazy Molly. Early on,
trying to survive after her natural parents had pretty
much abandoned her, she'd damn near destroyed the
school where she taught now. Aunt Eliza and Uncle
Patrick had transformed her from a dangerous punk
into family. Still, it was a good thing his mom had
plenty of leftovers. Molly could eat her weight in
homemade chili.

Zach climbed the steps a few at a time and pushed
through the B&B's front door. His aunt looked up
from the registration desk, sliding her hand through
salt-and-pepper hair that brushed her shoulders.

"Evening, Zach. Beth said you were on your
way."

"That was fast work, even for Mom. Which room,
Aunt Eliza?"

"Top of the stairs, immediate left."

"Thanks."

"Better hurry. Molly just took her some bath oil."

He ran up the stairs. At Olivia's door, he paused,
his hand raised to knock. Even through the thick

wood, he heard water running. He banged with extra force.

A moment later, Olivia opened the door, black hair flying, eyes wide. She opened her mouth in a throaty gasp. "Zach." Her hands went to the pale pink lapels of her robe.

It was hardly sexy attire, but he found himself imagining the warm body that curved beneath the terry cloth. By the time he met her gaze, a glacier had formed in the icy gray eyes that were quickly becoming his obsession.

"I want to meet Evan," he said.

The ice melted. She seemed to reach for him without lifting a finger. "Do you want to *know* Evan?"

"I'm his father. He's my son."

"That's not good enough. I've kept him safe—and happy enough—for five years. I need to hear plain talk."

"I want to be Evan's father for the rest of my life. I want to hear him call me dad."

Smiling, she let the robe go. He noticed the swell of lightly tanned flesh between the open lapels, but he was man enough to know their son mattered more than lust.

"We're in this together," he said. "I want to know Evan."

She grabbed his hand—to shake it of all things. He stared at her small, strong fingers. It was an odd way to start a relationship with your son's mother.

CHAPTER FOUR

THE NEXT MORNING, Zach followed Olivia back to the airport in Knoxville. All the way down the mountain road his heart hammered. Sweat beaded on his lip again and again. His body's natural response to an unnatural fear was about to reveal one of his most humiliating secrets to Olivia. Zach Calvert, former Navy pilot, was terrified of flying.

Forcing himself to ignore the fact he had to get on a plane, he concentrated on Evan waiting at the other end of the flight. Meeting his son was worth a couple of hellish hours.

At the airport, Olivia veered off to return her rental car while Zach parked in a lot. They'd agreed to meet at the ticket counter. Tall and confident as ever, she was easy to spot. Too easy.

They checked in without talking to each other and then headed for their gate. Walking at her side, he noticed how the other travelers stared.

Her poise and her flawless face, an aristocratic, elegantly drawn nose, and her intelligent gaze vied with the tousled confusion of long black hair. She drew attention partly because she didn't seem to know she was suck-the-last-breath-from-your-lungs gorgeous.

Zach had nothing to set on the security conveyor

belt, but he waited while Olivia pushed her briefcase and her purse through.

Her poise made him more aware of his Achilles' heel. A smart guy would have rejected her offer to arrange for seats together. A smart guy wouldn't let a self-assured woman who'd been in sole charge of his son for the past five years discover he was afraid of flying.

They cleared security with more than an hour to wait for their flight. Olivia was already fishing work out of her briefcase as they closed in on their gate. Zach held back. He couldn't sit there for sixty minutes without throwing up.

"I'm going to look for a paper," he said. "And a coffee. Want one?"

"Sure. With cream and sugar." Sitting, she pushed a pen behind her ear. "Wait— Will you make that half-and-half?"

Nodding, he turned, breathing easier the more distance he put between them. How was he going to pretend to be normal on the plane?

He took his time and passed the coffee shop twice before he turned in. A teenager in a cap and acne came to the counter and threw him a look that asked for his order.

"A bottle of water." Last thing he needed was caffeine. "And a large coffee. With half-and-half."

"The milk and stuff's over there," the kid said. "That'll be seven-fifty."

"Thanks. Do you have newspapers?"

"Beside the milk and the stir sticks. You pay here. That'll cost you another fifty cents."

Zach paid and tucked the paper beneath his arm.

He stirred sugar and half-and-half into Olivia's coffee and started back to the gate. She didn't look up until he sat beside her. Even then she just reached for the cup.

"Thanks." She sipped. "Perfect. I thought you wanted coffee, too." She might not be looking at him, but she saw too much for his peace of mind.

"I reconsidered." He unscrewed his water bottle's cap and guzzled half the contents. It didn't help.

Olivia checked the time. "We'll be boarding soon. Maybe we should discuss what we intend to tell Evan."

"Discuss what?" He felt his face harden. "There's no argument. We tell him who I am."

"From the start? What if you change your mind?"

He stared at her. Who did she see when she looked at him? "Did you ever change your mind about wanting Evan?"

She let her mouth open slightly, showing surprise. The moisture on her full lower lip made breathing a little harder for Zach.

"You can't appreciate what you just said." The joy in her smile made him glad, whatever it was. "I'm never sure I'm the best mom Evan could have. I have to work. He spends time in day care. Even my father assumed I wouldn't want to be a mother when I was so young, but you assumed I never considered an alternative."

His throat went tight. For a moment, it was as if he could almost remember her, as if the feelings they'd shared were there, on the fringes of what felt real to him now. "Maybe I can't imagine you not wanting to keep our son."

She widened her gaze. "Well, you'd be right." As if the subject had grown too personal, she busied herself with the pages in her lap.

"You're uncomfortable discussing your pregnancy with me."

She nodded. "It's all still as real as if it just happened to me, but to you I'm a stranger. I loved being pregnant, feeling Evan grow, even though I—" She stopped, her face pink with a blush. "I missed you."

"I was angry for a long time about what happened, but I thought I was getting over it." He wiped his mouth, his resentment an old, no-longer-welcome partner.

"Why did they give you so much training for one mission?" She was thoughtful. He was surprised she hadn't asked before.

He glanced at the empty seats around them. "I was assigned to do that kind of work from then on, but I was chosen for that flight because Kimberly Salva was a friend." His whole body seemed to tighten as he pictured Kim, idealistic, smarter than he'd ever be, full of fire for her own career. "We went to the Academy together."

Olivia drew back. "I don't mean to pry, but you're angry when you talk about her. You were just friends?"

He nodded. "She was a year behind me. I'm angry because I lost her. She had a husband and a two-year-old daughter, and she trusted me."

"And you're not over it yet?"

He considered lying. His own child's mother deserved the truth. "Maybe I never will be. I get to meet my son. Her daughter will never see her again. It's

not fair that I lived when I couldn't save her.''
Olivia's scratching pen drew his gaze. She was out-
lining the same abstract, many-pointed doodle so hard
the page looked ready to tear. "Are you having second thoughts?"

"No." But her glossy black hair hid her face from
him.

"I'm not going to hurt Evan. I only lose control
with people who want to kill the citizens I'm trying
to protect."

"You're joking, but people don't make jokes like
that without a little bit of honesty."

He curved his hand around her wrist, making sure
to touch only where her black blazer covered her skin.
"I'm telling you the truth. I wouldn't hide anything
that might affect Evan. I've explained my problems
with Helene. I don't want you and me to have difficulties. I'm a good father to Lily, and I'll be a good
father to Evan."

"I should have seen you with her. Not seeing you
together was a mistake."

"I didn't tell her," he said.

"Thanks." She sagged against her chair, clearly
deep in thought about how much fathering a wounded
man could do. He couldn't keep assuring her of his
reliable mental health. He'd start to sound crazy. A
sudden thought brought Olivia upright again. "What
if Lily or Helene find out about Evan through the
papers?"

"They won't. Helene doesn't read them, and I
never saw her watch the news."

"What if someone else tells her?"

"Leland—her husband—is a reasonable guy. He'll

figure out the facts and hold Helene back until I get in touch. He won't let her say something hurtful to Lily.''

''You trust her new husband more than you trust her?''

''We didn't know each other when we got married.'' How well had he known Olivia?

She turned away, leading him to believe she'd experienced broken trust. With a painful start, he realized he'd taught her that lesson. She'd trusted him.

''I didn't mean to leave you,'' he said.

''Your amnesia makes it no easier for me. I tell myself over and over that you won't just abandon Evan, but if you're not good to him, I'll—''

Ahhh. He understood rage. Though she sputtered to a halt, her vehemence drew him closer.

The vulnerable curve of her lips fascinated him. He'd made love to her and yet he had no memory of her mouth's firm, tempting texture. She knew secrets about him, about them together that he might never remember.

Her mouth twisted into a smile, and he dragged his gaze back to hers. ''Can't think of a threat?'' he asked. When she looked serious, he regretted teasing her.

''I won't need a threat if you hurt my son.''

''Our son.''

Her expression, stony, determined, and not in the least wary of him, was all too familiar. She like Helene did when she was about to announce he'd broken her rules and to hell with the ones in the custody agreement. He knocked back the rest of his water. They finished their wait in a troubled state of truce.

It was almost a relief when the attendant began to call their flight.

He stayed behind Olivia as they handed over their boarding passes and entered the jetway's gaping maw. His feet grew heavier, but he forced himself to keep walking.

Inside the narrow passage, his heart thudded in his ears. He felt as if he might plod right through the flimsy flooring. At last, the door of the aircraft came into view, along with a few precious inches of daylight around the gate's edges. He could see himself pushing through the plastic material and jumping to the ground. A broken leg or two would be worth escape.

The flight attendant eyed him with concern, but passed him through. To first-class. Which he couldn't afford.

He hung back when Olivia offered him the choice of aisle or window, with no idea he had a problem. Behind him, the rest of the first-class crowd began muttering at their unaccustomed delay.

"I can't pay for this." He grasped exactly how different their worlds were. How different they'd look to Evan.

"Fortunately, I can, so it's not a problem for either of us." She passed him her briefcase. "Could you put this…"

Before he answered, another attendant took her case. "May I take your jacket, sir?" she asked.

Olivia settled into the window seat. As if the cost of the ticket was no big deal. He'd bet on it being at least three of his car payments. He shrugged off his jacket and surrendered it. As he sat and latched on to

the seat belt with sweating hands, Olivia nodded
his way.

"You're doing me a favor. Forget about the cost."

"Being my son's father isn't a favor. I'm in this
for good—you'd better get used to it."

"I meant for now, coming with me when you don't
really know who I am. I probably would have asked
for a DNA test."

The idea startled him. "I didn't think of it. The
pictures... I can't deny his face." He rubbed his
hands down the thighs of his jeans.

She smiled and he had the feeling he'd passed
some test. Little did she know. She had no experience
sharing custody. They both faced plenty of tests to
come.

"I have videotapes we've been making since the
day he was born, and a library full of photo albums."

"I'd like to make copies." As he spoke the plane
rocked. He turned to the aisle, gripping the armrests
to hide his shaking hands.

"Sure." Olivia looked him up and down. "Are you
all right?"

Grunting an affirmative, he managed to ease breath
in and out at regular intervals. His humiliation was
complete when the kid in front of him sat up on his
knees to peer at Zach.

"You sick, mister? I always use that bag down
there." He slithered over the back of the seat to reach
for the one in front of Zach. "You'll be okay."

The kid's mom snatched him down so hard he
seemed to disappear. Zach glanced at Olivia, whose
close scrutiny made him feel weak.

He waved off an offer of wine and sensed Olivia

doing the same. The floor rumbled beneath them as the engines powered up and then down. Flaps opened and closed as the pilots went through their preflight checks. Zach's mouth dried like a desert in a drought.

He studied the stuff sticking out of the seat pocket. He might have to grab one of those bags.

At the first hint of movement he closed his eyes. When the jet jerked backward, his sweating palms slid off the armrests. A hand closed over his. He opened his eyes, biting back a shout.

It was Olivia, of course. She pulled his hand into her lap and deliberately threaded their fingers together. Her touch was more warmth and comfort than he'd known in six years. More than he had a right to know, considering.

"You don't have to pretend." Her low, liquid voice intoxicated more quickly than strong wine. "I know about being scared. When I heard you'd died, I tried to pretend I was strong, but I was terrified my dad would fire me and throw me out. He's terribly proud of our name, and I knew he'd be ashamed of me. I'd always lived a spoiled, easy kind of life, but food and clothing and car seats and immunizations felt beyond my reach. Can you imagine Evan or Lily going to bed hungry because you'd been foolish?"

"Why are you telling me this?" She'd hardly been an adult herself when he'd left her pregnant and alone. Not having known didn't seem to ease his guilt any more than it made her feel better.

"I told you because we don't trust each other yet." Each word came out under strain. "I can't forget you disappeared, and you've had a bad time I can't imagine and a bad marriage that makes you think a woman can't share a child with his father. I just learned something about you that you'd rather I hadn't, and I thought if I gave you something equally personal, we could skip a few steps learning about each other." She squeezed his hand with a shrug that didn't quite look casual. "And I know how it feels to believe every breath is the last one you're going to squeeze past the boulder on your chest."

He leaned toward her without turning his head. He didn't want her to see the terror in his eyes. "Even if your father came through for you, what you faced makes my flying phobia trivial."

A scent, half floral, half spicy, drew his gaze as he breathed in. Her smile, astoundingly sensual, confused him entirely about what he was doing here.

She shook her head. "I'd be afraid, too, if I'd crashed the way you did—if I felt the guilt you still feel. I won't tell anyone. Ever." She grinned, sharing a heaping measure of her self-confidence. "And I'd just as soon you didn't tell my father what I said. He and I get along better when he thinks I am as strong as I pretended to be."

"I wish I remembered you."

Her eyes blinked in slow motion. Her shrug implied she might have gone further than she'd meant to.

"And I'm glad Evan had you," he added.

This time she closed her eyes and averted her face. The moment had turned into something neither of them intended. They'd built a connection.

She didn't let go. He tightened his hand, finding compassion in the fingers wrapped around his.

AFTER THEY WERE in the air, Zach eased his hand away in a silent, "Thanks, but I don't need any more help."

Just as well. His too-familiar touch had taken her back to the brief months with him that now belonged to her alone.

Her impulse to comfort him had created an intimacy that spelled danger. She'd be crazy to let herself forget how difficult getting over him had been. She was too mature to assume they might feel something for each other because they both wanted the best care for Evan. Caution reminded her she'd only heard his side of his disagreement with Helene over Lily.

She turned her head on the seat back to sneak a look at him. With his eyes focused on a point somewhere in his own thoughts, he was ignoring the magazine he held.

"Will you ever remember the past?" she asked.

"I don't know. But that day in the bank—" narrowing his gaze, he seemed to decide to trust her "—I don't know if I remembered or responded—but I saw that guy's gun, and I knew how to disarm him and break down the weapon."

"Like pictures in your head?" Before he could answer, the boy in front of them cleared his throat. He'd squeezed his face into the space between his seat and his mom's.

"I have one of those bags," he said. "If you can't find yours or his."

"Thanks." She grinned. He made her count the hours till she'd be with her own son again. She glanced at Zach, who was also smiling. "We seem to be fine."

"My mom picks up an extra one for me before we—" The boy glanced at the seat next to him. "I'm not bugging her, Mom. She wants to talk to me." He listened for a moment and then looked back. "She says you don't."

Laughter rumbled low in Zach's chest. Olivia couldn't bear to look at him. She remembered that sound—how it had felt against her face when she'd lain across him, her cheek pressed to his skin. Sharp, sweet memory confounded her. She'd adored Zach with the innocence of first love. Maybe no one loved that way twice in a lifetime. She'd never felt anything half as intense again.

The boy popped up and this time, foisted an airsick bag on Zach. "Here you go. You won't get in trouble if you get sick in this."

His mother yanked the child down again, with a "Sorry" into the air.

"Is Evan like him?" Zach's voice startled her, moving wisps of her hair against her ear.

She tried hard not to shiver. "Sometimes. He might be shy with you at first. He's really polite."

Concern slashed a frown across his forehead. "You make it sound like he's too polite."

Zach didn't seem to sense the physical effect his closeness had on her, which was the way she hoped to keep it. "He spends a lot of time with adults." With her, her father, and with the bodyguard who drove Evan to school after he dropped her off at work. "I wish his life was more like other little boys'."

"What do you mean?"

"I should have mentioned the precautions before. My father's a little overprotective. I refused his bodyguards when I was in college," she said. Zach sat forward, clearly worried. She tried to explain, but it sounded weird to normal people. "When I was a baby, he received kidnapping threats and he tried to protect me. After Evan was born, the crazy stuff started again—you know, crank letters that said people like me thought I could go around having bastards and buy off the decent folk who knew I was a slut. Anyway, I took the letters about Evan seriously. He's always been around strangers who were paid to save his life. They get to be friends, but they also change jobs, so Evan deals with new people a lot."

"Poor kid."

His sympathy put her on the defensive. "I wish my son didn't have to live like that but you didn't see or hear the threats."

He lifted a hand in appeal. "I'm not criticizing you. I'm just trying to learn about Evan." For once, he opened his eyes and bared his feelings. "Does he get attached to these guys?"

"They haven't all been guys. His nanny when he was a baby could probably take you out if you brought him home late or you got something wrong when you helped him with his homework."

His mouth tilted at the corners, creasing new lines from his mouth to his nose. He'd been young and almost too beautiful before. Now he was a man.

"Bring the nanny on." He mocked himself, looking self-conscious as he had when she'd held his hand on takeoff.

Just as well he seemed clueless about her doubts. "Tell me about your ex-wife." She needed to know about Helene for Evan's sake, but she was also testing her feelings as she might prod at a tender wound. It smarted a little, but it wasn't fatal.

"We got married for the wrong reasons. It didn't work. We don't get along well, and she'd rather I broke contact with Lily."

"Why? I still don't get that."

"Because you have all the money you'll ever want. She doesn't." He turned a hard gaze her way. "I told you the truth before, and I'm not trying to offend you, but Helene will only see Evan when he's with me when I'm picking up Lily or dropping her off. I don't see why you need to know about her."

She didn't intimidate easily. "I want you to be a safe man for my son to know—and eventually to love, and I don't understand why Helene would choose money over a husband—over her child's father."

"She didn't just choose money. She traded up for the lifestyle."

"That makes no sense."

"To me either." Impatience glittered in his eyes. "But we've already covered this ground."

"I still need to talk about the changes I'm forcing on Evan. Like it or not, Helene is a big change for us."

"I love my daughter more than anything else in my life, and I'm prepared to love Evan as much. I'll protect him." His voice, almost a threat, certainly a deadly earnest promise, rode up and down her nerve endings. "But Helene isn't a monster. She wouldn't hurt him on purpose. She just has her own priorities. She grew up in poverty, and she believes the material advantages she gained through her new marriage offer

Lily a better life than I can give her. It makes sense to her. That's what I have to deal with.''

''It's no way to treat her child's father.''

''I hope you really mean that.''

His heartfelt plea annoyed her. She pressed her hand to his sleeve, startled to find her fingertips tingling on bare, hair-roughened skin. ''What if we both agree neither of us will lie?''

His gaze measured her. ''Deal,'' he said.

They shared silence for the rest of the flight. It didn't feel companionable, but neither was it hostile. As the aircraft began to drift downward, Zach tensed, clasping his hands in a white-knuckled grip in his own lap. Olivia kept her comfort to herself this time. As the wheels scraped the runway, he relaxed, but even Olivia was relieved when they finally taxied to a halt.

''As soon as we pick up our bags, I'll bring my car around,'' she said.

''You'll bring it?'' He took her briefcase and his jacket from the flight attendant. ''Thanks,'' he said and then turned back to Olivia. ''I have a memory problem, and I'm gutless about flying, but I'm not an invalid. If you need proof from a physical…''

''I may have one of your physicals in my file.'' She shouldered her case strap. Why let him get away with all the sarcasm? ''Courtesy of Brian, my very thorough assistant who thinks there'd be fewer thieves in the world if you trained the police forces to deal with them.'' She looked up sharply. ''You're not going to teach Evan any of that stuff, are you? He'll get expelled if he beats up a classmate.''

''You don't have to worry.'' Zach looked embarrassed. "If the guy had shot me, I'd have left Lily, and now Evan, fatherless. The consequences never occurred to me."

"Makes you wonder why they taught you to disarm someone with that much violence." She eased in front of him moving first into the aisle. "Almost as if you wouldn't ever need to worry about asking questions later."

When he looked down, his height made her feel smaller, more feminine. Not too many men stood tall enough to even look her in the eye. And not one other man had made her feel vulnerable since the day she'd read Zach was supposed to be dead.

"You sound like a reporter when you ask about my training." He followed at her elbow, close enough to converse. "You're not secretly planning a story?"

"You haven't noticed how paranoid I can be about Evan?" She grimaced. "Do you honestly think I want my son and you all over my magazine? That I want the other news outlets and the online upstarts to interview Evan about his long-lost daddy who just happens to kick bank-robbing butt for a living?"

Zach laughed with a quick downward glance that made her feel overdressed in khaki gabardine and her black broadcloth blazer. "The word 'butt' sounds odd coming from you." At her annoyed frown, he laughed again. His rich laughter had always been a sinful treat, but memories of naked play and sweet, sweet affection to the music of his voice unnerved her. He'd been generous with his laughter and his loving.

"It's not that funny." She pulled away to reclaim her own space, but not far enough to provoke more discord between them. "We'd better move."

She hurried up the jetway, anxious to get home to Evan, but also reluctant to feel foolish in front of Zach. By the time she reached the gate, she'd begun to regain her poise, but suddenly their situation took a turn for the dire. Amid the throng waiting for her fellow passengers, one man stood out.

Almost as tall as Zach, elbow-to-elbow with his own two bodyguards, James Kendall craned his dark brown head to catch a glimpse of her. He didn't seem to notice the stares everyone else directed at his famous face.

"Dad." Her father must have read her lips. He offered her a regal nod.

Zach stopped at her shoulder, his clean scent wrapping around her. "You didn't expect him?"

"I didn't even think I had to ask him to stay away. He'll draw every non-Kendall reporter in a ten-mile radius." People had stopped greeting each other to cast furtive glances at her father. It was a moment of pure desperation. "Let's try to ignore him."

"We'll be the only people in the airport who do."

"Do you have a better plan?"

"Why don't we cover our eyes and pretend he can't see us?"

Olivia grimaced. She looked foolish again—but she tried to recover. "You have raised a child if you know that game."

"Who knew how easily I could prove I'm a good dad?" He pressed his hand into the small of her back. "Your father won't let you ignore him. Let's just face him and find out what he's up to."

James Kendall parted the crowd and reached for her in a bone-crushing hug the likes of which she hadn't known since the day she'd survived giving birth to Evan. Olivia saw through his plan instantly. He was threatening Zach with a painfully obvious warning about hurting her ever again.

She broke away. "You're not a good actor, Dad. I'll bet Zach can guess you're on my side." She glanced at Zach. "Not that we've taken sides. Let's get out of here before someone figures out who you are."

"Maybe we want people to know," her father said. "We could leak a story that you and this guy had one of those two-week marriages that never works, an impulse you both regretted, but now you're older, wiser, and you're reuniting your son with his father."

"That story might work for you, sir." Zach vetoed the plan with confidence that matched and then raised James Kendall's. "But do you think the press would leave Evan alone just because he's a child?"

"You and I are going to talk about Evan."

"Not here and not now." Exasperated, Olivia clutched her father's arm and propelled him toward baggage claim. She nodded at the two men, one lean and dark, one buff and auburn-haired, who planted themselves on either side of her father. "Hi, Ian. Jock." They acknowledged her without taking their eyes off the crowd. She didn't bother to introduce Zach. They were too busy doing their jobs to acknowledge him anyway.

She turned back to her dad. "Don't try to challenge Zach. You can't win. He's Evan's father."

"I always win where my family's concerned." James Kendall spoke aggressively.

"We're talking about my family as well." Zach's steady gaze deepened her father's frown.

He squeezed Olivia's arm against his side. "Give Jock your keys, and tell him where you parked your car. I brought a driver so I could take you and Zach home."

"So you could orchestrate events." She glanced over her shoulder, prepared to see hordes of competing journalists. Not finding them, she borrowed Zach's calmer approach. "I'm not sure what you're up to, Dad, but we'll meet you at your house."

"I want to talk to you both before you introduce this man to Evan."

She dug her heels into the slick airport floor, but Zach took her arm and kept her moving through the stream of people.

He glanced at her father over her head before he spoke. "We have nothing to prove, Olivia. I'd be concerned, too, if a guy showed up claiming rights to my grandson."

He was right, but she didn't like being caught between two autocratic men. Especially since she needed to be the one in charge. She forced her head up and down again in a sharp nod and handed her keys to Jock, the stockier bodyguard.

They handed their claim tickets to Ian. While he waited for their things, Olivia's dad walked her and Zach straight through the terminal and out to the sidewalk where his long black car waited in a policeman's shadow.

The policeman actually tipped his cap and opened the far door for James. Her dad merely nodded in his best king-of-the-world manner, confirming Olivia's worst suspicions.

He had plenty to prove and territory to stake out. The limo provided two car lengths of luxury and evidence that showed Zach they lived in a different world than a sheriff from Bardill's Ridge, Tennessee, could hope to inhabit.

Zach didn't seem to get it. Apparently impervious to the undercurrent, he held the other door for Olivia to get in ahead of him. A cool, Chicago fall breeze tossed his blond hair.

He caught her shoulder as her father got in the car. "I can hold my own," he said close to her ear. "You don't have to fight for me."

"He's trying to run over you because he's afraid Evan will love you more than him."

"He's helped you and our son. Look, you didn't come to Tennessee because it was easy. You came on Evan's behalf. Your father obviously needs to show us I'm not going to take his place in your family. I can stand a jab or two if letting your dad have his say makes the rest of this easier."

"I guess that makes sense." She ducked in front of Zach, sensing the breadth of his chest as she got too close to him. Inside, her father had already sprawled across the larger seat. As Zach sat next to her on the bench that backed up to the driver, her dad reached for the Scotch.

She covered his hand. "It's hardly even noon."

"You sound like my doctors. Lay off."

"Dad, I want you to take care of yourself."

Zach took Olivia's briefcase and settled it on his

other side, uniting the two of them with a simple gesture. "Why don't we discuss Evan?"

Olivia's father widened his gaze at her while she tried not to show her own surprise. She was enough his daughter to resent being corralled with him. He smiled, waiting for an explosion.

Olivia hit the intercom. "Roger," she said to the driver, "can we turn the heat down a little?"

"Sure, Ms. Kendall."

She smiled at her father. He frowned, rubbing the top of the Scotch decanter.

"What plans have you made, Zach?"

"It's too early to plan." Olivia jumped in first. "Let's introduce Zach and Evan to each other and feel our way from there."

"Ridiculous," her dad said. "We don't make another move that exposes Evan until we know Zach's intentions."

"I intend to be my son's father." He settled his elbows on his knees, almost too tall to sit comfortably. "I appreciate what you've done—you and Olivia." His gaze raked her quickly, waking an unwelcome awareness that made her glad when he turned back to her father. "I'll never hurt Evan. I want him to be happy. I'd like to make up the past five years to him."

"You can't make up for five years. His mother and I are all the family he knows." James lifted one of the crystal glasses and set it down again. "We've been enough for him."

"Not after today." Zach sat back, his hair brushing the roof. "Our families just expanded. I want to get along with you. I intend to make our new relationship as easy as possible for Olivia and Evan, but make no mistake. I'm not going away.''

As Olivia gripped the leather seat with both hands her father tapped his perfectly tailored black serge knee. ''My wealth has nothing to do with your objectives?''

''My bank account doesn't stand up to yours, but maybe Evan has enough money. I didn't know about him, and I don't remember Olivia, but this has been a mistake we don't have to compound.'' Zach leaned forward. Pain crept across his face as if he were allowing them to see feelings he normally hid deep. ''I have no idea who my son is, and he thinks I'm dead. Even if he didn't need me, I'd need him. That makes me safe for your family.''

''And if I don't believe you?'' her father asked in a silky tone.

Olivia curved her hand around Zach's wrist. Her pulse faltered as she felt the heat of his skin, but she eyed her father as she spoke. ''You don't have to believe. I do.''

Zach covered her hand with his. ''I can't blame you for trying to protect Olivia and Evan, but I won't disappear again, and I'll never put myself before my son. I found out about him around twenty-four hours ago, and I'm here. How could I sound more like a parent?''

Her dad slid back in his seat. ''Okay. So now we know where we stand.''

His trembling voice stunned Olivia as he called a truce in the battle he shouldn't have waged. Behind him, the trunk popped open, and Ian stored Olivia's and Zach's bags inside. Then the bodyguard took his seat next to the driver, and they sped away from the curb.

"One last thing, Dad." She hated to doubt her own father's intentions, but he'd always done what he thought best, and to hell with the cost. "You didn't tell Evan about Zach, did you?"

"I thought about it," he admitted. "But I decided you'd want to, and I thought Zach had the right to tell him in his own way."

So ended the pissing contest…. She hoped.

CHAPTER FIVE

ZACH SCANNED Chicago as they drove through the town, but nothing came back to him. They passed strip malls and apartment buildings, houses and finally skyscrapers. Each structure, each turn in the road, each face that glanced at the long car passing, was chilling in its strangeness.

Apparently, he'd paid more attention to instructions for dismantling a miniature cannon than to directions home—or to a woman he must have cared for. What had made the gun stick in his mind when he'd lost Olivia?

He refused to believe he'd played with her. He wasn't built that way. He'd tried hard enough to make his marriage work with Helene, though they'd both realized early on that they weren't in love. Surely he hadn't made the same mistake twice in a matter of months.

He glanced at Olivia, trying to remember the texture of her hair in his hands, the soft, living warmth of her skin. This close to her, enveloped in her scent, every breath became an unexpected pleasure. He could want her now. What had happened between them six years ago?

As if sensing his gaze, she turned her head. She smiled first with her eyes, but the curve of her mouth seemed uncertain. She looked away almost in time to hide the color that washed up her throat. Zach turned too, but locked gazes with James Kendall, who eyed him with a mixture of speculation and suspicion.

"Anything seem familiar to you?"

Zach shook his head, going toe-to-toe. He couldn't blame Kendall for wanting to protect his daughter, but Zach wasn't out to hurt her. He pointed through the window, at nothing really, more to change the subject. "Do you live with your dad, Olivia?"

She shook her head with enough emphasis to splay her hair across her shoulders. "Evan and I have a condo. He's been staying with Dad while I was in Tennessee."

"You should still recognize something out here." James wasn't tactful about doubting Zach's memory loss. "Olivia brought you to our home a few times." The older man spread his arms along the back of his seat, a guy who owned his world. "I didn't trust you then, either."

"Dad," Olivia began.

Zach held out his hand to stop her. He didn't want to be a wedge between her and her cynical, overprotective father. "I can't explain what happened to me in that crash, but I don't believe I'm capable of abandoning Olivia—even if I didn't know about the baby."

Zach waited for Kendall's snide response, but the other man slid his gaze toward his daughter. The unhappiness on her face made him lock his jaw and turn to the window.

Zach followed his example, still searching for something he might recognize. High brick walls and stately trees planted at regular intervals between wide sidewalks and the street indicated a more exclusive area. Ivy climbed over the bricks into lawns well protected from the streets. Beyond the fences, houses that belonged to families like the Kendalls, rose toward the sky.

Some were brick, some stucco, some just glass-and-wood. All off-limits to a guy like him. James Kendall had wasted a lot of time. He hadn't needed to meet them at the airport. Even if he'd driven here with Olivia, Zach would have seen this wasn't his life. He wouldn't feel at home here, couldn't imagine belonging.

How would his son, a native of wealth and privilege, feel about a stranger who came from a place of cold streams and dark forests, where steel and glass and old money hardly ever showed up? Not only would Zach never make the kind of income the Kendalls enjoyed, he'd come back from the dead. He tried to imagine standing in his son's shoes. This situation was bewildering for an adult.

Kendall's driver turned in at the tallest walls Zach had seen yet. The car rolled to a stop in front of wrought iron gates and the driver put down his window to punch a code into the numbered panel on the intercom stand. The gates slid open on a drive that led through a winding tree-bordered lawn dotted with green shrubbery.

It didn't look much like a boy's playground.

The driveway widened, and a Tudor-style mansion hovered behind a long walk of precision-cut hedges. The whole estate could have been lifted out of the

English countryside, but it was as much Evan's world as the one he shared with Olivia.

For a moment Kendall's rudeness made sense. Zach couldn't compete. Sure, he had a huge family who'd love Evan to distraction. He'd already begun clearing the bike paths of his youth for Lily, and Evan, who'd been guarded from babyhood might enjoy the freedom of running free in primitive woods. But Evan probably owned a lot of Kendall toys Zach couldn't match.

A glance at James's self-satisfied reflection in the window told Zach he and Kendall were sharing the same thoughts. Olivia took her family's fortune in stride, but her father saw things Helene's way.

"It's not that big." Olivia looped her hair behind her ear. "Don't let Dad get to you."

Good advice. And he'd have to hope she'd kept her father from getting to Evan, too.

They parked in front of wide, stone steps. Immediately, iron-studded, double doors swept open and a dark-suited man floated somberly out, like a butler in an old black-and-white movie.

Ian opened the car door for his employer. James got out and Olivia followed him. Zach climbed out behind her, his heart thrumming with a shuddering beat as he waited for a small boy to burst out of the house.

"Where's Evan?" Olivia asked.

James looked surprised. "Upstairs, probably, with his nanny."

"Nanny?" Zach looked at Olivia, questioning. She'd said the nanny had helped her when Evan was a baby. A nanny now hardly matched Zach's image of trying to live a "normal" life.

Olivia took her briefcase and purse from Ian with a swift thank-you smile. "I told you about Mrs. Nedland. She retired when Evan started kindergarten a few months ago, but I asked her to help Dad while I was away."

He nodded. A more generous guy might be glad his son had access to so many people who truly cared about him.

"Let us show you our home again." James Kendall led the way up the steps, speaking in a tone as gratified as his expression.

"Dad, I want to see Evan, and I'd really like you to stop being rude to Zach."

"I'll ask Mrs. Nedland to bring Evan down." The older man sailed on, ignoring his daughter's frustration.

Zach stopped the second his feet touched marble in the wide front hall. The ceiling dwarfed them all. Pale, red-tipped white roses spilled over the lip of an oriental bowl on a huge, ancient table. Their perfect scent filled the air. Not too sweet, not too floral.

Footsteps on wood drew Zach's gaze. Ian was carrying their bags up one side of the curving, paneled stairs that split the back of the hall into two wings. Olivia dropped her things on the table as if scratches didn't matter. Her father, lord of this manor, spread his arms with a proud flourish.

Zach fought an intimidated urge to push past both of them and the bodyguard and find his son. This meeting needed to happen before Kendall and Zach's own doubts convinced him he might be inappropriate for his child to know.

"Let's wait in my study," James said.

"We could go up to Evan." To hell with patience. Zach didn't want to lose another second.

"I agree, Dad. I'm tired of your games."

"I'd like to talk to you both." The other man took a deep breath and looked as if he was making a great effort. "Please."

Zach suspected James of starting another game.

"Dad." Olivia's tone said she agreed with Zach again.

Zach shared a glance with her, but she fell in line behind her father. Seeing no other choice, he followed them through another tall set of double doors into a library.

Excess reigned here as well. Zach took in burgundy leather walls broken only by wide bookshelves stuffed with leather-bound volumes. Apparently, no one here read paperbacks.

A wooden staircase spiraled up to a balcony that bordered a second level of bookshelves. No paperbacks up there either. Just the Kendall collection of tomes last read by whom?

Zach stroked his upper lip, where sweat had begun to bead in response to a different kind of fear than his flying phobia. His farmhouse would probably fit on its side in this room. Evan's life here looked less and less compatible with a future in Bardill's Ridge.

James led the way to one of the leather sofas scattered between two man-size fireplaces. "Take a seat, Zach. Are you cold, Olivia? I can have a fire lit."

"No, thanks, Dad. Just call Evan."

James headed for the desk in front of ivory-draped, arched windows. Olivia loitered in front of a leather armchair, clearly too restless to sit. Kendall was trying to control her and Evan. He didn't want them stepping out of his reach. Zach recognized the symptoms because such maneuvers were all that remained of his and Helene's relationship.

Across the room, out of hearing range, James lifted a telephone receiver and spoke in a low voice. Zach crossed to his son's mother, his footsteps resounding on the hardwood floor.

She looked up before he reached her side. He searched her gaze, questioning again what they'd really been to each other.

He resisted a compulsion to touch her. They were planning to share a son, nothing more, but surely he could offer her comfort and gratitude in exchange for coming to find him, for the kindness she'd shown on the plane.

Forget James Kendall. Olivia was the one with the say-so around here, and she'd done everything possible to bring Evan and him together. With a glance at her father, he took her hand.

"Thank you." He needed to say it before Evan came or her father got off the phone. "You could have made this hard for me." Another thought sent an ugly chill down his spine. "You might have decided not to tell me at all."

Her half smile meant more to him than he wanted to admit. Unlike her father, she wasn't a gameswoman. She listened when he spoke to her, and she didn't seem to be planning her next move. With a start, he realized he wanted to trust her.

"I wouldn't hide Evan from you." She glanced over her shoulder. "Though I'm starting to think I should have taken him to Bardill's Ridge to meet you instead of dragging you here."

"I don't blame your father." That much was true. "I don't understand why he'd try to keep me away from Evan, but I believe he's trying to provide his own idea of protection."

"I hoped we'd all try to help you feel comfortable." She shrugged, looking younger, less assured. "Dad doesn't understand how I can risk letting Evan love someone else."

"I've grasped his territorial leanings, but I thought he was upsetting you. Don't worry about what he says to me."

"He'll get used to you. I won't give him any other choice." Olivia turned toward her father with a hint of his own arrogance in her posture.

"I'm not sure I could be as—unselfish as you in similar circumstances."

"Yes, you could. Have you ever wanted to cut Helene out of Lily's life?" She freed her hand. "No matter how difficult your relationship has been?"

"I haven't." He grinned. "Not seriously, anyway." He'd fought for every moment with Lily. He couldn't imagine having real time with his son without having to struggle for it. He was used to thinking twice about every word that came out of Helene's mouth, looking for her real demands in the undercurrents. The trick to getting along with Olivia would be learning to assume she had no ulterior motives.

"We're going to be fine." They just might be. Olivia looked up. "We are a kind of family unit from now on," he said. "And Evan's going to be fine. I promise."

A pulse quivered in the hollow where Olivia's collarbones met. Watching it, mesmerized, he clenched his hands to keep from touching her again.

"We can't turn back," she said.

"I don't want to." He hardly knew what he was saying. "I'm not the most diplomatic guy, and trust isn't my strong suit, but I'm grateful for the chance you're giving me with my son—that you were able to forgive me."

He got it all wrong of course. Being inept was his talent. He'd been the same with Helene, never grasping what she'd needed from him. When he couldn't be the hero she wanted, she'd held back love that might have saved their ailing marriage. Starving even now from that famine, it was too easy to be attracted to a woman who loved unselfishly.

James Kendall circled his desk, trailing his fingertips over the burnished top. "Evan's coming down." His suspicious voice injected reality into the charged atmosphere. Olivia stepped away. The movement made her father suspicious. "What do you think of the house, Zach? Not what you're used to?"

"It's great." He couldn't care less about a stack of bricks and expensive wood. He glanced toward the door, anticipating Evan's approach.

Olivia pushed her hands into her jacket pockets, facing her father. "Don't start again. Before Evan gets down here, let me make this clear. You have to stop trying to intimidate Zach."

"You don't want him to understand his son's life?"

"He's lived in a two-bedroom condo since the day we left the hospital."

"Your condo overlooks Lake Michigan. What can you offer him, Zach?"

A grandfather decked and laid out on his own marble floor. "Whatever Evan needs from me, I'll give him."

"You'll be there?" Kendall smiled, actually pleased with Zach's lack of specifics. "In Tennessee, while Evan's living here. You don't see the problem?"

"I don't want to cut you out of Evan's life, sir, but you're his grandfather. Olivia and I are his parents. You seem to be spoiling for a fight, and I can oblige, but Evan will be happier if we give him a united family."

In the ringing silence, small shoes slapped the hall floor and a boy appeared in the massive doorway. Wearing grown-up attire, khakis and a polo shirt, he looked tiny.

He had eyes for no one except Olivia.

"Mom!"

He flew across the room, launching himself at Olivia with so much force she staggered backward, laughing. Her smile, over Evan's pale blond flyaway hair seemed to change the room's light.

She looked at him for a moment, but then she closed her eyes. Happiness softened her face as she clung to their son. Though she'd spent only two days away from Evan, they both acted as if she'd been parted from him for a month or more. Sharing him would not be easy for her, and Zach vowed to cause her as little pain as possible.

Evan locked his legs around her waist. Spellbound, Zach felt self-conscious. The exuberant boy hadn't yet noticed him, and he had to ask himself if he was doing the right thing.

This was his child—not a baby. Evan had said his first word a long time ago, written his name the first time, had his first nightmare and needed comfort. He was full of five years of life Zach had missed, and Zach didn't want to screw him up.

"I drove a go-cart, Mom. And I ate three hot dogs. And Grampa says I can have a puppy."

"You're bribing him with dogs, Dad?" Laughter in her voice made Zach smile, too.

"A man does what he must." Even James softened around his grandson.

Evan slid down his mom's body. "Can I have the puppy?" When he touched the floor, he caught her hand and swung hard, but almost fell when he finally saw Zach.

"Hello, sir," he said.

Zach blinked. He'd never heard a five-year-old child call anyone sir. His closest cousins had no children, but a more distant cousin's daughter called most strangers by the generic "you." Lily managed the occasional "mister," but she usually needed prompting.

"Hi," he said. "I'm—" Words deserted him. He didn't want to scare Evan. He and Olivia hadn't even talked about what Evan would call him. The last thing he wanted was for this polite little boy to call him dad because he technically fit the bill.

"I'm Zach Calvert."

"Mr. Calvert." The boy stuck out a hand and

shook Zach's in a surprising grip. "Do you work for my mom? She can show you a picture of my puppy when I get him."

Zach glanced over Evan's head at Olivia. She curved her hands around their son's shoulders and then straightened to look at her own father.

"We could use a few minutes."

Indecision pinched James Kendall's nose. Zach knew a moment's empathy. Kendall had filled both his own and part of Zach's role for the past five years. It couldn't be easy to accept a stranger, especially when he'd thought Zach had deserted his daughter.

"I'll be down the hall," James Kendall said. "If you need me, Olivia…"

"Thanks, Dad." She left Evan and walked her father to the door, her hand on his shoulder, reassuring. Despite their tendency to bicker, they were close, this small family that couldn't be more different from Zach's own.

James flashed one last warning glance as he shut the doors. Olivia took her time coming back. Evan planted his feet a shoulder's width apart and locked his hands behind his back as uneasy as if he'd picked up some of the room's tension.

"Am I in trouble, Mom?" He peered at Zach, his expression wary. "Do you work at my school?"

Olivia laughed. "You're not in trouble, but since you're feeling guilty, I should probably give school a call."

"Are you mad at me?" Evan asked. "You sound weird."

"It's because I want you to like this man. He's

important to you but we don't seem to know how to tell you who he is.''

"You're right," Zach said. "We're making it worse, and it's not bad news, Evan.'' He wouldn't want to spring similar news on Lily, but they had to get it over with. He knelt beside his son so they could meet eye to eye. "At least I hope you'll be glad. Do you know any children whose moms and dads have maybe split up?''

"You mean like getting avorced?''

"Divorced." Olivia joined them, also on her knees. "But your daddy and I didn't get divorced.''

Right. Zach floundered. How did you come back from the supposed dead so that a five-year-old could take it in without being scarred for life? "I'm looking for a frame of reference.''

"Just get to the point.''

Evan made a slight strangling sound, responding to his parents' voices. Tears gathering in his eyes did the trick.

"Your mother and I knew each other a long time ago before you were born. We were together back then." So far, so good. "But I had to go on a trip, and when your mom found out you were coming she couldn't find me. I had an accident, and I didn't remember her—because I forgot things after I got hurt.''

"You forgot my mom?" Evan's eyes—as green as Zach's own—went round with shock. Zach couldn't help grinning. Olivia didn't seem forgettable to him either.

"Worse than that, I didn't know she was going to have you, so when you were born, I didn't know I should come and be your dad.'' He stopped to let it all sink in. He waited anxiously for Evan's response, which seemed to come after a slight delay.

The little boy's face wrinkled as if he might cry. ''My dad?'' Evan backed up. His hands slid to his sides, and he paled. ''You're my—''

Olivia caught him, looping her arm around his waist. ''Would that be so bad, Evan?''

He swallowed, his throat working. His pulse beat in the nest of his collarbones, just like Olivia's. ''I always wanted a dad.''

Zach smiled as the little boy deliberated. Evan leaned into Olivia's knee, but looked up at him. ''Where do you live now? Do you have an apartment like ours?''

''I live in Tennessee.''

Evan looked up at Olivia. ''Do you think we'll like Tennessee, Mom?''

She gasped. At the same time, the double doors at the back of the room popped open, and James Kendall all but fell on his face.

It was almost funny, a media czar listening at the keyhole, except Zach figured he might stand a better chance with his son if he got to know Evan away from his grandfather.

SHARING AN UNEATEN LUNCH with her dad, Olivia couldn't get her mind off Evan and Zach at their private repast in the nursery upstairs. She'd offered to join them, but Evan wanted to show his dad his ''stuff.''

''Can you believe he calls him dad already?'' she said.

Her own father grabbed her slight dismay as if it were a lifeline. "I thought you'd be pleased. You can always ask Evan to wait until he knows Zach a little better."

"No. I am glad." She picked up her fork and stared at her plate, never less hungry in her life. "But I thought he'd need me to help ease him over the beginning."

"Feeling abandoned again?"

"By my son, Dad, not by Zach." She carefully replaced the fork. "Feeling abandoned isn't healthy."

"It's human. What can Zach give him that we can't provide more of? Why didn't you stop to think before you dragged this man back into our lives?"

"I could think the whole thing through a hundred times and still come back to the same answer. Zach and Evan have a right to know each other, to love each other if they can."

"Zach is new to Evan—like that puppy he wants." Her dad harrumphed into his coffee cup. "My one comfort is the image of Zach with his knees around his ears at that nursery table."

Despite a reluctance to encourage her father, Olivia smiled. They'd both done time at that table. Evan considered the nursery his private domain, and he'd put together "entertainments" for them that included pitched battles between hundred-year-old iron soldiers, ABC lessons he taught on the chipped blackboard that had once been Olivia's, and a cool train set her father had bought for Evan because he'd always wanted one for himself.

"Zach's probably having as much fun as we do up there."

"So hoping he stabs himself with a utensil would be too extreme."

Olivia pushed back her chair. "You have to get a grip. Don't force Evan to choose between you."

"I've been with him since the day he was born. Do you actually want him to choose?"

"Please, I can't take another helping of your patriarch speech. And think about this, Dad. I moved to the condo in the first place because you kept trying to run Evan's and my lives. I was scared, even with Mrs. Nedland, and I could have used your help with Evan. I missed you and I missed my home. I'm determined to give Zach a fair chance with our son even if you don't think he deserves one, and you don't want to force him to do the same thing I did—move Evan away from you when he has him."

"He'll take him to Tennessee. We'll never see them together. And, by the way, have you forgotten he left you?"

She ignored the heart-twisting idea of her son spending so much time in Tennessee when she lived here. "Zach had no choice."

"So he says. I think he could have explained enough to keep you from worrying before he went."

"I would have worried when he didn't come back no matter what he said." She couldn't tell if her dad still believed Zach was lying about his amnesia, or if he needed an extra dose of anger to shore up his position. Sometimes her father was the small child in their family. "So stop trying to change my mind about him. Zach is Evan's father. Evan obviously needs him. I'm nearly as frightened as you of what I might be giving up, but you're not making this easier.''

"Nor am I required to until I believe Zach means you and Evan no harm. I've never ducked a responsibility.''

"I almost wish you would.'' She shook her head, exasperated and a little disappointed in him. "You always want to arrange life to your specifications. In your mind you and Evan and I are fine. Why fix what isn't broken?''

"Right.'' He was brazen.

"And Zach should pay because he didn't spill his guts before he was injured, but that's wrong. I'm asking you to be my dad. Don't make problems for Zach because when you do, you put me in the middle.''

He frowned. "I'd never hurt you.''

"You wouldn't mean to.''

"I'm being the careful one because you're making reckless decisions. What do you really know about Zach Calvert?''

"We beat this dead horse before I went to Tennessee, Dad. I know everything I could find out about him.''

"And his relationship with his ex-wife?''

He had no right to anything Zach had told her about his private life, so she glossed over her own concerns. "Helene tries to keep him away from Lily because she feels Lily could have a better life with her stepfamily's money.''

"I think she shows a little sense.''

"You wouldn't if you weren't afraid of Zach breaking up that empire you always brag about. Evan and I aren't your possessions or your subjects. We're

people, and he's a little boy who finally has a father."
She paused for a deep breath. What she wanted to say
next refused to come easy. They weren't the most
affectionate father and daughter. They often circled
each other with heads sore from their battles. "Just
the way I need you," she said.

"But I—" He stopped, planting his hands on the
table as he stood, his face tight with emotion. He
came around the table and knelt beside her, his knees
popping.

Touched—he'd never looked so distraught or so
loving—she pretended not to notice.

Without the least hint of ease, her father put his
arms around her and nudged her to lean close. She
relaxed against him. Funny how even such reluctant
reassurance still worked wonders.

"Thanks, Dad."

"I'd protect you with my life."

"I feel the same about Evan." It was a warning.
For her son's sake, she'd wreak havoc if her father
couldn't stop flinging challenges at Zach.

"I'd better let you in on something, Olivia."

"Huh?"

"I scheduled a press conference."

She stiffened, disbelieving—angry and hurt in
equal parts. His unusual affection had taken her in.
"You've got to be kidding. Dad—you planned to tell
them about Zach?"

He leaned back. Incredibly, he seemed surprised.
"Most of the invitees are from our own stations. Do
you want the world to make assumptions about
Zach's relationship to you and Evan, or do you want
us to tell them what they need to know?"

She sputtered, unable to speak, much less come up with an answer. "You're talking spin about Evan. How can you forget he's your grandson?"

"Why do I have to explain? Have you forgotten your prom pictures on the cover of our magazines and our major competitors?"

"I haven't forgotten you tipped off the photographers."

He had the grace to look embarrassed. "I knew your entry into college might become news, especially when you refused to go to Princeton as our family has done for generations. I wanted the other news outlets to accept a story we wanted, not chase you down on your first day of classes."

"And how'd you feel about the way it worked out?"

"If you hadn't dated a dope-smoking hophead, we would have had our prom story, and everyone else would have been sick of you by the time you started college."

"I'm not going to argue about one date with a guy I hardly knew. No one else wanted to take me to the prom because they knew you might turn up with a camera crew." She pressed her hands to her ears. "You always distract me with a ridiculous argument, Dad, but Tommy Pitt's single foray into pot illustrates my point. You can't control what anyone prints about us. Cancel the press conference. People will forget about me. I can't believe anyone will care."

"Stop trying to forget who you are."

She'd had enough. "Try to remember your grandson and put his happiness before yours."

"How can I forget Evan? I couldn't love him more,

but you know how long I've dreaded the truth splashing all over the news. I can't ignore the story, and you can bet no one else will. All our rivals will gladly spew pages and the longest on-air minutes I've had to endure about my daughter's illicit affair with a long-lost lover and the son he abandoned." He rose, rubbing his knees as they fired more angry gunshots.

This time his frailty didn't endear him to Olivia. "You're still ashamed?"

He stared at her, nodding at last. "I didn't raise you to make a mistake like that, Olivia, and I've protected you from most of the consequences since the day I found out you were pregnant."

"Consequences? Evan is the only consequence I care about and I'm not ashamed of him. You will not make a confession for me that makes you feel better in front of all your cronies and enemies."

"Stay out of my way for a change and see if I don't handle it right."

"You're betraying my wishes about Evan." A key phrase their counselor had taught them. "Cancel it."

"If I don't?"

"I'll take him away from here, away from you again. I've forgiven you every story you ever leaked about me, but I thought you understood about Evan. I thought you loved us both enough to let the past go."

He shook his head as if he couldn't believe what she'd said. "I understand reality better than you do. Let me protect my grandson. You seriously don't care if people find out the truth about his birth?"

She gritted her teeth. Time for a little havoc. "You aren't welcome in his life or mine until you find a way to take that back."

CHAPTER SIX

IN A CORNER of the dim hall near the nursery, Olivia turned her back to the wall. Control. Before she burst into that room, she had to get herself under control. She'd hidden here once before when she was barely in kindergarten herself. That morning, she'd panted just as hard as she did now.

Trying to sneak into breakfast before her dad noticed she was late, she'd overheard him warning his bodyguard du jour that someone had threatened to kidnap her. Her dad liked to pretend she didn't understand that his fame and their wealth made their family a target. But she'd known since that long-ago morning that her name could attract danger. She'd never liked being afraid, had refused to live in fear until Evan was born. To keep him safe, she'd live any way at all.

And if she had to take Evan away from his grandfather to keep him from finding out her dad had ever felt shame for his birth she'd be glad to do that.

She loved her dad dearly, but his feelings felt like a betrayal. At the best of times, he was difficult. She felt as if she was locked in an almost constant battle for power.

And now, this… To find out he still believed she'd disgraced him. Ridiculous.

She pushed away from the wall and smoothed her hands over her rumpled slacks. Two steps across the hall and she was almost herself. At the nursery door she knocked, unwilling to interrupt Evan's first private meal with his father. After a second, Evan opened the door, peering curiously around it.

"Mom?" He stepped back, not expecting to see her so soon. "Are you hungry? Did Grampa eat all your food?"

"No." Her father had robbed her of more spiritual sustenance—her trust in him. She gazed at Zach.

She didn't think he'd mind if she and Evan went to Bardill's Ridge, but consulting anyone about what she did with her son felt odd. The concept of sharing decisions had seemed less difficult in theory.

"You didn't have to knock," he said.

She closed her hands on Evan's shoulders. "I felt funny, barging in."

What she'd really come to say, "I'm taking my son away from here," refused to come out of her mouth. She had to speak up soon. Zach and Evan would notice, and time was short. Her father would no doubt carry on with his press conference.

Strangely, considering her father's feelings about her, she didn't want to expose the family's dirty laundry to Zach. As if Zach would be surprised. Her father had already flown his true colors, and Evan mattered more than misplaced family pride.

She nudged her son. "Could you get your soccer pictures? The ones beside Grampa's bed?"

Thank God for genetics. Evan laughed with joy at the opportunity to show off for his father. "I'll be right back," he said to Zach. He stopped a few feet away. "Don't go anywhere."

"Here to stay," Zach assured him.

Evan shot out of the room. Olivia hurried after him to close the door. A frown creased Zach's forehead as she turned back.

"What's up?" Perched exactly as her father had predicted, with his knees around his ears, Zach didn't look foolish. He looked vulnerable, like a man who'd do anything to build a loving relationship with his son. but foolish? No.

"My dad's arranged a press conference to give out a story about you. I can't stop him, but I don't want Evan here for it."

Zach clenched his hands. "Let's go to Tennessee."

"Thanks. I was going to ask if we could do that, but it might have taken me longer to be polite about intruding in your family's hometown."

"You thought I'd disagree? No way. My family will all want to meet Evan." Zach uncoiled from the table. "The town is quiet and small. We always know when strangers show up."

"That's what you said just before you knocked out the bank robber." She said it lightly, reluctant to let him see she was a little nervous about switching to his home ground.

A surprised smile curved his supple mouth. "You're safe." His glance roamed up her body and then down again, with a hint of possession that should have repelled her. She restrained a distinct urge to shiver as his smile deepened. "You're not sporting a gun," he said. "You have nothing to worry about."

"I have Dad. The ultimate loose cannon."

"He'd really parade Evan in front of a pack of reporters?"

She managed not to lift an eyebrow. He must have forgotten she was one of the pack. "Dad wants them to hear a suitable story." She shook her head in frustration. "The impulse wedding idea he tried out on us, maybe. Whatever—I'm not waiting around to let Evan hear."

"I still don't understand. What's the big deal to your father? This should be a good story. I'm grateful to find Evan. I hope he'll be glad to know me."

Subtlety wasn't working. "He doesn't want people to know how Evan was born." Her dad's embarrassment humiliated her. "People asked about his father, but I never answered, and finally they stopped asking. I've kept him away from anyone who ever wanted to talk about me or my work." She continued uneasily. "I never talk about him."

"What are you saying?"

"Dad doesn't want Evan to be labeled." Why should she try to protect her father? Even trying to explain his feelings dishonored hers and the life she'd tried to give Evan. Her face burned.

"James doesn't want anyone to know we weren't married?"

"I should thank you for putting it so delicately." She managed a nod. "So I'm getting Evan out of here before he finds out the strongest male influence in his life is spouting lies that make him suitable for the family."

Fury tightened Zach's features. He seemed to be searching for something to hit before he calmed down. "None of this was Evan's fault."

''No, it wasn't.'' She took a deep breath and jumped off the deep end, making her own intentions clear. She couldn't send her son away alone with him already. ''I'm willing to take Evan to Tennessee, but I *am* coming with him—and you.'' He didn't even blink, but she suddenly felt anxious about meeting his family when he hadn't wanted her to know them before. ''I have to call Evan's school, and I might have to pick up books for him so he can keep up with his class. We both need to pack.''

''You want to leave now?''

''I want out of this house as quickly as possible.'' She made no apology for her urgency. That her father cared what anyone thought of the circumstances of her son's birth made her sick.

''I'll make the arrangements this time,'' Zach said. ''For this afternoon?''

''Yes.'' In her mind she was already laying out Evan's clothes at home. ''My car should be in the garage.''

''Doesn't he have things here?''

''I'm leaving them.''

Zach nodded, looking up as Evan skipped through the nursery door. The tension seemed to escape him. He held out his photos to Zach, slipping his free hand shyly behind his own back as he danced from foot to foot.

''Look how strong you are,'' Zach said. ''You're the goalie?''

Evan nodded, his gaze solemn. ''I like soccer.''

''Do you think you could teach me?'' Zach asked.

Evan straightened, anticipation almost lifting him off his feet. He was enough of a Kendall to like being the head guy. "Sure," he said. "I have soccer balls at home." He grabbed Olivia's hand. "We could take my dad to the park."

"We could do that," Zach said. "Or you and your mom could come to Tennessee with me for a visit. I have a big yard."

Evan spun around to look up at Olivia, who forced herself to smile. "Would you like to visit Tennessee?" She almost asked if he wanted to meet Zach's family, but stopped when she remembered Lily. They still had to decide how to tell Evan about his sister.

"Sure, I want to go. Can we take Grampa's airplane?"

"That's a great idea," Olivia said. The company jet would be the quickest, most private way out of town. Olivia hugged her son close while Zach eyed her doubtfully over Evan's head. But he didn't argue. Thank God for a man who didn't argue. "I'll call from my car," she said. "Let's go."

As soon as Olivia parked in their building's garage, Evan jumped out of the car and skipped toward the elevator.

Zach leaned down, speaking quietly enough to defeat the building's echo. "I need to warn Helene," he said. "I want her to hear about Evan from me, not your father."

Olivia nodded. "We'll give you some privacy. I'll ask Evan to help me pack."

"C'mon, Mom, Dad!" Evan was holding the doors for them.

Olivia hurried. "There's only one elevator down

here from the lobby. I always picture a crowd pil-
ing up.''

Zach laughed, taking one step for each of her two.
Evan punched the button for the lobby floor as soon
as Zach got inside behind her. The car quickly rose
and then jerked to a halt.

"We have to switch elevators here," Evan said.

A doorman guarded the lobby. He nodded, showing
no curiosity as they strolled past.

"I always drive." Evan dashed inside the next elevator car. When they caught up, he jabbed the metal
disk embossed with the number twenty-three and the
doors slid shut. They rose again at rapid speed,
stopped more smoothly and exited into a parquet-
floored hallway. James Kendall had been right, Zach
noted as the oriental runner muffled his footsteps.
This was no apartment building he'd ever seen.

At the far end of the hall, Olivia fished keys from
her purse and unlocked the door. Evan sped through,
but turned back, just managing to clear the edge of
an inlaid cabinet.

"Dad, come see my room. It's cool!"

Laughing, Zach followed his son who powered
through a vast living room that was homelike rather
than the monument to wealth Olivia had lived in with
her father. Zach glimpsed fat couches and magazine-
strewn tables.

"Come on, Dad!"

"Wait." Olivia spoke softly as she bolted the front
door. "The phone's in here. You can take it to the
terrace if you want." Her smile looked a little shaky
at the corners. "I don't mean to push you, but we
should move. The jet's waiting for us."

"I want to make sure Helene understands she needs to protect Lily, too."

Olivia frowned. "I didn't think about that. I'm sorry."

He shook his head, not wanting to add to the pressure on her. Dealing with an ex-wife was all new, another complication she'd added to her life, so that he and Evan çould be together. "I'll try to keep this as painless as possible for you," he said. "Let me take a quick look at Evan's room, and then I'll call."

"You'll probably have to remind him we're on a deadline," Olivia said.

"Okay." Functioning as part of a two-parent team felt atypical. He and Helene had divorced when Lily was two, and they'd struggled continually since.

"Which room?" he asked. "I lost track of him." Because he'd been so intent on Olivia.

"Second on the right."

"I'll help him pack."

"I'd better do it. I know what he'll need."

"I'll start, and you can add the stuff I leave out." He'd like to make this escape easier for her, but her resources were the ones taking them out of Kendall's reach. Olivia could do everything she needed for herself.

At the bedroom door, Zach caught Evan just as he tripped over the man-size dragon he'd been hauling across the rug. "This is Burt," Evan said. "Grampa gave him to me. I sleep on him sometimes."

Big, green and threadbare at forepaw and sagging belly, Burt had been loved hard. "He looks comfy." Zach helped Evan carry the toy back to the bed on which he'd already laid out his soccer ball and shin guards and a red-and-white-striped shirt.

"Here's my soccer stuff. You really don't know how to play?"

Gazing at his son's small, upturned face, Zach felt an urge to smooth Evan's unruly blond hair back from his forehead. He held back, trying to make himself feel that this child was his, that Evan would be part of his life from now on. It didn't seem possible yet.

"We didn't play soccer in school when I was your age."

Evan frowned as if his newfound father might be a little on the crazy side. He tugged Zach toward the closet. "It won't be hard to teach you," he said.

Zach cleared thick emotion from his throat, grateful Evan didn't seem to share his grown-up responses to their situation. "Thanks," he choked out and then tried again. "Do you have a suitcase?"

Evan tugged him inside a closet as large as Zach's kitchen. "I left my dinosaur bag at Grampa's. That's the only one I like."

"Maybe we could choose another one together." But where to start? Enough clothing for three or four kids surrounded them on hangers and in drawers. Shoes for a classroom full of children waited neatly in racks at just the right height for Evan to reach. But not a suitcase in sight.

"Mom'll pack for me. Look at my hockey stick." Evan produced it from a corner, along with a scratched helmet. He pointed to a line of slightly crooked scrapes in the paint. "See? Tanya Randall tried to bite me, but she got my helmet instead."

"Lucky for you." Zach grinned.

"Yeah, she's pretty strong, but I can run faster."

Zach swallowed another smile. Smart kid. "She put you to the test, huh? You like sports a lot?"

Evan nodded his head up and down. "Me and Tanya are on a lot of the same teams." He peered at Zach through one considering eye. "Do you know how to play *anything?*"

How often did a guy's son ask him if he was a real man? "I'm pretty good at baseball, and I was a running back on the football team in college." He shared a look of commiseration with his boy. "I know a girl like your friend, Tanya." His cousin Sophie threw harder than the strongest boys they'd ever played with. "So I can run fast, too." Evan still looked unimpressed. Zach got desperate. He pulled out his trump card, the one activity that had fascinated him for most of his life. "I know how to fly airplanes."

Evan let his mouth drop open, staring as if he didn't dare believe. "Really? All by yourself? Could you fly us to Tennessee?"

He'd kept current. Even if the Navy didn't trust him with their equipment anymore and he felt sick when he got near an airport, he'd forced himself into the air to keep his licenses up to date. "I could, but your mom's pilot might not want to share."

"He probably wouldn't." Olivia sounded surprised.

As Zach turned, her gaze asked if he'd forgotten his little problem with flying.

He smiled, feeling foolish.

Olivia held out her hand. "Evan, you and I have to pack, and Zach wants to use the phone."

"Ours, though?" Evan tightened his grip and

begged with his eyes. Zach felt guilty for their missing years. "You're not going out to the car or somewhere to use a different phone?"

"He'll be right here when we're ready." Olivia reassured him, but his attachment obviously left her shaken.

Her pale skin and wary gaze troubled Zach. She must have known what she was asking for, but maybe she hadn't fully anticipated how it felt to have your child want someone else.

He'd always envied parents who managed to stay together. If he'd come back from that mission, would they have married? He'd certainly have asked her. He'd asked Helene.

How had he felt about Olivia? Had she loved him? Would they still have loved each other after an unexpected child and her father's disapproval? She would have tried to keep a marriage going. It might have been the same kind of battle he'd fought with Helene, but they'd both have been sincere about staying together. He knew, because she was so determined to be fair about giving him time with Evan now.

He resisted an urge to wrap his arms around her as he passed her on his way to the living room. Just as well, since she inched away from him. He reminded himself not to get carried away. She'd come to him for Evan's sake, not for his.

As he dialed Helene's number, Zach leaned back, listening to the comforting sounds of Olivia and Evan talking together as they packed. A stranger answered Helene's phone, a servant he hadn't met yet. He asked for his ex-wife.

Her greeting chilled the line. They'd long ago stopped trusting each other, but two days with Olivia had him wondering if he should have been able to salvage a healthier relationship with his ex-wife.

"Helene, I need your help," he said.

She didn't answer right away, and when she did, surprise colored her "What kind of help?"

"I have to tell you something that's a little hard to understand."

"I'm no idiot, Zach."

The one accusation they'd avoided before now. "I mean hard to understand because it doesn't happen often. After the bank robbery, someone in Chicago— a woman—saw my photo on the news."

"A woman?" Though she'd left him for Leland Nash, she could still sound upset at the thought of someone in his past.

"A woman I knew when I was training before that last mission."

"She was in Chicago?"

"I knew her well, Helene."

"So I assume. What are we really talking about?"

"I have a son."

Silence. Filled with hostility. But then she released a shaky sigh. "I guess that explains a lot."

She'd always contended he must have loved someone else. She hadn't necessarily believed it was someone in his past, but that was an old horse he didn't intend to beat anymore.

"My son's mother is Olivia Kendall. One of the Kendall Press Kendalls, and her father is holding a press conference tonight."

"Good God."

"Exactly," he said, relieved at her compassion. "So, Helene, could you keep Lily away from the television? And can you wait to let me tell her about Evan?"

"Evan would be her brand-new brother?"

"I'm hoping they'll like each other. Lily will be better off if you don't paint a bad picture of this situation before I can tell her."

"Maybe this works for me, too."

So much for compassion. "Forget it. Evan doesn't take Lily's place with me."

She sighed again, but he knew he was right. He'd tangled with Helene too many times to be naive about her tactics.

"When do you want to talk to Lily?"

"We're flying back to Tennessee this afternoon. I'd like to see her tonight, just to be safe."

"All right. Call me when you land. If she's awake, and she's finished her dance and piano practice, you can drop by."

Why did she have to keep Lily so busy at four years old? Annoyance tightened his grip on the phone, but what was the point of yet another argument? "I'll call you."

He'd barely set down the phone when it rang again. Instinctively, he picked up the receiver. The caller ID read out James Kendall's name. Not bothering to unlist his number went along with the older man's arrogance.

The phone rang again. Olivia came into the hall, her black hair swathing one shoulder, her eyes anxious.

"Your dad," he said.

"I guessed."

Without thinking, he clicked the phone's on button and lifted the receiver to his ear. Olivia took a few impatient steps toward him, and he regretted acting, but too late.

In his ear, James Kendall's voice spoke his daughter's name.

"Maybe you and I should talk," Zach said.

"What the hell—"

"Your problem is with me, not with Olivia. Maybe you and I should talk."

Olivia hesitated. Zach took her pause as permission to proceed.

"I'd drop the press conference plan if I were you."

"Fortunately, you're not, since I know how to run my business and my family and you don't."

"I'm making this suggestion because I see how upset Olivia is." Zach went for broke. "I already told you I don't want to take your place with my son, but I'm afraid you have to make room for me. For Evan's sake."

"You don't understand who you're talking to."

"I'm talking to my child's grandfather. I've kept your relationship with Evan in mind from the first word you spoke to me, but understand I'm not going anywhere. You and I might as well get along."

"Put my daughter on the line."

Zach hadn't expected miracles. He'd just wanted to state his position. He carried the phone to Olivia, who half smiled as he handed her the receiver.

"Sorry," Zach said, and he actually meant it. "I hope I haven't made it worse, but Evan will be better off if Kendall and I can share the same breathing space.''

Olivia shrugged. "I've been trying to explain since I found out about you. He always assumes I'm still his little girl and I need direction."

"I doubt I'll ever see Lily any other way, but maybe your dad is teaching me to keep my mouth shut when the time comes."

OLIVIA WAS ASLEEP when Evan hitched himself into the leather chair next to Zach's on the Kendall jet. Evan pointed to his mom, sprawled on a tan couch, her feet crossed at the ankles, one hand across her face as if to block out the light with her slender, splayed fingers.

"Mommy's snoring."

Evan's long-suffering tone made Zach laugh. "I didn't hear her."

"She scared me. I was falling asleep, too, but I thought she was choking on something." Evan bounced against the cushion at his back. "You don't have to wear your seat belt on this plane."

The plush surroundings Evan took for granted only slightly eased Zach's compulsion to grip the nearest stable object. He tucked his hand around the seat belt he'd securely fastened before they took off. "I like wearing seat belts. You should put on yours, too."

"Mommy's not wearing one."

Even in her sleep she swayed with perfect balance against the jet's slight movements. "Your mommy's used to flying."

"You are, too," Evan said.

"Oh, yeah." What the hell had he been thinking?

He hadn't thought at all. He'd simply run down a shortcut into his son's heart. "But I'm also used to wearing seat belts. Do you like to fly?"

"Well, sure." Evan stuck out both his arms and tilted back and forth, whining an engine sound. Suddenly, he leaned across the chair arm. After a quick glance at Olivia, he pressed his cheek to Zach's shoulder. Clearly on the verge of confessing a secret he wanted to keep from his mom, he made Zach want to wrap him in a bear hug.

"I *really* want a horse," Evan said. "My mom said maybe I could get a pony, but they're for babies. I want a real horse—as big as you. And I bet I could ride better than those cowboys my grampa watches on TV."

Zach tried to picture James Kendall watching John Wayne movies. He couldn't. He weighed his answer to Evan's revelation. Evan had obviously talked to his mom about his cowboy dreams, and she'd put the kibosh on them.

"You know those guys on TV are a little older than you?"

Evan flopped into his seat, disgust written large all over his face. "You're just like my mom, but I'm big enough to have a horse. I'll ask Grampa."

Did that manipulative bent come from his Calvert side or the Kendalls? "Better stick with your mom's word on the horse, Evan."

"You're my dad, right?" He studied Zach with disappointment that hurt. A responsible dad shouldn't bribe a boy with horseflesh.

"I am your father."

"Then you can say I get a horse."

It never worked that way with Lily. And maybe this was a good time to bring her up. "That's not the way parents figure out what's best for their children. A lot of times dads or moms who can't live with their kids full-time want to give them more presents, but sometimes the children don't need those gifts. I already know that because I have a little girl, too."

"A girl?" Evan flicked a quick look at his mother. "Why doesn't she live with Mommy and me?"

Zach cringed inwardly. Would he ever look himself in the face again? He'd made a lot of mistakes all at the same time. "Lily lives with her mom." Helene was harder to explain, so he directed Evan's attention toward his new sister. "My little girl's name is Lily."

"But she's not my sister even though you're my dad?"

"She is your sister." Zach abandoned the concept of halves or steps. No way did he want Evan or Lily thinking the other meant more to him, or that they shouldn't love each other wholeheartedly.

"I always wanted a sister," Evan said. "Mom said she didn't think I'd have any—or a brother either." He grinned. "You don't have any more boys anywhere?"

God, he hoped not. "I only have you and Lily."

"How old is she?"

"Four. Do you think you'll like being an older brother?"

Evan straightened. His earnestness brought an ache to Zach's throat. "I'll take care of her, like Grampa and Mom take care of me."

Zach rested his hand on his son's nape for the first

time without wondering if it was all right to touch him.

"Lily's going to be as glad as I am that I found out about you." He pulled his boy toward him. "And I'm awfully glad, Evan."

His son pushed his elbow across the armrest to lean against Zach's side. "Me, too." He looked up, beaming with absolute, humbling trust. "Dad."

CHAPTER SEVEN

THEY LANDED at Knoxville and picked up Zach's car in the parking lot. Darkness had covered the mountain roads before they reached Bardill's Ridge. Evan nodded off just as they reached the town, his head braced in a hollow in the back seat.

Olivia glanced at him as Zach navigated the narrow streets to The Dogwood, his aunt's bed-and-breakfast. "Evan?" She hoped he wouldn't answer. He didn't even twitch an eyelid.

"He's asleep?" Zach asked.

"Seems to be." Moonlight gleamed in Zach's hair. His sharply drawn profile reminded her of nights long past, but she steeled herself against a need to touch the bright strands. After all this time, she couldn't remember if his hair was the same soft texture as Evan's.

She shook her head. Overhearing his conversation with Evan on the jet, she'd bided her time for a private moment with him. "I don't know how to start this."

He tightened his mouth. "You've changed your mind?"

"About coming here? No, but the next time you have something as important as Lily to talk about with Evan," she lowered her voice, "I hope you'll let us tell him together or at least that we'll talk about it beforehand."

He searched her face, his too-expressive eyes glinting with relief.

"I can't believe you don't know I'm not going to change my mind," she said.

"Yeah, well, I'm trying. You were awake on the plane?"

"Sort of, at first. I was wide-awake once you said Lily's name."

"I thought he needed to know before we got here. I asked my mom to keep the family away tonight, but my aunt and uncle might slip up and tell him."

"I agree, but a sister's news that should come from both of us."

His deep, patient breath annoyed her. "He seemed fine. You're sure this isn't you being afraid to let him go a little?"

Suspecting he might be a little right, she stiffened. "Don't condescend to me, Zach. I am afraid, but I'm capable of objectivity."

"Who can be objective about her own child?"

"Don't confuse me with—anyone else." But now that he'd brought her up… "You don't plan to talk to Lily without Helene?"

His extended silence wasn't quite an apology, but he avoided looking at her. "No."

"What makes it all right for you to talk to Evan without me?"

"You're not like Helene." Lowering his voice, Zach checked Evan in the rearview mirror. "I had to tell Helene first so I could judge how she'd react in front of Lily. You're more…''

She waited, but he didn't finish. Dancing in the minefield of his former marriage was tricky for both of them. "More what?"

"You put your child first. Helene isn't always capable of doing that." He hit his indicator switch and turned toward the brightly lit courthouse on the square.

"I'm not questioning you about Helene." At least she hoped she wasn't. She didn't much care for the pictures in her head of him with someone else. "She's none of my business, but you shouldn't assume I don't care just as much about Evan as she cares—as you care—about Lily."

"I wasn't trying to take over. The moment seemed right, so I told him. I didn't have an ulterior motive."

"But we're in this together as much as possible, right?" She'd better find out now if they thought about shared child care differently.

Zach nodded. "Sorry," he said in a curt tone.

No doubt thinking he hadn't chosen the most amenable moms for either of his children. "Maybe I'm blowing this out of proportion, but I'd rather make sure we sort out our problems before they turn into brawls."

"We're together on that, too."

The car didn't feel as comfortable after that. She followed the gleam of the courthouse lights on the wrought-iron fence around the square. This town, picturesque but terribly quiet, was going to be her son's part-time home from now on. With luck, he'd enjoy visiting here, but she couldn't help hoping he'd love Chicago more.

She gazed at Zach again, regretting her part in putting the remote expression on his handsome face. She had to get over the feeling he might disappear if they argued.

His eyes glittered as they passed beneath a streetlamp. She remembered him, on a night in her bedroom, when her father'd been out of town. The memory was so intense she felt as if she was back in that room again with the night sky behind his head as she'd gazed at him from her pillow. His eyes had shone in the moonlight that crept through the window. Shone with love, she'd thought.

She'd changed in the past six years, and so had he, but his green eyes could take her back to that time. She remembered too well when his broad lean shoulders had looked like the safest place to lay her head.

If she indulged in too many of those memories, she could get herself in trouble, and the prospect of falling for him again frightened her. Evan was the one who'd really lose if things went wrong between Zach and her.

As soon as he stopped his car in front of the bed-and-breakfast, Olivia shoved her door open and sprang to her feet. Gripping the cool door frame, she met Zach's curious gaze as he rose more slowly.

"What's up?" he asked, their discord already forgotten.

With plenty of valid reasons for being scared half to death, it wasn't hard to choose one. "I'm a stranger to you, but you're my son's father. You're going to want Evan to yourself, and I'm trying to imagine how I'll manage.''

With a wary gaze, Zach nodded. "Makes sense."

"Since I saw your picture," she said, leaning into the car's roof, "I've been thinking of Evan, of what and whom he needed. I've never been away for him for longer than five days. I've never had to listen to anyone else's opinion before I decided what was best for him.'' Well, except her father, but that wasn't so much listening as fighting a pitched battle.

Alarm filled Zach's eyes, but to his credit, compassion quickly followed. "I'm not asking you to leave him or to hand him over to me. I do want my share of time with him." He joined her at the front of the car. "But for now, I think you're telling me we won't have a formal custody agreement?"

Her throat went dry. She tried to swallow. "Thanks for understanding.''

"For now, you come with him when he comes to me. We'll work it out." He moved close with the impossible grace that had always made her want him. She looked away, but he curved his index finger beneath her chin. "You'll learn to trust me, and I'll figure out who you are," he said. "Because no matter what you say to me, or how you try to keep me at a distance that makes you feel safe, I can't believe I forgot you.''

"I'm not trying to keep you at a distance."

"You are." His assumption perturbed her, but he didn't seem to think it was important. "But it makes sense. I hurt you—accidentally, but I did hurt you— and I'm sorry for that.''

"That's all over now." She didn't want to talk about the past he didn't even remember. Slipping out of the pool of Zach's body heat, she reached for the back door handle. "We'd better take Evan inside. He's had a long day."

Zach caught her wrist. "Let me say one more thing. You don't have to be afraid." His gaze held her with the force of his promise. "We're not competing for Evan. I don't want him to love me more. I'll never try to make him choose me over you."

He understood her fears too well. "You've been through this with Lily."

"Often." A wry tone thinly disguised his regret.

"But was she so desperate for this Nash character that she called him Dad the second she met him?" Why not just undress all her fears? "Has Lily spent so much time with you that you're as familiar as a piece of her furniture? Do you wonder if Nash is new and more fun and a whole lot less strict? So that she won't want to come home to you again?"

Zach tugged her close, and she thought her skin might have caught on fire. Zach didn't understand all her fears, not the ones that focused on him.

But his large hand around her wrist spread comfort into her very bones. "A child needs his furniture around him. Stability rates much higher with children than they think." Zach's smile, though clearly meant to offer ease, lent his mouth a sensual curve. "I can't imagine thinking Evan would be better off with me. He's a great kid, and you're a great mom. Obviously."

"Do you really feel as if you're in competition with Helene?"

She had no right to ask, but she hated the pain that had changed him.

"Helene loves order." He shrugged. "And she believes in a caste system. I'm an untidy mess she'd like to forget, and my family is an embarrassment in her current station."

"Why?" She flushed at the squeak she couldn't control. A sheriff wouldn't spring from felons and murderers.

Zach laughed. "Don't worry. You won't come across us in the wanted posters behind my desk. But Helene's husband Nash and his family own half of East Tennessee. We Calverts are content to settle here on Bardill's Ridge, most of us. I didn't want more than that."

"Ever? You were homesick in Chicago, but you never said you were biding your time to escape the Navy and go home."

"I loved my job." His mouth quirked in a...familiar expression. Half the charm of this big, powerful man had been his ability to laugh at himself. "I just wish I could remember loving to fly."

"Is sheriffing as exciting as being a pilot?"

"Not until the bank robbery." Changing the subject, he opened the back seat. "You should probably wake Evan. I'll carry him, but I don't want to startle him."

She wanted more details. Her son would be spending a lot of time with his father the sheriff, but Zach, who'd told her more about himself than she'd expected, seemed to be setting boundaries where his job was concerned.

She leaned across the back seat, pulling Evan into her arms as Zach popped the trunk.

"Mom, are we home?"

"We're in Tennessee."

"I didn't dream about my daddy?"

His plaintive question put a lump in the back of her throat. "Your father's real." Backing awkwardly out of the car, she met Zach's warm gaze. She couldn't hold back a grin. The three of them together like this made her happy, even if her place in Bardill's Ridge was only temporary.

The Dogwood's front doors burst open. Olivia jumped, and Evan spun, tossing his longish hair in her face. A woman hurried down the sidewalk, her face strained with worry.

More gray streaked her dark chignon than had shown in the picture in Zach's apartment, but she was Zach's mother. Olivia's pulse strummed a nervous beat. Meeting Beth Calvert would have meant everything to her six years ago. The other woman shot into Zach's open arms, speaking in a Southern voice so distraught Olivia couldn't understand her.

"Who's Helene, Mom?" Evan asked.

"Helene?" Had he heard her talk with Zach?

"She said Helene. And James—that's Grampa?" Evan kicked to be let down. "Is my grampa here?" he demanded.

Olivia rubbed her mouth, feeling almost sick. Her father must have given the press conference after all.

"It's all right, Mom." Zach hugged Beth. "We expected him to do it. Look who I've brought."

Beth Calvert turned to Evan. Her face, a softened version of Zach's, crumpled, awash with tears.

"Oh," Olivia said, taken aback.

"Evan?" Beth added about three lilting, Tennesseean syllables to his name. "My grandbaby?"

Zach held out his hand to Evan. "This is your grandma Beth."

Their son hung back. Zach shifted his gaze to Olivia's. She smiled an apology at his mother. "He might be a little shy."

"It's okay," Beth said. "We have plenty of time now."

"My mother, Beth Calvert. Mom, this is Olivia Kendall."

Moving to shake Beth's hand, Olivia accidentally dragged Evan along because he'd clenched his fingers in the hem of her shirt.

"Nice to meet you, Mrs. Calvert." Olivia hugged her timid child. "This is Evan."

Happiness and anguish mixed in Beth's mobile features as she dropped to her knees on the cold, hard cement. She tucked her hands behind her back, but beamed with genuine affection at her newfound grandson.

Olivia restrained a strong urge to hug Zach's mom, herself. Beth had come prepared to love Evan. Surely the rest of Zach's family would feel the same.

"We finally get to meet." Beth lifted her hands to Evan's face, but then dropped them just before she touched him. "Do you know how much you look like your daddy?"

Evan opened a smidgeon of space between himself and Olivia's thigh, leaning around Beth to silently quiz his father.

"We have all kinds of pictures," Zach said. "I'll show them to you tomorrow."

"Okay." Evan drew out his assent, still holding on to Olivia's blouse. He might have craved a father, but grandmothers seemed to be more iffy.

"Speaking of photos." Beth stood to give Evan all the room he needed. Her glance at Olivia expressed more conditional approval. "I was telling Zach that some people might be on the way down here to take a few pictures."

Olivia closed her eyes. The sins of the fathers... "I'm sorry. I asked him to cancel the press conference."

"He did." Beth looked from her son to Olivia. "At least they said he did on the news, but his butler was taking out the trash when the reporters accosted him. He was so startled he just spilled his guts right there on TV."

Zach laughed. "The butler did it?"

"On purpose." Olivia had no doubt. "My father must have told him what to leak."

"Why would your father expose Evan to the journalists?" Beth shut her mouth as if she hadn't meant to say that in front of her grandson. "I told myself to be careful."

"Don't worry." Olivia had no illusions about

James Kendall in media tycoon mode. "Evan has to know something's up."

"What, Mommy?" He tugged her arm. "What's everyone talking about? Did Grampa's butler do something bad?"

"He talked to some people about us, and now those people might come down here with their cameras. They might even want you to talk to them, but remember what I told you. No talking to strangers. Don't even answer when a stranger talks to you." She leaned down for emphasis. "And don't talk to anyone who works for Grampa."

"Not even Ian and Jock?"

"You can talk to them." Hopefully, they hadn't sold their souls to the kinds of devils who chased down little boys. "But only Jock and Ian."

"Not Brian?"

"Brian's okay. He works for me."

"I'll memem—*remember*."

She grinned at the mistake he'd made since he'd first learned to talk. "You're my good guy." She hugged him close and met a more indulgent gaze from Beth. Olivia didn't know whether to be self-conscious about having to hold a private conversation with her son in public or apologetic because her father couldn't get a clue about not trying to control his family's life. "Dad believes in giving out the story you want before someone digs up the ones you'd rather keep to yourself."

"The Knoxville stations have already called," Beth said. "Along with some local paper editors. A couple of them claimed to work for the Kendalls. For you, I mean." With a shake of her head, Beth turned to Zach. "I don't know how much you've discussed with Olivia, but Helene saw the report, and she thought you should—" Beth interrupted herself to gaze at Evan uncertainly. "She brought someone with her."

Lily. Olivia's hand tightened of its own volition on Evan's shoulder. She glanced up at the moths circling in the streetlights over their heads. It seemed like such a mundane place to fall upon the point of no return.

Lily and Evan, both children, would now be bound to each other forever. Once brother met sister, she and Zach couldn't part them again.

"Helene's right." With a quick survey of the street, Zach yanked the suitcases out of his trunk and steered them all toward the B&B. "We should go inside."

"I'll get the other bags." Olivia released Evan's hand, expecting he'd wait for her. Instead, he dashed to Zach's side.

"Leave those, Olivia," Zach said. "I'll come back for them."

"I'm fine." She hoisted a shoulder bag onto her back and hauled the other two canvas roller bags out of the car. Doing something physical released a little of her disgrace at her father's behavior.

"Wow, you're strong." Zach's joking voice cut a deeper wedge out of her embarrassment. "I'll put my money on you if anyone comes over the fence with a camera."

He took her back to the summer they'd shared,

teasing in bed and out, trust that had turned out to be more fragile than a cobweb.

Stick with the present. Their son was their only connection now and in the future. "Evan, let's go inside. Maybe we can ask for a fireplace in our room."

She ignored Zach's doubtful look as he turned with Evan and the largest suitcase toward the B&B. Nothing felt normal with Zach. She couldn't seem to find her place in a present colored vividly by that long-ago summer—but only for her.

Dragging the bags up the uneven sidewalk, she felt as if a billion eyes followed her every move. She had to be imagining it. No one who'd found them would waste time hiding in the shrubbery.

She fumed, adjusting her hands around the heavy handles. Even James Kendall should know better than to set his hounds on his own grandson.

Beth held the door for Zach and Evan and then for Olivia. Olivia smiled a thank-you at the other woman.

"I'm glad you came," Beth said. "Thank you for finding my son."

Olivia's tongue tied itself in a knot. Beth's smile, full of love for her own son, connected one mom to another. One generation to another. Olivia, only child of an only child of a family rich in everything except normal attachments, eased in a breath and finally produced sound. "He's Evan's dad. I had to find him."

Approval warmed Beth's smile. She took one of the bags from Olivia's hand and nodded for her to follow Zach and Evan, her simple gesture allying them all in this predicament. It was the connection Olivia had dreamed of sharing with her dad.

"HERE'S YOUR ROOM KEY, Olivia. I'll take Evan to the kitchen, Zach. You help Olivia carry their things up to the rooms."

Meaning, she'd occupy Evan while he talked with Helene and Lily. "Thanks, Mom." He looped an arm around her shoulder. "I appreciate your help."

"No problem. I want to get to know this boy."

Evan peered up at her. "Are you really my grandma?"

"I sure am, buddy." Shifting away from Zach with a heartening glance she hugged Evan as if it never occurred to her he'd have to get used to her. Smart woman.

"I never had a grandma before."

"I never had a grandson, but I think you and I will get along."

"Do you have a puppy?"

"I have a great big old cat." She patted his head. "And I bet I can find milk and cookies for you in your aunt Eliza's kitchen. How's that for a start?"

"Well, I like puppies." Evan slid his hand into hers as Zach watched, bewildered. "But I like choplit chip cookies, too."

"Choplit chip? They're Aunt Eliza's specialty."

"See ya, Mom." He waved over his shoulder, and Olivia waved back.

"Bye." She sounded stunned. Still holding her bag, she started toward the stairs. "Your mom is a pied piper."

"The cookies help." He glanced at the closed study door where Lily and Helene waited. "Imagine what she could have done if she'd actually had a dog."

"It'd be the heck with a mom and dad."

"Yeah." He followed her up the stairs, reaching around her to take the suitcase. "Will you give me that?"

"I'm no weakling."

"I've noticed." She seemed to understand he was complimenting more than her ability to move luggage. In silence they trooped to the room she'd had on her previous visit.

Olivia opened the door, but waited while he preceded her. "Thanks," she said, reaching immediately for the zipper on the first bag as he set it down. She always had to be doing something.

"I have to go back down," he said.

"I know." She stilled, her sudden cessation of movement as powerful as a stop in a loud conversation. "I just don't know what I'm supposed to do."

"Come on down in a few minutes. We'll see how things go." If Helene was in a territorial mood, he'd give her time to cool off before he introduced Olivia and Evan.

"All right. I was going to offer to explain for you since you don't remember, but that's a hideous idea."

"Probably." He smiled to show her he was teasing. "I should go. I don't know what she told Lily about waiting for me to talk to them."

"You're right." Anxiety painted a storm in her

gray eyes. "Good luck. It went well with Evan. Maybe Lily will be glad of a brother, too."

"I hope so." More than he'd ever hoped for anything in his entire life.

He left her, taking the worry in her gaze with him. She was capable of taking care of herself, but he didn't want Helene messing with her.

He hurried down the stairs with no idea of what he should say. As soon as he opened the study door, Lily leaped off the fat, chintz couch.

"Daddy!"

"Hey." Catching her in midair, he scooped her into his arms. "How ya doing, doodle-bug?"

"I'm up late. Mommy says I have to go home soon, but we wanted to see you." She twisted to examine her mother. "Why did we have to see Daddy tonight, Mommy?"

Helene looked frozen into her armchair. Too worried to rage. Compassion replaced his wariness toward her.

"I have to tell you something, Lily." He set her down. "And Mommy wanted to tell you tonight. It's big news."

"What?"

He walked her back to the couch and sat down beside her. "Helene," he said. "Thanks for bringing her."

"She wanted to listen to the radio."

"Mommy made me practice." Lily pointed to Eliza's piano.

Helene shrugged. "It was all I could think of."

"Eliza would have given you a coloring book or something."

"I didn't think to ask." She'd resented his family since the day she'd left him for Nash. As if they'd pushed her out. Maybe she was embarrassed. Who knew?

"Lily." Just as with Evan, he didn't know how to go on. The direct way had worked before. "How would you like to have a brother?"

"Daddy!" Lily bounced to her feet on the cushion, and Helene reached for her automatically.

"It's okay," he said. Eliza's chintz was childproof.

"Mommy said I couldn't have any bruvers, but I can if you have one for me." Lily bounced again, and he caught her, pulling her onto his lap. "Daddy, did you get married?"

His four-year-old daughter saw things James Kendall's way. He felt so much guilt that he could believe he deserved Lily's question and Kendall's judgment.

OLIVIA DRAGGED OUT the process of unpacking, not quite sure how long Zach needed to explain to Lily and Helene. She put away Evan's things in the room adjoining hers, setting a much-mended tyrannosaurus on his pillow. On her way back through her own room, she passed a mirror on the dresser and had to go back. Falling asleep on the jet had made a rat's nest of her hair.

Oh, great. She'd met Zach's mother looking like this. Surely Evan or Zach might have mentioned she had a strong case of flat head going on. If either of them had noticed.

She brushed her hair and then her teeth and decided twenty minutes was long enough. She didn't have to interrupt Zach and Helene and Lily, but she'd like to make sure Evan was getting along all right with Beth. She left the room, turning back to lock the door behind her.

"I've always wanted to meet the ghost who haunted my marriage."

Olivia whirled, already on the defensive. Tall, blond and furious, Helene looked ready for battle. Except for sadness in her gaze that locked Olivia's irritated response inside her—where it belonged. This woman was not her enemy.

"You must be Helene." Offering to shake hands might be a mistake, but she stood her ground.

"You finally found Zach."

"I never looked for him. I thought he was dead." Olivia faced the other woman, straight on. "And he didn't remember me."

"So he claimed, but I knew someone was between us."

Once she would have liked to believe she'd stay in his heart, but from the maturity she'd gained in the past six years, it didn't seem likely. "He married you. He must have loved you."

"He married me for the same reason he would have asked you to marry him. I was pregnant." Her short laughter sounded as if it hurt. "Zach was busy for a few months, wasn't he?"

Olivia tried to swallow a sour taste in her mouth. Bitterness must be catchy. "I loved him, Helene. Back then." She wouldn't have married Zach if she couldn't be sure he loved her, too. Not even for Evan. "But I didn't exist for him by the time he met you. I don't know why you're angry."

"We could never say whether his memory loss came from emotional trauma or his physical injuries."

"You were one of his nurses. I forgot."

"He told you?"

Olivia shrugged. "I investigated him before I came here."

"Him or us?" Her voice was sharp as a knife.

"Him. All I know about you is that you divorced him."

"Well, he may have blocked all the memories that make him feel he did something wrong."

Olivia stared at Helene. Zach hadn't put it that way.

Helene went on. "Which means he probably still felt something for you on a subconscious level, even if it was a reluctance to betray you. I always knew something kept him from wanting me." Her mouth twisted. "Which means I and my daughter never stood a chance of creating a family with him."

Did she really believe that? Her side of the story didn't jibe with Zach's. "If he'd loved me, he would have remembered me. I wasn't part of his problem. We parted on good terms."

"In these cases the good gets swept out with the bad. You're here now, aren't you? He asked you to come back with him."

"He didn't ask me. We came because of my father's plans."

"He told me."

Olivia nodded. "So you know I'm here for Evan. I couldn't just turn him over to someone he didn't know, even though Zach's his father. You have Lily. You must understand."

"I'm not in the mood to understand anything tonight. You prove all my worst fears about my marriage were correct."

Lily's existence proved Zach had wanted Helene, but Olivia wasn't unselfish enough to say so out loud. Even now she couldn't bear the image of Zach with another woman. She'd been so convinced he cared for her, but by his own admission, he hadn't wanted her to get as close as she'd wanted to be. Maybe Zach didn't know how to commit. Maybe she'd been his distraction from the work that had taken so much of his life away from him.

"Helene, you've remarried and you're happy. Maybe you should forget about the past." Immediately, she wished she could take back the words. Who was she to advise anyone?

"Like you've forgotten?" The other woman's voice taunted. "Your past with my ex-husband means nothing?"

Not to Zach, though it still had the power to make her wish she'd stayed in Chicago. Obviously, both she and Helene still had a lot to learn about letting go. Olivia prayed she learned before she didn't mind exposing such bitterness in front of strangers.

"We shouldn't discuss this. It doesn't matter anymore, and you and I don't need to be upset with each other. Evan's late for bed, and I assume Lily is, too.

Why don't we go downstairs and get tonight over with?''

Helene planted her hands on girlishly narrow hips. ''Fine. Evan's already with Zach and Lily, but I wanted to tell you to call off your father. My daughter shouldn't have to worry about reporters.''

Olivia's breath caught. ''I'm sorry about my dad. If I could make him see sense, I already would have.'' Needing to reach Evan, she pocketed her room key and started past Helene. ''Aren't you coming?''

''You'd better believe it. You and your son are another reason Zach should stay out of Lily's life. She's a Nash now, and that's all I want her to be.''

Olivia said nothing, not believing Helene for a single second. It might be the mantra she used to whip Zach, but no one could be so annoyed because she wanted to forget a man. Side by side, in tension-filled silence, they went downstairs.

At the bottom, Olivia tried again, her heart banging hard in her chest. ''I wish I could assure you I don't want to hurt you or your daughter. I'm sorry my father set the media on us, but our children matter more to me than anything else. I hope Evan and Lily will learn to love each other.''

Helene's delicate face flushed with color. ''I'd never try to harm your son. I just wish I'd known about you. I wouldn't have wasted nearly three years of my life with Zach Calvert.'' She slid in front of Olivia to reach for the study door. ''This is our business. We'll send Evan out after we've explained.''

Olivia was halfway to the door when it shut. To hell with being fair or compromising. Her only thought was to rip the other woman a brand-new throat. She stopped, breathing hard.

She could barge in, grab her son and set Helene Nash straight, or she could let Zach take care of Evan and tell him about his sister. She'd never let anyone else take care of her son when something so important was happening to him.

She sucked in a breath and examined Helene's behavior. Though the other woman had been annoyed, Olivia had thought they were getting along until Helene made her move at the study door. If Olivia pushed into the room now, Helene was unpredictable enough to make a scene that might put a wedge between Lily and Evan.

She trusted Zach to protect Evan, and she didn't want her son to see Lily's mother in a rage.

"Want a coffee, Olivia?"

She spun around. Beth and Eliza Calvert stood arm in arm behind the registration desk. Beth was a little ahead of her dark-haired companion, as if Eliza had dragged her back.

"You heard?" Olivia asked.

They nodded with tight mouths as if they'd sworn not to say anything.

"She hoodwinked me with that part about meaning Evan no harm," Olivia said.

"She doesn't realize she had a part in the marriage not working. She blames the breakup on Zach, so anything she does is justified by her suffering."

Beth's frank diagnosis made Olivia uncomfortable, but she'd probably be the same if it were Evan. "You don't have anything stronger than coffee?"

"Some tea our mother-in-law brews," Eliza offered. "It's supposed to soothe pregnant women in labor."

"I was thinking moonshine, but if you don't have any…" Olivia smiled. After the confrontation with Helene, smiling felt like a relief. "Are moonshine jokes all right around here?"

Eliza beckoned her toward the kitchen. "I wouldn't talk about a still too loudly unless you're running one. You don't sound like one of us, so you might be mistaken for a 'revenuer.'"

By silent agreement, the three women brewed their tea in the B&B's kitchen but sipped it around a small, round table in the entrance hall. They sat on three sides, all with a view of the study door. Olivia wasn't sure what to expect, but she was glad they didn't hear shouting.

"Eliza," she suddenly said, "do you think we could light the fire in Evan's room? Just a small fire—he likes to pretend he's camping out. He sleeps in front of our fireplace at home sometimes."

"I'll be glad to." Eliza shared a glance with her sister-in-law. "The boy likes to camp."

"Lily and Zach spend as much time as they can up at a spring on the ridge," Beth said. "Are you a camper, too?"

"I do it for Evan when I have to, but I prefer room service and a shower." Olivia smiled ruefully as the other two women looked snakebitten. "It's not that I'm a city girl. I just don't like having dirty hair and washing in cold water."

"Sounds familiar," Eliza said in a voice as dry as

dust, but then she locked her own hand around her throat. "Sorry."

Olivia eyed both women. "I'm not here to pick up where Zach and I left off."

"No," Beth said, but the look she shared with her sister-in-law suggested they'd discussed the tidiest future available.

"Zach and Lily will want to take Evan up to the spring. No man should have to care for two kinder-garteners on an overnight," Eliza added.

Just then, the study door opened. Evan came out, shyly smiling at the sandy-haired girl who skipped to keep up with her taller brother.

"Where's your mom?" Lily asked.

Evan pointed, and Olivia met deep green eyes, astoundingly like her own son's and Zach's. "Hi, Lily." The little girl in bell-bottom jeans and a brown-and-green peasant blouse, was another small replica of her father. She smiled with bashfulness so like Evan's Olivia ached for the years the brother and sister had already lost. She splayed her hand across her chest.

"Hello," Lily said, her voice light, yet unwavering. "I don't know what to call you."

"My name is Olivia."

"Miss Olivia." Helene came out behind her daughter. "That's how children address adults down here," she said.

Behind her, Zach shut the door, his gaze uneasy as he caught Olivia's eye. "I thought you'd be in."

She flicked a glance at Helene who smiled, waiting for Olivia to turn snitch.

under a brighter sun, anticipating a whole morning with his two children. And Olivia?

Would she leave him with the children as she had the night before? He'd expected her to come back into the study with Helene. Helene had surprised him, offering to go find Olivia and bring her down. The next morning, he still didn't understand Olivia's reasoning, and he'd rather not acknowledge his own disappointment when he'd realized she wasn't going to appear.

Lily grabbed the door handle, and he helped her. Then he helped her into her booster seat and got behind the wheel. "Are you starving, Lily?"

"Nope. Mommy made me eat toast and oatmeal."

On her way to breakfast? He bit the inside of his cheek to keep from swearing. "Maybe you can have some hot chocolate while we eat."

"Evan and I have to play in a hurry."

He grinned at her, but she was right. They had to pack a lot of playing into about three hours. "You'll have other days with Evan, you know. We'll ask Aunt Eliza if we can eat outside on the garden terrace, and then you and Evan can play in the yard."

Aunt Eliza was ahead of him. She'd already set a table outside where Evan and Olivia were waiting patiently in front of coffee for Olivia and juice for Evan. Lily glimpsed them first through the dining room window.

"There's my bruver, Daddy. There's Evan."

"Go ahead." He lifted her hand and let it go. "I'll find Aunt Eliza and let her know we're here."

She shot through the terrace door at Lily speed, and Zach smiled as she stopped like a girl in a cartoon, almost rocking to a halt beside Evan's chair.

They beamed at each other, both obviously happy to be together, both wordless. Olivia pushed her chair back and flashed an indulgent look through the window as she helped Lily into the seat beside Evan's. Zach pointed toward the empty reception area, and she nodded.

He met Eliza carrying a tray from the kitchen. Laden with French toast and fresh bacon she bought from a local farmer, she had almost too much to carry.

"I'll take that."

"Would you?" She handed it over. "I'll go back for the fruit salad. Strawberries and mango, Lily's favorites."

"Thanks." Zach pressed a kiss to her cheek as he took the tray. "And thanks for letting us take over your terrace this morning."

"My other guests thoughtfully took themselves off to the Museum of Appalachia in Norris, and I'm having a fine time with your Evan. He asked for a taste of grits, which he then nearly spat on the kitchen floor." She shook her head with the dazed look so familiar to all parents of small children. "We decided on French toast and fruit."

"Maybe he'll acquire a taste for grits on his next visit."

"After he was almost sick, Olivia turned down a bite."

Zach nudged his aunt's arm. "If she'd spat, she might have died of embarrassment. You wouldn't want to clean up a body."

Eliza arched her eyebrows. "Is she that delicate, Zach?"

"She's that determined to keep a low profile."

portion before Lily said the words "swing set," and both children tore around the side of the walled garden for the play area.

"You can stop eating that now." Zach topped off Olivia's coffee cup.

"Thanks." She slugged some back. "It grows on you."

He laughed out loud, actually relieved to let it out.

"Really." She sounded affronted.

"It was nice of you to try. Did you see Lily watching you? She felt better because you ate it."

"I don't know what came over Evan."

"He's little. They're both excited at seeing each other."

She looked a little dazed. "All of a sudden, I wonder how long this charmed period will last. Lily's bound to realize Evan's going to take more of your time, and Evan wouldn't be human if he didn't hope you'll love him as much as you love Lily."

Zach nodded, picking up his own coffee cup. "Funny, you immediately know how to love your child." It was true. He felt as if he'd loved Evan all his life. "What I wonder is how I'll ever make up the past five years to him."

Olivia frowned. Her hand trembled as she reached across the table. "You don't have any reason to feel guilty. Evan seems perfectly happy with things the way they are. He checked the clock every fifteen seconds or so until you and Lily drove up, and he kept interrogating your aunt about what she was making. He wanted the perfect breakfast. I was sort of startled she didn't stuff him in the oven."

Zach shook his head, smiling. "We're not big oven

stuffers around here. How do you feel about all the family you just picked up?'' Right away, he realized asking was a mistake.

Olivia straightened in her chair in an apparent effort to back away from him. ''You're all Evan's family. I'm glad to meet everyone, but I'm not part of the deal. You guys aren't stuck with me.''

''You all, or just plain y'all.''

''What?''

''Not you guys. Y'all.''

A smile hovered on her lips. Her moist lips, full and red, defining temptation. ''Y'all,'' she said.

She looked away, and strands of black hair flitted into her eyes. As she batted it, he imagined her hands sliding over his chest. ''And it's too bad you didn't know how Southern family works before you came down here,'' he said.

Was he flirting with her? He wasn't sure, and she didn't seem to be either.

''You mean because everyone just accepts Evan and me? I've noticed,'' she said. ''Your life is so different than mine.'' She met his gaze again. ''I always wondered why you didn't ask me here.''

''We didn't know each other a long time.''

''No, but you visited once after we were—'' She stopped, a blush coloring her cheeks. She meant after they'd become lovers. She smiled, her mouth curving self-consciously. ''You ignored all my most blatant hints that I'd like to come along.''

Was *she* flirting?

He had no time to find out. At that moment, Evan's voice shouted, ''Sister!''

Zach was on his feet, an urge to kill what or whomever had put fear in his son's voice. Evan flew around the corner, towing Lily by her hand.

"Sister, come on. That was a bad girl." He flung himself at his mom. She almost toppled as both children wrapped themselves around her waist.

"Cameras," Evan said, heaving for breath. "And some lady who wanted to know Lily's name."

"Take them inside." Zach was already on his way to confront them.

"You come inside, too. They'll go away if they have no one to talk to."

Rage had such a grip on him he couldn't talk. Only the children, watching them as if they were Ping-Pong balls, kept him sane. At times like this, he believed his worst fears—that he could have killed Salva on his last mission, and that was why he'd chosen to forget.

Through a maze of guilt, one thought surfaced. He had to take care of his children and get rid of the reporters who'd dared frighten them. "Olivia, do as I say."

Her frigid expression showed disdain for his tone and his suggestion. "Listen to me. I have experience."

He didn't give a damn about her skill with the scavengers who'd trespassed on his aunt's property. "Take Evan and Lily inside."

Waiting for no further argument, he pushed through his aunt's flower beds and rounded the corner to find two cameramen and three reporters clinging to the brick wall. Anger swept him back to that day in the bank. In his head he saw cameras and bodies flying, and he began to plan the best way for making it come to pass.

How dare they interrogate his son? How dare they try to use his daughter to paint some story about Olivia Kendall's family? Animals, feeding on babies.

"Get the hell out of here."

"Are you Evan Kendall's father?" the female reporter asked.

"I'm the man who's going to—" *snap your neck in two* "—throw you all in jail for trespassing if you don't get off this property."

The woman opened her mouth as Zach flexed his fists. No one scared his children. No one.

The woman glanced from his hands, exposing barely controlled fury, to her colleagues. "Back to the easement, boys."

Red hazed over Zach's eyes, but he couldn't legally push them any farther away. They slid off the wall, and he backed into the house.

His heart was trying to spring out of his chest. His reaction had been completely out of control, but his temper jacked up every time he thought of Evan's sad cry of "sister."

"God," he muttered as sweat poured over him.

"Zach?"

He turned, still on the attack. Wariness flickered in Olivia's eyes.

"Eliza has the children."

"You shouldn't have left them."

"We'll both go back as soon as you don't look like a hired killer."

"What?" But he knew what she meant because he felt like a killer who'd work for free.

"Actually, in the movies, the hired guns are always calmer than you."

"I'm calm."

"You've got death in your eyes." She glanced toward the wall. "Are they all okay?"

"Setting up on the easement, probably with some good shots of me threatening them."

"How often do you lose control?"

Now that accusation scared him. He stepped away from her. "Never. I said those idiots are all right."

"I know you had to put the bank robber down, but these people are just doing their jobs." A tremor of unease vibrated in her voice. Used to Helene's methods, he steeled himself, but Olivia wasn't looking for a reason to part him from her son. She really didn't understand. And he couldn't ease her concern because he had no idea why anger was leaking out of his bad dreams into his real life.

He forced himself to feel calm so that he'd sound calm when he spoke. "You understand those people because you work at the same job. I believe they were threatening my children. They're too young to deal with tabloid writers."

Olivia inhaled quickly and began to choke. "Is that how you see me?" she asked between coughs.

Great. "No." Turning, he started back to the dining room. "Drop it. I want to see my son and daughter. We can discuss anger management later."

"We're going to."

Fear did a little dance down his spinal column. Not fear of Olivia. Concern about skills he didn't want, that taught him how to present a convincing calm facade, or take a man apart. He couldn't trust them. They hadn't saved his friend's life.

BETH STARED through the window over her kitchen sink, searching as far down the driveway as she could see. Zach and the children and Olivia should have arrived by now.

Zach had asked if they could come by long enough to duck the reporters who'd picked the Dogwood as their only stop on a tour of Bardill's Ridge.

Beth assembled her materials for the evening's crocheting class, then she checked the toys she'd set up in the living room. Zach's beloved Lincoln Logs and the race car and track that made the house smell like an electrical fire. She'd found two paint-chipped yo-yos and a jump rope that must have been Molly's or Sophie's. Did kids play with toys that didn't include video screens these days?

She'd do anything to help Evan feel at home here.

She bit her thumbnail, scanning two back copies of *Relevance* that stuck out above the other magazines in the rack beside her chair. Should she shove those into a drawer? Having the magazine's top editor in for cookies felt odd.

The phone rang, and Beth left the magazines, breathing a sigh of relief. It had to be Zach, explaining where they were. He knew how she worried.

"Hello?"

"Zach Calvert, please," said a man with no time for anything except business. Probably a reporter who thought she'd sprang stupid from the Smoky Mountains.

"He doesn't live here."

"I believe he's brought my grandson to visit a Mrs. Beth Calvert? That would be you?"

"I'm Beth." She considered cussing at the man who'd brought extra pressure to bear on her son.

"I need to talk to Zach. Now. Put him on, please."

Who'd died and made this guy supreme being? "He hasn't arrived yet. May I give him your message?"

"What do you mean he hasn't arrived? My daughter and Evan are with him. They left their hotel half an hour ago according to another Ms. Calvert I spoke to."

Eliza. "We've had some reporters in town," she said pointedly. "He's probably trying to shake them so they don't follow him here."

Silence and static came over the line. "Ms. Calvert, my daughter won't take my calls or e-mails right now. Perhaps you'd also give her a message for me?"

"I might." As long as it wasn't some pompous order to call him the second Olivia stepped out of Zach's car.

"Tell her I fired the butler."

His officious attitude annoyed her, but Beth laughed in relief. "I'll gladly tell her. And would you still like Zach to call?"

"Yes. His former commanding officer just placed a call to me, and I'm willing to entertain Zach's thoughts on the information I should give the admiral."

Her forehead knotted in an instant headache. "I'll pass that message as well."

"Thank you, Ms. Calvert."

"Beth." She didn't mind a truce since he'd fired the big-mouthed butler.

"Thank you. Beth."

"You're welcome, Mr. Kendall."

"Please call me James. Have you seen Evan?"

"He's a bright, funny, loving little boy. He hauled his sister away from the reporters as if they were the hounds of hell."

"Trust me, they most likely are. I suppose you wouldn't believe me if I told you how sorry I am that I've caused this problem for my daughter and your son."

"For some reason, I do believe you, but I don't much matter. You'll have to make your peace with Olivia and Zach. And Evan. He was scared for his sister."

"My daughter ignores my advice about hiring a bodyguard when she travels with Evan. I'm sure the guy who takes him to school would welcome the extra salary."

The idea of Evan needing a bodyguard made her wish she'd hung up while they were ahead. "I'll pass your messages along, James. Good afternoon."

She thought he wished her a formal goodbye before she put the phone back in its cradle. She got scared, thinking of the lifestyle that demanded bodyguards. How would Evan be happy with Zach who couldn't give him half as much excitement?

"DAD," EVAN SAID, from the back seat, "Lily says you're going to build her a tree house."

"It'll be yours now, too," Zach said. "Do you want to help us with the plans?"

Olivia turned in time to see her son arm-pumping in unison with his sister. Helene wouldn't care for such an unladylike expression of excitement.

"You may have to come back for the tree house, Evan. I'm not sure how long we can stay."

"We'll start in a couple of days." Zach kept his tone even, but his gaze reflected the plea on Lily and Evan's faces.

Olivia could have kicked herself. At the talk of long-term building plans she'd panicked, but she shouldn't have mentioned time frames in front of the children. "I have a job. I have to go back before Brian quits on me."

"Who's Brian?" Lily asked in a whisper Zach and Olivia couldn't help hearing.

"This guy. He plays soccer with me sometimes."

Remembering Zach's apparent anxiety about sharing sports with Evan, Olivia glanced at him. He turned his head, meeting her gaze with a rueful smile.

"Yeah, it bugs me." He whispered more proficiently than Lily. "But I can learn to play, too."

"Brian's a good guy. He just tried to—" She didn't want to imply Zach had been deficient. A man couldn't be lax in caring for a son he didn't know about, but Zach's conscience didn't always seem to consider the circumstances.

"Brian took up the slack. I get it." Zach veered onto a gravel road. "And I also get you're not complaining because I wasn't there. You don't have to sift through every word before you talk to me."

This wasn't a conversation the children needed to hear either. But in the back seat, Lily claimed she could "run quicker than Grandma's cat," and Evan couldn't resist claiming he was faster. The argument would keep them occupied.

"It's a tense situation." Olivia eased toward Zach, just far enough to speak, but not draw attention. "I don't know how you feel about what happened before, and I don't want you to think I'm holding a grudge."

"I'm not sure why you're so forgiving."

She straightened. "You didn't leave on purpose. I'm a reasonable woman."

"More than." While her heart pounded, Zach glanced into the rearview mirror again. The car brushed overhanging shrubbery as they took a curve on Olivia's side. "Here we are, buddy," he said. "That house on the hill was my mom's when she was a little girl."

"I want to see your house, Dad."

"We'll do that, too, but Grandma has some toys for you and Lily to play with, and Lily thought you might like to make cookies."

Back at the B&B, Olivia had agreed with his real reason for visiting Beth. Once they'd escaped the reporters on a road too narrow for a dog sled to navigate, Zach's house had to be the first place someone looking for them would go. He didn't think anyone could find it, but he'd wanted to be sure before he took Evan and Lily to his home.

Olivia slid her hand into her coat pocket, touching the cell phone she hadn't turned on in a day and a half. Her father would have flooded her voice mail by now with more of his rationale for sending the journalists after them.

At the top of his mom's driveway, Zach parked

behind a spreading green shrub that looked a lot like a spaceship in disguise.

"You should see this in the spring," he said. "It's honeysuckle, Evan."

"You can drink it," Lily added.

"Really?" Her son asked before Olivia could.

"Uh-huh. Grandma Greta showed me how." Lily pointed at their father. "She's Dad's gran."

"Do I know her, Dad?" Evan asked.

"You will." The many Calvert faces were apparently already blurring.

Olivia got out of the car and opened Lily's door. After she unfastened the booster seat, the little girl slid out and slipped her hand into Olivia's. Olivia stared from the trusting little grip to Zach, but he only smiled with happiness that erased the usual strain in his face.

"Are we sneaking up on Grandma, Daddy? I didn't know you liked to play hide-and-seek with cars."

Zach laughed. "Why don't you go ring the doorbell?"

She ran and Evan hurtled after her. Olivia rubbed her fingers together. "She held my hand."

"I saw."

"She's a sweet girl, Zach. I know you and Helene have problems, but she shows no sign."

"We both love her, and even Helene professes to want the best for her."

"You don't think she does?"

"In most things, maybe."

"Helene's still angry about your marriage."

"My mom said she was rude to you last night."

The children banged on Beth Calvert's door. As

Olivia debated how much to tell Zach about his ex-wife's accusations, Beth came out and scooped both children into her arms.

"Helene said what she thought." Olivia watched Evan swing in his grandmother's embrace. "He's going to be spoiled after all this attention."

"My mom likes having another grandchild better than Christmas. And what does Helene think?"

"We should go inside. Hiding the car won't do any good if someone sees us out here."

"They'd have to come up the driveway to that last curve, and we'd hear them before they caught sight of us."

Playing spy games came too easily to him. Did he realize? When she tried to talk about the past, he tended to be defensive, so she didn't ask. Today was for family, not for explanations Zach couldn't provide. Olivia climbed the porch steps to the door that had closed behind her son.

Zach's body heat startled her as he reached past her and turned the doorknob. "You don't have to knock."

"It's not my house."

"I remember that much." He touched the small of her back, urging her inside.

The scent of apples and fresh baking wrapped her in homey warmth that surely didn't exist outside the movies. They entered a living room filled with chintz furniture and so many family pictures she didn't have time to take them all in. This was the kind of home she'd always wanted.

She was most drawn to the photos. "Evan couldn't look more like you."

"I knew he was mine the second I saw his face."
Movement across the room attracted his eye. "Lily,
Evan, let Spike off the television."

Olivia followed Zach's glance. A huge gray cat
stood on a wide console TV, arching and hissing at
Evan and Lily.

"Evan." He'd never cornered a cat before. "You
love animals. Leave the kitty alone."

Zach's mother came out of a tiny kitchen, two
mugs in her hands. "He doesn't like to be patted,"
she said. "If you two drink your chocolate and play
quietly, he'll jump down and sit near you."

"That's not much fun." Evan sounded just a touch
spoiled in his disappointment. He turned to his sister.
"How can you run with him?"

"Maybe I chase him." Lily grabbed her grandma's
pant leg. "But only a little, Grandma Beth, and sometimes I let him get away."

"As long as you don't scare him, it's exercise. But
don't scare him, okay?" Beth herded the children toward a stack of toys. "I don't have any video
games."

"My mom hates 'em," Evan said. He tapped the
top of a tin of wooden logs. "What's this?"

"You build stuff with 'em." Lily copied her big
brother's lax pronunciation. Olivia turned away to
hide a smile.

"Can we," Evan asked, "Grandma Beth?"

The name sounded sweet on his lips. She'd never
thought he'd have a grandmother.

"Absolutely," Beth said. "Your mom's been pre-
paring you to visit me so you wouldn't be bored."

Evan's smile made him look exactly like the boy

in pictures all over this room. "I'm not bored. Everyone likes me in Tennessee."

Less than comforting words to a mother's ears. Olivia moved toward him. "Evan, does someone dislike you in Chicago?"

He looked as if he wished she'd stop embarrassing him. "No, Mom, but you know what I mean."

"Yeah, Mr. Grown-Up, I guess I do." She ruffled his hair in a small head lock. "You're a gift to everyone you meet here."

"Mo-o-m." He tried to flop his hair back into place, looking anywhere except at his sister.

"Olivia, I need to talk to you and Zach."

Beth made the chat sound serious. Olivia peeked back at her son. "Can you open the logs?"

"I'll help," Lily said.

Zach just popped the lid. "We guys have to stick together." He also ruffled Evan's hair, but their boy grinned at his dad and left his hair on end.

Olivia tried not to grimace. She'd anticipated at least eight more years before her son decided she was too humiliating to keep. Trying not to mind Evan's minor switch of allegiance, she followed Beth into the kitchen.

Ceramic cow creamers and cookie jars and a collection of flower-strewn teapots littered the shelves and the window ledges with homey clutter. "Thanks for having us." Olivia took care of manners first.

"I'm glad you came."

Olivia was surprised anyone ever willingly left Beth's house. "Did something else happen? That you have to tell us about?"

"Your father called."

Olivia stopped smiling. She should have known he'd try someone else when she refused to pay attention. "I'm sorry. I guess this is why he's king of the newshounds, but I should have picked up his messages. I'll make sure he doesn't—"

"He didn't bother me." Beth included Zach in her gaze. "Admiral Gould called him."

Olivia turned to Zach. His skin had paled. Something in his past remained to torture him, whether he admitted the pain or not.

"Can I use your phone, Mom?"

"Sure."

Both women waited, Olivia feeling as if she should leave the room. Zach jabbed a number into the phone, and after a moment, said, "I'll call you later, when I'm at home." He waited long enough to hear an answer. "Nothing's changed. Same story." He glanced at Olivia, his eyes troubled, yet somehow warm. "I explained, and I'll tell her. No, don't worry." And he hung up.

Olivia crossed the linoleum floor, laying her hand on his forearm before she considered whether she should. "Are you okay?"

"Fine. He just wanted to know if I planned to talk to the journalists." He looked over her at his mom. "None of us is talking to them." He turned back to Olivia, covering her hand with his. She liked his touch so much she nearly pulled away. "And he asked me to apologize to you. If he'd known about the baby, he would have told your father the truth."

She lifted her head, smiling though it hurt to. "Thanks."

"Speaking of your father..." Beth's reluctance was obvious.

Olivia held her breath. It was bound to be a set of instructions.

"He said to tell you he fired the butler."

"Oh." She slid her free hand inside her jacket pocket and closed her fingers around her cell phone, often her only physical tie to her dad. "What a relief."

Zach and Beth shared matching puzzled gazes.

"He wasn't lying," Olivia said, "when he claimed the butler leaked the story. I hate being lied to." And should she offer them any soap with that heaping helping of her family's dirty laundry? Moving toward the living room, she avoided the compassion that smoothed Zach's sharp features. "I'm dying to build a log house."

CHAPTER NINE

THE DAY AFTER they made cookies at Beth's house, Evan and Olivia shared breakfast in her room over a picture book about dinosaurs. A knock on the door interrupted them.

"Hold on." Olivia pushed her napkin into the book to mark their place. "That's probably your dad."

"And Lily?" Evan's hopeful little face wrung her heart.

"I doubt it," she said gently. "Her mom will probably want to spend time with her today." Olivia climbed off the bed, tucking her pajama T-shirt over the top of her flannel pants. She'd never liked robes and her pj's covered as much as sweats would, but she felt in need of a cover-up.

She padded across the thick carpet, took a breath and opened the door. It was Zach. Olivia tried not to notice the way his dark leather belt accentuated a narrow waist lovingly surrounded by faded denim.

Olivia's mouth dried. "No uniform today?" she asked.

He'd shown up yesterday dressed as the sheriff, because he'd had to work a shift after he'd taken Lucy home. The jeans made him look more raw, more dangerously like the man she remembered. She'd hardly ever seen him in uniform.

He tugged at the loose knit of his long-sleeved olive T-shirt. "I asked my deputy to take over for a long weekend."

Olivia digested the news. She shouldn't be so glad to see him. Evan, plagued by no qualms, yelped from the depths of the puffy comforter. "We get you the whole time, Dad? What's a long weekend?"

"Four days." Olivia felt herself blushing, but she couldn't help a weakness that seemed to be growing stronger. She liked being with Zach and Evan.

"Four days?" Evan asked. He lifted his hand and counted. "One—three—four. No— One—two—th— One—two—three—four."

Zach grinned, and Olivia had to smile. "His math gets a little rusty when he's excited."

Zach's gaze clung to her as if something on her face kept him from looking away. She lifted her hands, feeling for a smudge. He caught her wrists, and the concentration in his gaze deepened until she forgot to breathe. At last he curved his fingers possessively around hers and pulled her hands down without saying anything.

He turned to Evan, but Olivia felt dizzy. He'd touched her as if he had a right, and she'd forgotten to remind him he didn't. She'd forgotten she shouldn't feel the way she had in the past. Fighting for poise, she focused on his conversation with Evan.

"I thought you might like to see the aquarium in Chattanooga," Zach said. "They have this path that takes you through the whole Tennesseean ecosystem."

"Huh?"

Olivia worked her hardest to conceal a grin, but

Zach just cupped the back of Evan's head, and hugged him. "You walk down a path that makes you feel like you're outside. The trees and the flowers change as if you were following the Tennessee River from the mountains all the way to the Gulf of Mexico."

"Is that fun?"

"Too much fun," Zach said.

"Oh, yeah!"

"Evan, careful of the tray." Olivia dashed across the room, imagining Calvert gossip about Kendall crumbs in the bed. "Maybe we should have eaten at the table."

"We're picnicking," Evan told his dad. "You want some toast? Mom ate the muffin, and the crescents are all in here." He puffed out his belly and pounded with true, masculine pride.

"I'll have a piece of toast if you have any to spare," Zach said. "What kind of jelly do you have left?"

"Just this yucky orange stuff." Evan lifted the small jar of marmalade vigilantly as if it might bite him.

Zach helped himself, laughter in his eyes, and Olivia decided against helping her son pronounce "croissant." That could wait.

Zach's plans pushed every other thought out of her head. Did he expect to take Evan to Chattanooga by himself? "What time do you think you'll have Evan back here?"

Zach looked puzzled. "What do you mean?" He wiped marmalade off the corner of his mouth pressing one thumb to his lip in a precise, curiously male gesture that left her aching to help him with the smear of preserves.

Breathing grew difficult again. She was going to have to tell Brian he'd been wrong in his article that claimed women didn't respond to visual stimuli.

"Olivia?"

Her inappropriate response to him had to be as obvious as hell. "I thought you might want Evan to yourself."

"I thought you might both be ready for a break from the Calvert horde."

She might have been before she'd discovered she could want him simply because of the way he wiped marmalade off his mouth. "It's a long drive, isn't it?"

A chill came into his gaze. He moved so that Evan couldn't see his face. "You don't have to join us."

On any other man, that look would mean rejection, but she already had plenty of experience reading Zach wrong. The time might be right to cultivate a new approach.

Maybe he was offended because she'd sounded reluctant. She was only reluctant because she kept seeing the Zach she'd loved in him. But forget about self-preservation. She should go with them because he was still too new to Evan to send them on their own.

"Come on, Mom." Evan decided for her. "Ya gotta see the fishies."

She glanced from her pleading son to Zach, who'd become decidedly noncommittal. "I'm a sucker for turtles." Who cared for caution? Besides, her son had invited her. "And I read in a brochure on Eliza's desk that there are seahorses, too."

Cheering again, Evan took another bounce on the bed, while Zach smiled as if he was glad to have her along. "Good," he said.

Olivia felt inappropriately happy. She was along for the maternal part of this ride. Nothing more.

"If you're finished with breakfast, Evan, put your book away. We'd better change clothes."

He leaped for the open door to his room, and Olivia started toward her bathroom, but Zach cut her off.

His scent, spice and grown male, washed their past over her in a series of high-speed memories—simple moments when they'd gazed at each other across clasped hands, heated hours when his lingering touch had made her believe he was claiming her for all time. Carefree times, like the day they'd carved their initials in his Halloween pumpkin and somehow both survived, fingers intact.

"Why are you smiling?" Zach's soft tone made her feel warm.

She backed away from him, opening her closet to search for clothes. "Just thinking." He wouldn't want the details. However he'd felt then, his concern was for Evan now.

He came after her. Taking her hand, he turned her to face him. "I would have invited you if Evan hadn't."

What did he mean? She tried to read the emotion in his eyes, but she didn't trust herself. She didn't even have the nerve to ask.

The explanation hit her with painful force. He was trying to be friends. He didn't want another messy relationship like the one he had with Helene. He liked her well enough. She could tell that much, but she'd

be crazy to assume he felt anything more than gratitude to her for asking him to be part of Evan's life.

"Thank you," she said stiffly. "I'll be a minute."

Composing herself, Olivia put on jeans and a
sweater. After she brushed her teeth, she leaned into
Evan's room. Cross-legged on the floor, he and Zach
seemed to be engrossed in deep conversation.

For a shocking moment she wanted to know what
they were talking about. Seeing her son so willing to
attach himself to his father became more difficult as
her feelings for Zach tried to resurface. She wiped
perspiration born of shame from her upper lip.

"Ready?" She strove for a bland tone.

Neither of them noticed anything amiss as they
sprang to their feet and went into the hall. She must
be a better actress than she thought. She locked both
rooms and then clattered down the stairs several steps
behind Zach and Evan. Eliza looked up from doing
paperwork at the reception desk.

"Off to play?" she asked.

"In Chatta—" Evan consulted his father. "Where,
Dad?"

"Chattanooga." Zach reached for one of the bro-
chures on Eliza's desk and handed it to Evan. "To
the aquarium. The pictures will show you what it's
like, son."

"Oh, you'll love it, Evan. So many things to see.
I wish I could close up and go with you."

"You can," Evan said politely.

"Gotta work." His great-aunt leaned over her desk.
"But thanks for the invite."

"How about Grandma Beth, Dad?"

"I think Grandma Greta locked her up for the day."

Evan was clearly appalled. "Not in your jail?"

"No, at Grandma Beth's house. They're planning that party I told you about, the anniversary party."

"Oh. Then she'll let Grandma Beth out sometime. Maybe we should go see them." He grabbed his dad's hand. "And make sure my grandma's okay."

"You don't have to worry about her. She'd call us if she needed help." With his free hand, Zach held one of the front doors, and Olivia and Evan passed in front of him. Knowing Evan's propensity for darting into trouble, Olivia grabbed his shoulder.

Her protective grasp made him forget his grandmother's plight. "Mom." He tugged, escaping her, and then skipped down the sidewalk toward Zach's car.

"Evan, don't run into the street."

He looked back at Zach as if to say "See what I have to put up with?"

Zach laughed, and Olivia was tempted, but just then a rumbling like a fleet of battle tanks rose from the direction of the square. Slowly, a massive mobile home nosed into their street.

Gleaming silver-and-metallic-blue, as large as a blimp, it must have room to sleep a Cub Scout troop. Antennas of all shapes and sizes bristled on its roof.

"Oh, no." Olivia suffered a genuine and profound sinking feeling. She'd bet her last word processor her father was driving the overgrown toy.

"Man," Zach said.

"Dad," Olivia corrected him.

"Grampa? When'd he get that, Mom?"

"He probably ordered it the second we left home."
She glanced back at the B&B, hoping Zach's aunt
Eliza wouldn't see her dad's showpiece. Zach's family would surely despise hers before long. "What
next?"

"You have to admit it's big," Zach said.

"Everything about my father is big except his
sense of tact. I can't believe he'd follow us."

"Can I have one of those, Mom? When I'm old
enough to drive? I'd look really cool."

"You can probably have that one. Grampa will get
tired of it by then," Olivia said with reckless ill humor.

As the mobile home drew close enough to reveal
the driver, she recognized her father. Naturally, he
couldn't trust Jock or Ian to drive his brand-new le-
viathan. He couldn't fit the thing in the street's angled
parking, but Ian opened the door and dropped loose-
limbed through it. Jock followed him, limping a bit
on landing. Olivia shook her head as the two bodyguards directed her father into about eight parking
spaces.

"Can't you ticket him for that?" she asked Zach.

He didn't even glance her way. "I don't think so.
Don't you already have enough family trouble?"

"Mom." Evan danced in front of her. "Does this
mean we don't get to go see the fishies?"

"Maybe not today," she said. "We have to figure
out where Grampa can stay."

"We have a park, just to the west of town." Zach
started toward the huge vehicle. "Give him a break,
Olivia. He's worried about you."

She stumbled over perfectly smooth pavement,

feeling as if he'd patted her on the head and suggested she get over it. "I could use a backup. He's interfering, and your family's going to think we're nuts."

"They'll know you care about each other. Why did you come with Evan? You want to make sure your child is with good people. Your father's no different."

"I'm twenty-seven years old, Zach."

He turned back, looking her up and down. He started with amusement in his gaze, but slowly, languor clouded his eyes as he acknowledged each curve, each nerve that quivered in the wake of his glance.

"Oh, yeah," he said, in a huskier tone. "I forgot. You are all grown up."

An independent, self-supporting, completely-not-in-need-of-a-man-to-make-her-whole woman should have been offended. Instead, Olivia stood stock-still, trying not to tremble.

JAMES COULDN'T SEEM to understand why Zach couldn't allow him to appropriate several parking spots. Zach tried to explain, with an eye on Evan, who'd forgotten both his parents and the trip to Chattanooga because he had so much room to search for fun at Grampa's new place.

"You can make an exception for me, Zach. You're in charge of this town." Completely without shame for the trouble he'd caused Olivia and Evan so far, James Kendall tried to flatter his way into getting the favors he expected as his due.

"You know, our mayor thinks he actually runs

Bardill's Ridge," Zach said. "And you can't park here because it's illegal."

"Tomorrow starts the weekend. You won't need all these extra spaces for business people." Kendall's sidelong glance toward the square suggested there would never be enough professionals in Bardill's Ridge to use up the available parking.

"People park here while they shop on the weekends, and the people who stay at the B&B use these spaces, too."

"The Dogwood." James looked pleased with himself. "Owned by one Eliza Calvert, whom I assume is some relation to you. I already know Bardill's Ridge like the back of my hand. I've made it my business in the past few days."

His business? Zach hated the possibility of offending Olivia, but he had to back James Kendall down on the dictator wattage. Evan's voice, whooping with joy over a video game inside, made him hesitate. Evan idolized his grandfather.

"Dad, you and everyone else with a TV or a newspaper knows this town now." Olivia spoke in a low tone, punctuated by Evan's descriptions of a TV and computers and a bowl of his favorite candy bars. "Why are you here?"

"You're my daughter. I didn't want you to think I told anyone to talk to the press. I took what you said to heart and I tried to call the whole thing off."

James flashed Zach a look, as if he was suggesting the sheriff-turned-traffic-cop should offer his family privacy. Besides a tendency not to take orders well, Zach found he couldn't leave Olivia to face her father alone. She felt James had betrayed her, and Zach was too aware of letting her down himself to walk away.

"Sir," he said, "you may not have instructed your employee to talk to the press, but your presence here means the journalists will stay."

"Your presence in my daughter's life brought them here in the first place. If you'd done the right thing, and by that I mean keeping your hands off her, none of us would be facing this problem."

Zach couldn't argue. He couldn't remember Olivia at twenty-one, but he'd probably had no business getting involved with any woman until he'd finished his training. He was more responsible than that. Why hadn't he talked to anyone else about her? His silence had forced Olivia into a solitary pregnancy and five years of single motherhood. "You may be right."

"Dad." Impatience splintered Olivia's tone. "Stop trying to throw the blame on Zach. You're going to make this worse because no one will find a hotter story while you're lurking."

The two Kendalls squared off. They were well-suited for a family battle. James turned her away from Zach. "I don't want you to go through this by yourself. I know you hate it when I try to help you, but Evan has been my responsibility all these years as well, and you'll always be my daughter."

Zach distrusted Kendall's earnest tone. He'd proven he knew how to spin a story. Zach would have liked to warn Olivia against her father's attempt to coerce her back into the fold.

But he saw her make a decision. Her expression firmed in a patient smile that acknowledged twenty-seven years of emotional tug-of-war between them.

She gently detached herself from her father's hand. "You'd like me to run home every time something bad happens because you think you can fix all my problems. I'm glad I can ask you for advice, but this time I know what's best for my child."

Zach admired the effort she made to avoid hurting her manipulative father. Kendall saw himself as the patriarch of their small family, but Olivia was the source and the flow of the bond between Evan and her father. She protected her son and gave her dad room to run until he crossed the boundaries she'd set for Evan.

She slid her hands into her back pockets, and Zach's palms burned as if he were tracing the firm flesh that filled out her jeans. Only one thing seemed to be missing in Olivia's life. Why hadn't another man fallen in love with her? Why hadn't she, so capable of love, fallen for someone else?

What had he and Olivia been to each other? Every time he passed within arm's length of her, he fought an urge to touch her, to wrap himself in the sound of her voice, the passion of her arms clinging to him.

He backed away from her and her father. He had to be careful. He couldn't afford to fail again with a woman who'd given him a child.

He'd bent over backward trying to be a good husband to Helene—until she'd gotten sick of his trying so hard. After the accident he'd gone a little crazy, driven too fast, forced himself to fly, though he was so frightened he'd made mistakes. He'd loved too quickly, needed too much. He'd stopped taking those kinds of chances the day he'd known he was going to be Lily's father. She'd mattered more than his own loyalty to the Navy or his confusion about the past that felt like a gaping wound.

He turned his head, mesmerized by the slide of Olivia's black hair over her shoulder. The strands curled around her full breast as she turned her father toward the front of the mobile home.

His aquarium plan today hadn't been all for Evan's benefit. He'd wanted to be alone with both of them. His son and his son's mother. He heard himself breathing. He'd wanted to know how she felt about him—not as Evan's father, but as a man.

She slid her hand over her forehead, dragging her hair into one smooth section at her back. Her breasts rose, and he could almost imagine cupping their full weight.

His pulse ratcheted to a near stop. He wanted her. She'd belonged to him once. Had Helene been right about his unconscious feelings for Olivia?

"Let's get this thing out of here," she said to her dad. "Zach, you said there's a place he can park it?"

Her tone was normal. He tried to sound natural, too, as if her generosity of spirit in the face of her determined father's tyrannical ways hadn't made him see her in a whole new light. He cleared his throat.

"Follow my car. They have gas and electricity hookups."

"You're sending me to a public campground?" James's shock was almost laughable.

Zach eyed the gleaming vehicle. "Looks to me as if you've got yourself a glorified camper there."

"Dad, Mom, come look!" Excitement surged in Evan's voice. "I can see you on TV."

Olivia scanned for the short-circuit cameras her fa-

ther would use for security. "Dad." The edge returned to her voice.

"Well, you may not be worried about safety, but
I'm vigilant."

And maybe his extra care was a good thing. James
Kendall had helped Olivia raise a normal, happy little
boy who didn't seem to demand or take advantage of
his privileged life. All Evan seemed to want was a
family, a real one with a mom and a dad and his
"grampa" and himself. He had all the pieces.

For the first time, Zach wondered if he and Olivia
might have married and made it work when she was
so young.

He forced himself to step away from that mystery.
Thinking about what might happen could put ideas in
a man's head.

What kind of dad would risk disappointing a son
as happy with life as Evan?

OLIVIA HID A YAWN behind her hand as Zach stopped
his car at the B&B that night. In the back seat, Evan's
head lolled, too.

"He's asleep again," Zach said.

"Yeah. You guys were both pretty tolerant."

She felt a little guilty. After they'd checked her
recalcitrant father into his camping space, she'd used
the extra equipment he'd brought along for her to
catch up on some work. Zach had kept Evan busy,
racing astoundingly dexterous dinosaurs in colorful
cartoon cars over a variety of video racetracks. And
when they'd been ready to leave, Zach had stowed
the laptop and scanner and fax machine in his trunk.

She'd protested against appropriating the new laptop, but her father had smugly replied that the one she'd brought with her wasn't strong enough to handle the workload if she intended to play in the Smokies indefinitely.

And she couldn't say how much longer she'd be staying.

"Did you finish your work tonight?" Zach asked.

"Not really, but I left an e-mail list of tasks for Brian, and I can take care of a few more things after Evan goes to bed. The work's never done."

Zach shrugged, a picture of nonchalance—so perfect a picture, he made her suspicious. "Lily and I have some stuff to do in the morning. I could swing by for Evan on my way to pick her up."

Olivia formed the word "no" on her lips, but managed to swallow it before it escaped. Zach wanted to take their son with him. A morning without her might make a good start for him and Evan. The more time Evan spent with Lily, the better for both children. And she could use a few more hours to work on the current issue.

"Okay." She dragged the word out unintentionally. "But you'll take my cell phone number?"

"Olivia." Amusement deepened his tone. "I have a child. I'm checked out on caring for humans under aged ten."

His claim brought the past back like a slap in her face. "Now that's Navy talk."

"Yeah, I guess so." He sounded wistful. "Sometimes their terminology works best. Yes or no?"

"Yes." She couldn't help a touch of caution. "But you'll be careful with him?"

Zach's only answer was a low chuckle that chased

along her nerve endings as if he'd actually touched her.

"Why are you laughing?" She shifted, trying to distance herself, but her body responded slowly, as if its yearning were stronger than her reluctance to get involved again.

"I'm always surprised you survived your father," Zach said, "but you have a little of him in you."

"Just his tendency to overprotect."

And not to like being laughed at. And one other thing. If she could control Zach's every movement on his first outing alone with her son, she would have. Gladly—which meant one thing more. She wasn't wise enough to be ashamed.

CHAPTER TEN

THE NEXT MORNING Evan flew down the steps to greet Zach the second he parked at the B&B. Olivia waited in the doorway, tall, deceptively fragile-looking and alone. When Evan turned back, she lifted her hand in a halfhearted wave.

Evan stopped with an exaggerated sigh. "Girls worry too much," he said. "Mom," he bellowed, "I'm fine."

Olivia's pinched face kind of bugged Zach. Did she think he was going to run off with their son? He waved over Evan's shoulder, giving her room to panic. This was as new to her as to him, and they'd both have to adjust.

Putting on his confident sheriff's face, he lifted his voice. "We'll come back for you, and you can help us feed the animals."

She nodded, and a stronger smile lightened her gaze.

Evan flapped his hand at Olivia again before scrambling into Zach's car. "How long do we have to drive before we get to Lily's house, Dad?"

"A few minutes, but I need to stop at the post office first. Do you mind coming with me?"

"Nope." He gave a little skip. "But don't you have a mailbox at your house? We have one in our building. It's a little gold box in the wall, and Mom lets me open it with our special key."

It sounded magical. "I live up on the mountain, and it's easier for the post office to deliver my mail down here."

"Oh. Okay." Evan moved his hand so Zach could open the car door and then climbed across Lily's booster. After he put on his seat belt, Zach shut the door and went around to the front.

They drove around the courthouse to a small, square, clapboard building. Zach opened the door marked "In" for Evan, but the boy stopped on the threshold.

"It's dark in there, Dad."

He eased his hand into Zach's, and Zach squeezed. "There's a light on the counter." Mrs. Banks, the elderly postmistress angled it to shine on the patron's faces as if she was an investigator for a secret government agency. "You'll be able to see better as we move up in the line."

About then, Evan bumped into the backside of Mike Henderson.

"'Scuse me," Evan said, shuffling into Zach. "I didn't see him, Dad."

"Wait a minute and your eyes will adjust." Zach dropped his hand to Evan's head.

"Hey, buddy." Mike wrung Zach's hand. "I want to thank you again for saving my wife at the bank."

A sharp memory of his rage that day made Zach glance at Evan. He didn't want anger like that to touch his son. "It was just my job, Mike. Hey, Evan and I are going to pick up Lily and then head to your store after we leave here."

"Are you planting?"

"Picking up seed for the animals on my land. The weather's getting colder."

"Good idea." Mike Henderson stuck out his hand to Evan. "Nice to meet you, young feller."

"Hi." Evan shook Mike's hand, but his usual self-confidence seemed to ebb. The dark post office and the big man might be scary to a little guy. Zach gripped his son's shoulder, trying to give him comfort. Evan glanced up and leaned into his father's leg in a gut-wrenching gesture of trust.

"Mr. Henderson," Mrs. Banks said, "I have a few things for you."

The other man turned around, and Evan eased away from Zach's leg. As Mike turned from the counter a second later, he tipped his UT Vols ball cap and patted Evan's back. "See you later. Maybe Tammy can find some apple fritters for the young ones. She's been picking apples all week."

"I think we're doing that next Saturday at my grandparents' anniversary party." Zach eased forward.

"Smart of Seth to put you bunch to work."

Behind them, Mrs. Banks cleared her voice. "See you later, Mike." Zach led Evan to the counter.

Mrs. Banks tilted her banker's light until it shone on Evan's face, painting him paler than he was. "Good morning, young man."

Evan nodded. "Hello."

"Looks like you, Zach."

Mrs. Banks waited for him to speak, her pale blue eyes glittering behind large, old-fashioned glasses. If

she and James Kendall ever got together, they'd put
the rest of the news services out of business.

"Thanks," he said.

She still waited. So did he. Evan reached for the
papers fluttering from Mrs. Bank's bulletin board.
"Kitties. Does this say they're giving kitties away?"
he asked. "I'd like a kitty, Dad."

"We'll have to ask your mom." Answering to
"Dad" should give Mrs. Banks plenty to chew on.

She must have thought so too because she finally
resorted to doing her job. "Not much for you today.
Couple of bills and an ad from that home repair center
over in Knoxville. You planning to do something to
your house?" She passed his mail through the rusty
screen that blocked her from her patrons and her patrons from their mail.

"I don't know how they got to me way out here.
You wouldn't think they'd bother with someone an
hour and a half from the store." He started to leave,
but plucked a lollipop from the bowl Mrs. Banks
stocked on the patron side of her counter. She wasn't
all ruthless snoop. "For Evan."

"You take another one for Lily and give both your
little ones some sugar from me, hear?"

"I'll do that." Turning, he handed the candy to
Evan.

"Thank you," the boy said to Mrs. Banks.

"You're welcome, son. Now save that and eat it
when you give your sister hers."

"I will," Evan said quietly.

"Thanks again." Zach pushed through the door
and trailed Evan, blinking, into autumn sunlight that
had burned off the twisting whorls of haze that gave

the Smoky Mountains their name. "What do you think, Evan? Pretty country?"

"Yeah, but scary mailmen." Evan scrunched up his eyes. "What kind of sugar are you supposed to give me and Lily?"

"That's Southern for a kiss."

Evan rubbed his face with both hands. "I don't need any. I'm a boy, you know."

Zach grinned with pure happiness. His son was easy to love. "Let's go pick up your sister."

OLIVIA WAS so deep in next month's layout she didn't hear the phone ring at first. On the second ring, she picked up her cell, but then realized it was the room telephone. She typed a last quick note into the e-mail she'd been putting together for Brian and then picked up the receiver. "Olivia Ken—Hello."

"Zach told me he'd be here at 9:00. It's now 9:13, and he's interfering with my plans for the day. Where is he?"

"Helene?" Steeling herself for battle, Olivia pulled off her glasses.

"Of course. How many ex-wives can one man have? Except, of course, you weren't a wife."

Olivia refused to be annoyed or offended. "He and Evan left here a little while ago. I'm sure they'll be with you soon."

"How long ago?"

Long enough that Olivia felt a little concern he hadn't made it to the posh side of Bardill's Ridge yet. She looked at her watch. He'd been a little early for Evan. She couldn't be sure how long they'd been gone, and she didn't want to make more trouble for him. "Maybe he stopped somewhere on the way."

"How long are you and your son staying in town?"

"I don't know, but Helene, we have nothing to do with you. We never did."

"Don't kid yourself. Unless Zach has a commitment phobia, something—or someone—held him back during our marriage."

Helene could be right and wrong. Sheriff in his hometown, deeply involved in his sprawling family's life, and most of all, trying desperately to father his children, Zach seemed to have no problem committing. In fact, he took on enough to keep him busy every second of every day. Since she'd known him—even six years ago—he'd always been on his way somewhere to do something.

But he'd never truly committed to her, and obviously, his commitment to Helene had broken down. "Let's be honest with each other, Helene." She wasn't a Kendall for nothing. "I don't know what went wrong between you, and I don't want to know. It's none of my business. I just want to get along well enough with you to keep both our children happy." The silence lasted so long she suspected the other woman had hung up on her. Just as well. Her pulse seemed to be hammering in her ears. Her head could explode any second now. "Helene?"

"Don't get me wrong. I'm happy with Leland and my life now, but I wasn't the bad guy with Zach, and his family thinks I was. I never stood a chance with him, and I see him trying harder with you already."

"Maybe—because of Evan."

"Then Lily must not matter as much to him. He didn't try as hard with me."

"That's ridiculous. He just learned from his problems with you. He does love Lily, and you know it. I hope he'll love Evan as much."

"Aren't you a Goody Two-shoes?"

If she were, this woman would try her character beyond saving. "Not particularly, but you lose nothing if Zach and I manage to be friends."

"I'll have a problem if Lily loses something."

Stunned, Olivia didn't know what to say. Helene must have changed her mind about wanting Zach out of her life. Unless that had always been face-saving.

"I need to know Zach's a good dad—to Evan and to Lily." Olivia pushed her finger around the telephone's keypad. "And I'm thrilled Evan gets to have a little sister. He loves her already."

Helene hesitated again. "She's glad to know him, too."

Olivia quickly forgave her grudging tone. "So that's where we stand. On the same side."

"Honestly, I can't say I want to. I always knew there was someone else, and I've built you up into a monster."

Olivia took a deep breath. Was Helene willing to change her attitude? Olivia figured she should be the angry, suspicious one. Helene had gotten everything Olivia had dreamed of back then. "I know I'm a horrible shock to you, but I want Lily to be happy, too," she repeated. "I'd no more hurt her than I'd risk causing Evan harm."

"Zach's just driven up." Anger edged back into

Helene's voice, but she inhaled deeply, too. "I guess you and I declared a truce?"

Olivia bit back the protest that she'd never wanted to argue in the first place. "I'm glad."

"I don't think I'll tell Zach we talked."

"I have no problem with private conversations." Zach had kept plenty of secrets before and this one couldn't hurt him.

ZACH PARKED in front of the blue clapboard feed store with its sign swinging on rusty hinges and the usual crowd of farmers passing the time of day. How would Evan compare the place to James Kendall's expensive bit of paradise on wheels?

Zach helped Lily out of her booster seat while Evan came around the car trunk. Straightening, Zach took both his children's hands.

He surveyed the hardwood trees nestled among pines on the ridge across the wide road. Yellow and orange seemed to weight the leaves, dropping them to the ground. Cold was coming. Even the tardiest tourists would soon abandon their leaf peeping.

He breathed in a lungful of air absorbing the scent of several Bardill's Ridge fireplaces pressed into early service. It was a smell he remembered from his own childhood—one that represented the continuity he craved. He'd come home six years ago, feeling as if he'd failed, instead of completing his duty in the Navy, as if he hardly deserved to live.

The pattern of life among his family and overly interested neighbors had helped him begin to believe in himself. Why not believe in Evan, too? A boy could love this town. It was Evan's heritage as much as Lily's or any other Calvert's, and Olivia seemed eager to help their child feel at home here.

Even Helene had been semiapproachable today. "Your mom's in a good mood," he said to Lily. She'd hardly harassed him at all for being late.

"She was talking to someone on the phone when you got here. She was mad before that."

"Oh." He hadn't meant to fish information out of his little girl. He turned Evan and Lily toward the slightly peeling front door. "You all stay close to me inside, okay?" Some of Henderson's wares might be dangerous to a boy who usually shopped in department stores.

"What kind of seeds are we buying?" Evan asked.

"Feed," Lily said with a touch of importance, because she knew better than her brother. "For the deer and the squirrels and the possums and the—what else, Daddy?"

"Rabbits, I guess, and some chipmunks." He arched an eyebrow at Evan. "The occasional skunk."

"'Cassional?" Evan asked.

"He means skunks come round once in a while." Lily made a less than delicate gagging sound. "I hate 'em. They'd be cute, but they stink so bad."

"I've seen them in movies. I want to see a real one." Evan pulled on Zach's hand, itching to charge the stairs. "Let's hurry."

"They aren't inside." She tugged back. "Daddy, can I show Evan the whistles?"

Mike and Tammy stocked carved wooden train whistles and animal calls near the counter. Zach's uncle Ethan, a cabinetmaker, had made many of them.

"Let me ask Mike if he'll keep an eye on you while I load the feed."

"Cool." Evan stopped struggling.

Inside, shelves ran floor to ceiling, where a line of old-fashioned fans wafted the pungent smells of seeds and animal feed. Evan stopped for a moment, obviously not a big fan of the strong odors. Lily patted his arm.

"Stinks almost as bad as a skunk," she said in a voice full of sympathy. "You'll get used to it."

"Everything's weird down here," Evan said. "We went to this place to get Dad's mail and it was dark."

Zach was pulling the lollipop out of his pocket as Lily whipped her head around to interrogate him.

"Did Mrs. Banks give you suckers?"

"I saved mine." Evan pulled his out of his pants pocket, too. The stick was all bent, and he blew lint off it. "Dad said we could eat them after we feed the deer."

"Is it cold enough to feed the deers yet, Daddy?"

They usually waited until after the first frost. "We might be a little early, but Evan's never fed animals outside of a zoo before."

"We throw the food down, but the deers hide till we go inside," Lily said. "But I'll show ya."

Zach handed the lollipop to his daughter and walked past the kids to the counter. "Mike."

Mike Henderson turned from doing a crossword puzzle on the other side of the cash register. He pushed his pencil behind his ear. "Hey." He leaned over the counter to smile at the two upturned faces. "Hello again, Evan. How are you today, Miss Lily?"

"Hi," the children chorused.

"I'm fine, Mr. Henderson, but I need to show Evan your whistles," Lily said.

Evan bristled. "I know about whistles."

"Not like these ones."

Those two were going to duke it out in a power struggle before long. "Mike, do you mind if they hang around here while I—" Zach stopped, noticing the silence in the tin-roofed, wooden-floored building.

He glanced to the end of the counter where a couple of old codgers lounged in jeans and flannel shirts with fat tobacco wads tucked inside their bottom lips. The Larsen brothers had stopped settling the world's affairs to gape at his growing family. Sometimes living in a small town worked against you.

"Go ahead," Mike volunteered. "We'll be fine up here." He leaned back on the squeaking, red vinyl stool his own father had perched on day after day. "Tammy, bring out those apple fritters for Evan and Lily."

Zach glanced down the other side of the counter. No one in the store seemed to be interested in planting or feeding all of a sudden. Neighbors he'd known all his life stared at him as if he'd grown a spare head. Or brought home a spare child.

"Mike, don't let anyone…"

"You don't have to say it. They couldn't be safer."

"Okay."

At least he knew all the staring faces. None of the reporters had planted himself in the local feed store. Zach hoisted a sack of deer pellets to his shoulder and hurried out to his car. He loaded the rest faster than he'd ever run this errand in the past.

He paused only to make sure none of his friends

stopped to have a word with Evan. They were well-meaning, but he didn't want anyone questioning his five-year-old. Maybe he should have given Mrs. Banks more facts to post along the Bardill's Ridge grapevine.

He'd finished loading the car as Evan came out of the store with Lily on his tail. "Dad!" Evan's voice slurred around the edges of a wooden turkey call.

And Lily was blowing a train whistle behind him.

"Don't run with those in your mouth." He slammed the trunk lid and then reached to pluck both the call and the whistle from between their lips.

Evan let his call go. Lily held on to her whistle. "Dad, I sound just like a train."

"I wanna call turkeys." Evan clearly craved a pet of any species. "Can I have it?" he begged as the wind pushed light blond hair away from his forehead.

"Not if you're going to run with it." But God, he wanted to give his son a present. And Lily played another train tune, dampening the whistle until even Mike wouldn't take it back. Helene would kill him. "Lily, the same goes for you."

"We'll only run when we're holding them in our hands," Evan promised. His earnest look reminded Zach of James Kendall telling Olivia he had only her best interests at heart.

"Do you know how to use the call?" he asked.

"Mr. Henderson showed me how." Snatching it back, he popped it between his teeth and gobbled, his eyes flinging sparks of pride.

Zach flinched at the volume. The boy had skill. "You learn quick."

"You'll scare the deer," Lily said.

"No, I won't. Deer aren't scared of turkeys. They're both animals." He tried to gobble again, but something on Zach's face made him grin. "Don't make me laugh, Dad." Zach nodded, but a slightly hysterical note entered Evan's next gobble. "Can I have it?"

He might not have a Kendall-type budget, but he could afford the cost of a wooden turkey call. Maybe he should find out how Olivia would feel about Evan calling turkeys in her condo. The heck with common sense. He gave in and encircled them both with his arms as they climbed the steps. "Come with me so I can pay."

Evan and Lily heaved the screen door wide, running inside, and Zach turned his head, catching the door just before it would have slapped him in the face. But he noticed a man he didn't know, leaning against the stanchion at the end of Henderson's porch.

Zach stopped. A stranger, dressed in khakis and a polo shirt. Could be a tourist. More likely a reporter—if he judged by the man's interest in his family. Zach started toward him, and the guy jumped off the high porch.

Zach gripped the rail and leaned over the edge of the wooden structure, but the stranger had already disappeared. He waited, scanning the road in both directions, and then the ridge above him. No flash from a camera lens. No sound of voices, even whispering. Sound carried well in the valley beneath Bardill's Ridge.

If the guy was a reporter, maybe he'd gotten the message. It didn't seem likely. He'd be wise to hurry out to the B&B for Olivia and then run Evan and Lily up to his house—hopefully out of camera range.

Feeling jumpy, he crossed the porch, listening to the echo of his own footsteps. His instincts weren't always reliable since the accident. Something in those empty years sometimes pressed him to take action against a threat that didn't exist.

"Dad," Evan bellowed, as close as Zach had ever seen him to being a perfectly normal kid.

Forget about the reporters. Focus on the children. Zach pushed inside the store. Evan and Lily dragged him back to Mr. Henderson's pocked aluminum counter.

Lily slapped her small hands on the surface. "Dad has to give you some dollars, Mr. Henderson. My brother wants that turkey thing, and I *need* this whistle."

"You taking the boy hunting, Zach?"

"No," he said, before Evan could get excited about the idea.

Evan had his own ideas about wildlife. "I won't kill no turkeys," he said. "You don't kill turkeys, do you, Mr. Henderson?"

"Not a chance." The older man smoothed his overall bib over a portly belly. "I say we ban guns in this county and save all the turkey and deer and skunks as long as folks like you and your sister and dad buy your feed from me."

Evan and Lily giggled. Zach bent to examine the porch through the gleaming windows while Mike rang up his bill. No one came up, but he couldn't see the road. "What do I owe you, Mike?"

The other man pointed at the total on his cash register. "You've got the wind up, Zach."

"I'm probably wrong." He'd rather not scare the kids, but he didn't want their faces all over the evening news or the late paper. He fished his wallet from his back pocket and counted out the dollars Lily had talked about. Tapping his wallet on the counter, he waited while Mike figured his change and Evan gobbled and Lily whistled.

Mike's other patrons couldn't even pretend to be interested in their own business now. All interest turned to the smallest customers.

Zach herded the children toward the screen door, but stepped in front of them at the last minute. Halfway across the porch with Evan and Lily in his wake like ducklings, he stopped. A sea of faces and cameras waited below. Rage blew through his head at the bastards who kept chasing down his children. He counted without thinking. Their numbers made them more of a small pond than a sea, but who the hell wanted to stalk babies for a living?

Zach walked the children back to the store's doors, out of camera range and took his cell phone out of his shirt pocket. He dialed Olivia's number and she answered on the first ring.

"Reporters." He moved Lily out of the way as Mike opened the door behind her.

"Where?" Olivia needed no explanation.

"At the feed store. I won't come back for you. They'd just follow us. Do you remember the way to my mom's house?"

"I think so."

Conversation rising behind Mike's screen drew his

gaze. The inquisitive Bardill's Ridge farmers were spilling onto the porch.

"Dad?" Lily sounded scared.

"You're fine." He hugged her tight.

Evan also looped his arm around his sister's shoulder. "I can handle it. Don't worry. We'll just do what Dad tells us."

Even pissed as all get-out, Zach fought a lump in his throat, grateful and appalled at the same time for Evan's maturity, his instant inclination to protect his sister. He held on to both children, but spoke to Olivia. "Ask Aunt Eliza the way to Mom's house to make sure, and ask her if you can borrow her car. Meet us at Mom's, and then I'll take you all home to my place. They won't find us out there if I can get out of their sight before we leave town behind." He knew a couple of back roads.

"Don't drive crazy with Lily and Evan."

"Olivia," he said. As if she had to caution him. "I'm going to call Sherm as soon as I get in the car. He may be able to run interference."

The men from the store had also begun to ease around him and the children.

"Sherm?" Olivia said.

"One of my deputies. Get going."

As he hung up, he slid in front of Evan and Lily, while his neighbors began their slow, threatening march down the steps as if to confront the reporters who refused to back off. The advantages of small-town, family feeling. This was why he'd come home. People looked after each other.

"Mike," Zach said, grateful but fearing he might

have to arrest his own rescuers if he didn't stop them. "I'm calling Sherm."

"If you think we can't handle it." Mike planted himself in front of the guy Zach had first seen on the porch. "I think we can."

He'd like to handle a few of them himself. His arm and leg muscles jumped in anticipation. "Stop and think about the situation. Let's not ask for any more trouble." He sure didn't want to expose Lily and Evan to a riot. "I'm going to drive the children away, and these jokers will all *disperse*." He lifted his voice on the last word, offering it as a suggestion.

"We won't touch them unless they try to barge after you, and no judge in these hills is going to take these boys' part against us."

He had a point. Zach wasted no more time. "Thanks." He lifted both children. "Let's move."

Evan tucked his face into Zach's shoulder. Lily saw and followed suit. "You're well-trained, Evan." Zach's temper fired up again because his son had been forced to learn how to avoid the media.

"Grampa says to keep my face private," Evan said, his voice muffled.

Camera shutters clicked, and Lily whimpered. Zach held her even tighter and thanked God he'd left his car doors unlocked. He checked the back for stray reporters before he put the children inside. Lily climbed into her booster seat, shaking her hair in front of her face.

"I'll buckle it, sister," Evan said.

"Make sure it's tight," Zach said, "and then put on your seat belt."

The townsfolk had managed to contain the reporters and Zach started the car. Gravel sprayed as he peeled out of the lot. Not one reporter escaped the crowd of his neighbors.

"Lily, you all right?"

"Yeah, Daddy." But she sounded dazed, and tears dampened her green eyes.

Evan patted her shoulder with a little too much force, as Zach reached back and tugged on the protective shield on her booster seat. "Thanks for fixing that, Evan. We'll be at Grandma Beth's soon," he said.

"And you can play with Spike," Evan told his sister. "And maybe we'll build another log house with my mom."

Now that the danger had passed, he could almost hate his son's maturity. Evan had a long time to be all grown up. He shouldn't have had to start before he was five.

"I thought we'd all go home and scatter food for the animals," Zach said.

Evan nudged Lily again. "See? We're going to have fun. You don't have to cry."

"Not crying," she said. She lifted her whistle and blew a weak blast. Evan answered with a turkey gobble that sounded like a bird with asthma.

"I'm sorry, guys," Zach said. Helene was going to kill him when she heard about this. For once he might deserve it. He should have been more vigilant— should have picked up the feed himself and then picked up the children.

Evan and Lily made stronger efforts on their purchases and eased his guilt a little, but Zach didn't feel better until he turned the last curve through the shrubbery at his mom's house.

She flew out of the house, worry all over her body. After he parked, she jumped into the back seat and hauled Lily and Evan into a big hug.

"My poor grandbabies. Come inside. Spike and I made you some hot chocolate. You need to warm up."

"It was scary," Lily said, still spooked, "but look." And she whistled so loud Zach and his mom reeled out of the car.

He'd have to remember to caution her about busting eardrums later. He unlatched her booster seat and his mom helped her out. Zach opened Evan's door.

"Thanks, buddy," he said, leaning in. "You took good care of your sister."

Evan pulled his call from his mouth as he clambered out, his gaze mystified as if he didn't understand the big deal. "I love her, Dad."

Zach's eyes burned. His mouth trembled as if he were the young girl. For a second, he saw Salva, passing around pictures of her newborn daughter in a class they'd both attended about a year after she'd left the Academy. Zach dropped to his knees in the gravel and hugged his boy tight. "I love you, Evan."

CHAPTER ELEVEN

THE AUTUMN SUN WAS straight up in the sky as Olivia eased Eliza's old but obviously beloved car around Beth's overgrown shrubbery. As desperate as she was to see her son, he was with his father, and she wasn't about to scratch a vehicle that belonged to one of Evan's new aunts.

She peered greedily up the driveway at the house. Zach was kneeling in the gravel, hugging Evan. Fear jetted through Olivia's body.

Had something happened to her son? Had she been crazy to trust a man who took bank robbers apart with his bare hands, whose ex-wife claimed he didn't know how to commit? What if he couldn't even commit to taking care of their son properly? Helene's fears about Lily certainly hadn't matched Zach's explanation of her concerns.

Olivia hit the gas. As rocks spewed behind her, Zach rose, shoving Evan behind him, and his mom straightened on the other side of the car. Olivia slammed on the brakes, stopping at the top of the hill. She threw the door open and ran to her son, taking quick inventory of Beth and Lily, who stared at her openmouthed.

Olivia tried to sound calm to keep from scaring Lily. "Are you all right, Evan?"

"Huh?"

She searched him for broken bones, already realizing she'd overreacted, already embarrassed to meet Zach's gaze.

"Mom, you're tickling me." Evan pushed her away and then lifted a small, wooden whistle. "Look what Dad gave me."

That was it? She sat back on her heels, her heart beating at the walls of her chest, her blood so heavy in her head she felt like fainting. All that scare—complete with Sherm the deputy letting her know he'd scattered both Zach's friends and the "mob" of reporters—and "Look what Dad gave me" was all Evan cared about?

"That's nice." She licked her dry lips. "What is it?"

He blew it, and she fell backward onto the driveway. "Is that a bird call?"

"Yeah—for turkeys."

"And I gotta train whistle." Lily piped up behind her just before the whistle shrilled.

Olivia barely managed not to cover her ears. She'd hate to insult the children. "Wow, Lily. That sounds just like a real train."

"Come on, let's not deafen Olivia."

Zach held out his hand, and Olivia stared at his broad palm. Even the lines were familiar. She put her hand in his, though she was perfectly capable of dragging her own behind off the dirt.

Zach hauled her into the air with impressively little effort. "Can you hear me?" he asked.

She laughed, glancing down at Lily and Evan. "I guess they're all right."

"Mr. Henderson helped us," Evan said.

"Maybe we should go inside." Beth spun Lily toward the porch.

"No, Mom." Zach let go of Olivia to take his mother's arm. Olivia's hand felt cold, and she tucked it into her back pocket. Zach went on. "We'll wait to see if any other cars come along, and then we'll head to my house. I need to let Helene know what happened in case anyone uses the pictures they took."

"You can call from inside."

"I just want to make sure we don't have to deal with them again tonight, Mom." He bent a meaningful look toward Evan and Lily. "It was kind of scary."

"I thought so, too, Daddy." Lily held out her arms for him to lift her and ducked her head against his shoulder.

Guilt dropped heavily on Olivia. "I'm sorry. Maybe we should have stayed in Chicago. I did call my father and ask him if he could do something. He said he'd look into it."

Zach frowned. "What can he do?"

"He's bigger than any of the other guys." Olivia didn't enjoy talking about her family's influence. She'd always avoided using Kendall power—maybe she'd even tried to convince herself it didn't exist, and she and Evan were just like any other mom and son. But now, if he and Lily were going to be camera targets, she'd set her father on anyone who tried to harm the children.

"Doesn't that make him vulnerable? Don't the other 'guys' want to beat him?" Zach asked.

"Dad has this theory. Give the others a little of

what they want—photos, or the press conference, and they won't be ambitious enough to go for more than you want to give. That's never been the way he worked, so I don't know why he thinks it's effective, but that's the way he manages the competition, too. He can't put everyone out of business, so he makes a little room for them, the stories, the territories he deems expendable. He has more resources, so he always looks better.''

Zach also seemed to doubt the process her father had perfected for getting his own way. He checked his watch. "We've waited long enough. I'm going to put you back in the car now, Lily. Evan, do you want to ride with me or your mom?"

Evan's sigh was a heavy gust of wind. "I'd better go with Mom. She might need me."

Olivia was taken aback. "I'm perfectly fine, son. Ride with your dad if you want to."

"Okay." He scampered around her and climbed in beside Lily.

Olivia watched, nonplussed to take a back seat in her son's priorities. She thought she'd steeled herself. She was the adult. She possessed a sound mind.

She still wanted her son to pick her first. Which no doubt made this a desirable lesson in character building.

"I'll back up over there." She pointed to the far corner of Beth's driveway. "And then follow you down."

"Sounds good," Zach said. "Go slowly because I'm going to ease out after I make sure no one's waiting for us."

She nodded and then turned to his mom. "Thanks, Beth, for letting us meet here."

"I'd rather you stayed awhile," she said, in the way of a grandmother, "but I understand, Zach." She forestalled her son's explanations and then leaned into the back seat of his car. "Evan, Lily, I'll see you at the orchard on Friday."

Evan stopped inspecting his turkey call. "Orchard?" Excitement perked him up.

"For Grandma Greta's party," Beth said. "You can pick apples."

"On a ladder?" Lily bounced in her seat, forgetting her earlier scare.

"We'll have to see about that." Zach's reluctance boded ill for Lily and ladder-climbing. "Ready, Olivia?"

"Sure." She crunched through the gravel, then backed Eliza's car away from his. She tried her father's cell phone, but received no answer. With any luck, he'd be busy working his evil magic on their behalf this time.

She dropped her phone back in her purse and concentrated on following Zach. They rolled slowly down his mother's driveway, entering the highway only after he made sure no one was waiting for them.

He turned north and they began to meander up the ridge on narrow roads. Zach would have to lead her out of here when she and Evan started back to the bed-and-breakfast tonight. She'd never find her way back to town unless Bardill's Ridge glowed as brightly as Chicago.

Finally they turned down a paved driveway that turned into small pebbles in front of a white farmhouse. Dark green shutters and empty window boxes bordered the upstairs window. A tall porch wrapped around the lower floor.

Olivia imagined colorful plants in the window boxes and in the flower beds that Zach had left barren. She saw Evan and Lily and maybe a couple more children swinging off the porch rail to land on the run in the neatly mowed lawn.

Those nebulous, faceless children brought her up short. Imagining him with Helene hurt, no matter how deeply she didn't want to care. But it was far too easy to imagine him with someone else—someone who could make him happy, settle him down where she and Helene had failed to make him care enough to stay.

Heat filled her face. Talk about a fine time to panic, with reporters all over the hills, and her son falling under the spell of his brand-new father. It'd be a better time to remember this was almost exactly what she'd wanted six years ago, two parents for her son, and Zach, safe and sound.

She parked the car behind Zach's and cleared all dangerous thoughts from her mind as she joined the others. Zach got out of his car, but Evan and Lily stayed in their seats. Olivia leaned in.

"Not coming out?" she asked.

"We're driving to the barn to unload the stuff we bought at Henderson's." Zach took a key off his chain and handed it to her. "Go inside. Check out the fridge. Get a drink. We'll be back in a few minutes."

"Where's the barn? I don't know that I want Evan out of my sight any longer today."

"I didn't think of that." He led her to the rear of

his car. "See that road?" A continuation of the pebbled drive, it wound around the house. "It leads to the barn. You can see it from the kitchen." He held out the key. "Or you can come with us."

She hesitated. She would have gone if he'd asked her. It was silly, but in her present, uncertain state, the invitation mattered.

"Okay. I'll see you later. Watch him. Evan hasn't been in a real barn before."

He dropped the key in her hand. "He's been in a fake barn?"

"At a petting zoo. I don't know if it was real."

As Zach looked bemused, a train whistle blasted the air. A turkey called in response.

"I'd better go before they hurt themselves."

Shouldering her bag, she stepped back as he started the car again. She climbed the porch steps, listening to his engine fade. A gust of wind blew her hair into her eyes and her mouth and a shiver ran up and down her body. Under the covered veranda, she wished she'd brought a jacket.

She put the key to the door. This was Zach's home. She hadn't walked into a fairy tale where everything was going to end all right and they'd find the love they'd lost. She'd loved. He'd been careful not to tell her too much about himself.

She'd quizzed him about every family member in every picture he'd kept. She'd needed more than he could give, and she'd searched for more information every way possible.

With those past interrogations in mind, she couldn't seem to turn his key in the front door lock now. Going inside without him would feel like snooping. She no longer snooped—except at work.

Smiling wryly, she dropped into a rocker beneath a wide picture window. She tucked her collar close beneath her chin and rocked slowly.

The view took her breath away. Straight ahead, beyond the line of spruce that blocked Zach's property from the road, the ridge continued to climb. The trees looked as if someone had picked up a bucket full of autumn and painted the ultimate fall landscape. To the east a glimpse of the courthouse cupola, and the church's spire peeked above more forest.

The Calverts who'd lived in this home must have felt like kings. As Olivia turned her head, the low brush of wind rustled in her ears. Nothing could have been more different from the museum she'd grown up in or the decidedly contemporary city dwelling in which she raised her son.

She felt good rocking on Zach's porch. This land accepted anyone, enfolded even a lonely woman in ancient, rugged beauty. Her name and her bank account meant nothing here.

The door opened behind her, and she bolted upright, a scream on her lips. Zach came outside, his eyes questioning her.

"What are you doing?"

She stood. "Rocking." Thinking. Being. Something she hadn't done a lot of lately in Chicago. "When did you move to this house?"

"I lived here until my father died. My mom hated the farm for taking him from her, so we moved to her family's home."

"How old were you?" He would have avoided that

question in Chicago. It was too specific, and if she'd had unpleasant intentions, she could have used the information to work out the kind of man who grew out of a boy who'd lost his father so young.

"He died about a week after my eighth birthday."

"You tried to become the man of the house. You took care of your mother."

"When she'd let me." He trailed the backs of his fingertips across her cheek, and it didn't seem like an inappropriate gesture. She had to stop herself from leaning into his hand. "You look cold." He retained a talent for fending off personal questions. "Come inside, and I'll start a fire."

"Where are Evan and Lily?"

"Scattering food in the back." He held the door wider. "Want some coffee? Something to eat?"

"I'm fine." He still wanted to take care of people, but he didn't want more. Though the sound of his voice double-timed her heartbeat, she couldn't let herself forget they had a son who needed them to be natural together, not attracted.

She tucked her purse between Zach's body and hers. Still, she couldn't avoid his heat against her uncovered hand. Crossing the threshold in the long, lean shelter of his body, she resisted confusing urges. She wanted to run, to keep herself from caring again. But she wanted to stay, to play make-believe again, because make-believe with Zach had been so much better than aching for him after he'd gone.

She no longer trusted her memories, the hard, hot texture of his thigh beneath her hand, the strain of his flat belly against hers as he'd gulped air. For him, those times had just been sex.

Tripping on a Berber rug brought Olivia back to the here and now as she slid across the polished pine floor. Zach reached for her, but she evaded his touch.

"I must be colder than I thought." Cold explained the low pitch of her voice, too. If Zach was gullible enough to believe her.

"Come to the kitchen. I'll make coffee. You shouldn't have waited on the porch, Olivia."

She doubted he was gullible. But now wasn't the time to discuss feelings and his compulsion to protect gave him a to-do list to make her comfortable. She went along with it.

The wide farmhouse kitchen held a table for six in its center. Six. But one man lived alone here.

Zach took coffee from a cabinet and set it on the butcher-block counter. As Olivia drew closer to the square kitchen window, she heard laughter. Lily.

Olivia leaned across the sink. Outside, Evan ran across the sloping lawn, a blue plastic bucket in his hand. Chasing behind him, Lily threw as much animal food at him as she scattered on the grass. As they reached the edge of the woods, they slowed, to spread the feed with more care.

"Evan's hoping he can persuade a deer to live here." Zach spooned coffee into the filter. "He'd really like a pet."

"I know, but we're so busy I've never been sure we could take care of an animal. We had a fish when he was a baby." She pushed back from the window. "But I don't like to talk about that."

Zach's mouth curved. Even from the side, his smile softened features that were tighter than she remembered. The years between them hadn't made him happy either.

Olivia shifted away from him to the end of the counter, pretending she needed to look through the square-paned windows in the kitchen door.

"You have a deck." Two stories of deck, open to the clouds streaming over the ridge and to the breeze that was picking up in the swaying pine boughs.

She pressed her forehead to the door's cold glass. A gas grill stood near the kitchen. On the lower level, a dark green table and cream-padded chairs waited for company.

"My uncle Ethan and I redid it this summer."

"Ethan? He's—Sophie's father?"

He looked up, surprise widening his eyes. Her heart started bumping instead of beating. "How did you remember?"

She almost looked away, but why give in to a challenge? "Remembering is my job."

He lifted his head, his gaze careful. "So it is." He turned back to the coffeepot, but nodded toward the window. "Did they run out yet?"

"The buckets may be empty, but they look happy. Evan's chasing Lily now."

"You and he should stay here tonight."

Had she just imagined an invitation? She turned her head. Her hair tickled beneath her chin, raising a shiver.

"The reporters can't find you." Zach took two cups out of the cupboard. "If they knew where I lived, they'd be here already. No one in town is going to give us up, and if they can find my land in the courthouse records, I'll hire every last one of them as investigators.''

"Kendalls don't hide out."

"Maybe this Kendall should, if hiding means Evan and Lily get to know each other without cameras chasing them around the yard.''

"They're going to find us here, Zach." And she didn't want to stay. She didn't belong here. It was too simple, too homey, too much the kind of place she'd tried and failed to make for Evan. Being in Zach's house unnerved her, not least of all because she didn't know how to build a home like his.

"I promise you no one will find us. If I can't find Buford Taylor's family still, and I grew up in these woods, no outsider is going to find a house that isn't even listed in the phone book.''

"I don't want to confuse Evan."

Zach pulled cream from the fridge, but she thought his shoulders stiffened. "Confuse him?"

"He might start to see the three of us together as a family. I could let him stay if you want." As much as she hated the idea. What if Evan loved this home better than his own?

"If you leave, someone may see where you've come from.''

"That's not likely, Zach."

"Those reporters are your colleagues. You know how resourceful they are. We got away without being caught this time.''

"I didn't bring any extra clothes."

"I can lend you something. Sweats and a T-shirt to sleep in. Evan can borrow one of my shirts, too.''

She pressed her forehead into her palm. A headache had begun to build back there. She pushed her fingertips into her hairline. What should she do?

Flee any dwelling where being alone with Zach felt so right? She let her hands fall to her sides. Zach lifted both brows, waiting for an answer. She couldn't give in and say the words, so she unzipped her purse and plucked out a plastic bag that held shorts and a T-shirt and underwear for Evan.

She set the bag carefully on the counter. Zach picked it up. The plastic crackled in his fingers as he twisted it for a closer inspection of the contents.

"I *know* you didn't plan to stay." He stared, trying to read her mind.

At twenty-one, she would have bared herself gladly, soul and all. Now she knew better.

"Evan is five. I'm his mom. He often needs a change of clothes."

"Good idea. I'll have to remember that for Lily. I don't know how many ice-cream cones she's worn home."

"We should call them in now."

"Also a good idea. I didn't expect you to let Evan stay with me so soon, so I don't have his room ready yet."

She glanced toward the living room through which they'd entered. The last thing she wanted to do was help him clear a room and get it ready for her son. Working together would stick in her head for the rest of her life.

"Does your couch fold out? Evan and I can share."

He nodded. "Why don't you share my room, and I'll take the couch." She started to say no. Zach lifted his hand to rebuff her arguments. "My way is the most sensible. And you'd want more privacy than you'd get on the couch.''

''I meant to say thanks.'' Clearly she hadn't, but a peace offering might ease them back into more neutral territory.

Zach opened the kitchen door and stepped onto the deck. He shoved his hands into his pockets, tilting back on the heels of his hiking boots. ''We should have called them sooner. I think storms are coming.'' He raised his voice. ''Evan, Lily, time to come in.''

''Awww!'' Lily shouted.

''Awww,'' Evan echoed.

''Hot chocolate might warm you up,'' Zach said. ''Lily, you have to help Evan pick a mug.''

''A mug?'' Olivia asked.

''Every night she's here, Lily and I have chocolate milk before she goes to bed. Cold or hot, we drink from the same mugs. I think Evan's going to want his own mug.'' His smile acknowledged the way brother and sister copied each other when they weren't fighting for top-dog spot.

''I hope you have another one to match Lily's.''

Zach came back into the house, leaning a fraction of an uncomfortable inch too close. ''You'll probably have to pick one, too.''

''I'm not—''

''Part of the ritual? Might as well be while you're here. You have nothing to lose.''

He could say that. He didn't remember last time.

BETH LOCKED her doors and windows. All afternoon she'd felt as if someone were staring in at her. She hadn't even gone out to cover her plants, and the weather felt cold tonight: She was turning out the lights when someone pounded on her door.

She shrieked. Whoever it was had slammed his weight into the door, obviously intent on getting in. Where was a shotgun when you needed one?

"Are you all right in there? Mrs. Calvert, do you need help?"

She went to the window beside the porch and caught Olivia's father, searching for a way in. Before he could toss a planter through her window, she opened up.

"You scared me out of my wits. I didn't hear your car."

"But you're all right?"

She nodded.

James Kendall brushed his flying white hair out of his eyes. "I'm sorry. When you screamed I thought you might be hurt." He looked disgusted. "Why play around? I thought someone had broken in. I haven't been out without Ian and Jock in so long—never mind—where's my daughter?"

"Putting Evan to bed, I assume."

"I've just been to the B&B. That woman wouldn't let me see Olivia and Evan, and she wouldn't tell me a thing. I had the feeling they weren't there."

"Eliza's helping us hide Evan. Hasn't Olivia called you?"

"Then it's true." His face expressed true dismay. "She's staying with Zach tonight. She and Evan."

He couldn't expect her to share his consternation. "They're safe. Would you like coffee?"

"No, I don't want coffee. I want my daughter to stay away from a man who's hurt her in the past. No one will say where your son lives. You're going to tell me.''

''I don't think so.'' His arrogance, despite its flavor of frustration and worry, drained all her sympathy. ''And I think you need to leave my house. I don't normally accept visitors this late.''

He opened his mouth and then closed it, forcing himself to act calm. ''I might have come earlier, but I spent all afternoon buying up film that made every man in this town look like a thug.''

Her respect for him rose. ''Why would you do that?''

He seemed to lose enthusiasm for his story. ''They used their pitchforks to keep the reporters off Zach and the children.''

''Your rivals let you buy them off?''

His egotism flooded back in a smile that suggested he was no mortal man. ''You'd be surprised how much money I have.''

She tried not to laugh. He seemed so earnest. She wouldn't laugh at Evan for showing off. ''I thought the rich didn't talk about their bank accounts.''

''You look as if you need impressing.''

He was probably right, since wealth didn't often impress her. ''I owe you for protecting my town, and probably my son, since I assume those others would have said he instigated the misuse of the farming implements.''

''There weren't any pitchforks. I may have exaggerated.'' The truth made him uncomfortable. ''A problem I have.''

She liked a person who could turn human when

THE SECRET FATHER

you least expected it. "Step inside. I already have the coffee made."

"Maybe I will."

"But I'm not going to tell you where Zach lives."

"Maybe you will."

She'd reacted to no such challenge since Ned's death. But this man needed setting straight.

CHAPTER TWELVE

ZACH HAD ALREADY wished Evan good-night. While he was singing "Mary Had a Little Lamb," which Lily simply called "Mary" and required each time he put her to bed, her eyes drifted shut. He kissed her forehead, thanking any power listening for the generous little girl who'd so happily welcomed her older brother.

She'd forced Evan to take her ceremonial mug for hot chocolate—a thick stoneware one Zach's gran had made for her in the kiln up at the baby farm. She'd then claimed her second-favorite mug, the one that matched hers, except for a slight chip in the rim.

Zach tucked the quilt beneath her chin and turned off her lamp. He left her door open just a crack in case she needed him during the night. Neither child seemed as upset about this afternoon's confrontation as he and Olivia were, but he'd be sleeping farther from Lily than usual in the living room and he wanted to make sure he could hear her if she called out.

Unusual darkness blanketed the hall. Olivia had shut his bedroom door. Through the thick wood came the murmur of her voice and Evan's sleepy-sounding responses. Now would be a good time to call Helene.

When she came to the phone, her hello sounded

surprised, which meant none of this afternoon's photos or film had leaked into her house.

"It's me," he said.

"So I was told. Is something wrong with Lily?"

"She's fine. She's already asleep, but we ran into some trouble at Henderson's today, and I wanted to tell you about it myself."

"What kind of trouble?" she asked almost before he could finish.

"Nothing too serious, just the reporters again. Mike Henderson and some of the old boys who hang out there helped us."

"Boys? Those guys are ancient. How could they help you?"

"They surrounded the reporters while Lily and Evan and I left." Or fled, but he didn't want to scare his ex-wife any more than he had to.

"This won't do, Zach. Why don't you face them and stop running?"

"It's none of their business. This isn't the same thing as six years ago, Helene." He wasn't about to discuss his future with Evan outside his own convoluted family.

"If you don't do something I'll have to make Lily a prisoner in her own home."

His fingers tightened on the phone. "Don't threaten me. You can't take Lily away from me just because you're angry. How many times do I have to remind you we share joint custody?"

"Unlike the Kendalls, I can't afford bodyguards to keep strangers off her back. When I drop her off at day care or at a lesson, she's on her own. You tell your concerned little girlfriend about that."

"My—huh?"

"Olivia Kendall. She's all talk about making Lily happy, fitting our daughter into a family with her son. Well, if her son causes my daughter problems I don't want that boy in this town."

"When did you talk to Olivia?" Had Olivia gotten in touch with Helene in a Kendall preemptive strike? "Did you call her?"

"Give me a break. I'll call your sweet Olivia if I want to. She doesn't need your protection, Zach Calvert."

Her resentment was clear, but he was still unraveling the steps of her chat with Olivia. "I'm asking if Olivia decided she'd fix any difficulties by talking to you."

"No." Helene breathed hard. "But you can tell her for me I won't believe she's worried about Lily until she insists her reporter friends leave our child—*our child,* Zach—alone."

"If she could make them leave any of us alone, she would have stopped them already. That's the problem. And Helene, *I* won't let anything happen to Lily."

"So far you're reacting to the problem. Do something about it."

"I'm trying to become Evan's father, and in the meantime, he and Lily are learning to be brother and sister. Talking to reporters along the way won't make them less curious."

"Not good enough. I don't want to see Lily running from cameras."

"Neither do I, so we're going to hang around up here all weekend."

Her silence asked if "we" included Olivia. Well—ingrained guilt wouldn't let him tell her. He'd lived with Helene, tried with Helene, for nearly three years longer than he should have. He'd done her no favors trying to love her, and she'd probably hate him till he died for trying and failing.

"You'll return Lily to me on Monday morning before you go to work then?"

"Yes. Helene—I'm sorry."

"I don't give a damn about sorry. Sorry never did any of us any good." She hung up.

He turned off the phone and set it on the counter. That Scotch in the cupboard sounded pretty good again.

"Maybe I should go back to town."

He froze. He couldn't will himself to love Helene, but even the sound of Olivia's voice started a storm in his bloodstream.

"You heard?"

"I tried to walk away, but you covered a lot of ground before I could go."

"We're like that." He turned to face her. Holding Evan's jeans and sweater and shirt, she looked anxious, like a maid who'd spilled something on the laundry. Not like the confident newswoman who'd swept into his office. "You also spoke to Helene?"

"I told her exactly what I've said to you, that I want us to make things good for the children."

"This situation is turning us all into—"

"I know—a crazy kind of family. I never dreamed I'd have to consider another woman's feelings when I make decisions about my son."

"She said something similar." Only she'd added

the instinctive jealousy she couldn't contain toward Olivia. How could he have forgotten Olivia if he cared for her? God knew he wouldn't have intentionally hurt Helene, tying himself to a ghost.

"I can't persuade her she's wrong about you and me—although Evan and I seem to have made her realize she does want you in Lily's life."

He nodded, also puzzled by the change. "She wanted the divorce, but she's still angry about our marriage. I don't think she's ever said anything to Lily, so I put up with whatever she says to me."

Olivia narrowed her gaze as if she could sense the leftover pain from his bad relationship. "Maybe you married too soon after the accident."

"Worse than that," he said, "we had Lily too soon, and I just hope she never figures it out." He loved his daughter as unconditionally as he'd wished he could have loved her mother.

Olivia stared down at Evan's things, which she'd begun to crumple in her hand. "Could I wash Evan's jeans in case it's too cold for shorts tomorrow?"

"Sure." Her discomfort spread tentacles to him. She already knew more than enough about his past. She'd raised their son on her own while he'd tried to make his marriage to Helene work. Burning inside, he realized he didn't want to know about men Olivia might have been with after he'd left. "The laundry room is back here." He started across the kitchen. "Do you want to wash your own clothes?"

She hesitated, but then threw off her reticence. "I'd be grateful."

"Let me get you something to put on." She nodded, and he eased into his room where Evan rustled beneath the bedclothes.

"Dad?"

"Sorry, son. Were you dreaming yet?" He took gray cotton sweats and a white thermal pullover out of his dresser.

"Not yet." Evan held up his arms and Zach went to hug him. "Did I hear you singing to Lily?" Evan asked.

Zach nodded against his clean, boyish-scented head. "We sing 'Mary' together every night."

"Will you sing 'Frosty' to me?"

Evan sounded a little less sleepy. A bad omen, since Zach wanted to sing the song he'd asked for, but he could hardly make up the words if Evan was alert. "Do you know how it goes?" Zach asked.

Evan started belting it out, and Zach followed along, meandering off course a few times. Evan didn't seem to mind. At the end, he hugged Zach so tight he might have been making up for lost time.

"Why 'Frosty,' Evan?"

"It's my favrit." Slurring the last word, he rolled over, immediately falling asleep again.

As Zach stood, Olivia moved back from the open doorway. He followed her down the hall, mesmerized by her slender, unhurried grace. "You didn't have to leave," he said in the living room.

"I suddenly realized I was watching you and I felt nosy." She smiled, and her mouth, which he'd thought perfect, tilted a little crookedly.

He couldn't look away from the slight flaw that made her even more beautiful, but he didn't know he was staring until she covered her mouth. She gazed at him as if she were seeing him through a haze of the past.

"You always said I had a crooked mouth." Her voice, low and husky, played on his nerve endings.

Tension woke between them. He felt its touch in the muscles that tightened in his legs and arms. Olivia shuddered as it reached for her. A deep inhalation lifted her breasts, and he matched his breathing to hers. He took a step toward her, but she reached for the clothes in his hands and he released them from nerveless fingers.

Was this memory or longing? Born of attraction or loneliness? Or both, buried in need so deep he never let himself feel it. But now was not the time. Zach searched the room for something he should be doing.

"While you change, I'll bring in some firewood."

She didn't seem to hear him at first, and then her gaze faltered. She swerved her head toward the open woodstove.

She'd probably never seen anything so primitive. He nodded. "It looks decorative, but it heats the house." Maybe this idiotic conversation would distract her, too. "My great-grandfather built the place, and my dad added vents from the stove for central heating."

"I have no idea what you're talking about."

The low tenor of her voice pulled him back to the desire he was trying to ignore. If he didn't do something else, he was going to touch her. The firewood. Carrying firewood took a man's mind off impossible situations. "We'll be warmer tonight if I bring in enough logs to keep the fire going."

She nodded, but irritation slowly fed into her gaze.

Surely she understood he was trying to protect her and Evan as much as himself. He headed for the woodpile, willing to be a coward if he kept from hurting Olivia or anyone else ever again.

SHE CHANGED in the bathroom, yanking off her jeans and shirt. Her socks came off and flew toward the toilet, fluttering to safety at the last possible second.

She must be out of her mind giving Zachary Calvert one more chance to reject her. She stopped as those moments in the living room washed over her again. She swore as she felt herself swaying toward him. And she should have sworn out loud when he'd started rambling about firewood and heating.

She glanced at herself in the mirror, naked except for the blush that spread from her breasts to her throat to her cheeks. Tomorrow she'd call up Helene and ask if she wanted to start a damn club for women the sheriff had dumped. For tonight she'd better stop herself from blasting him from his own bathroom in case she woke both their children.

She put on his sweats, refusing to imagine the slide of thin cotton against his taut skin. While she hauled his thermal shirt over her head she held her breath for fear of catching some faint remnant of his scent.

She'd never known such a weak woman. What was wrong with her that she couldn't stop thinking of him that way? She splashed water on her face and ejected herself from the bathroom's safety. Stiffening her spine, she marched down the hall. Kendalls gave way for no man.

In the laundry room, she loaded her clothes and Evan's jeans into the washer. Water sloshing into the machine blocked all other sound. With any luck at all Zach would brain himself with a log. Short of that, maybe he'd finish his chore and resort to the cliché of a long cold shower.

She helped herself to detergent and shut the washer lid. Restless, knowing she'd whirl like a dervish and disturb Evan's sleep if she tried to go to bed, she opened the kitchen door to the deck and stepped outside.

Clouds floated past the face of the moon. Olivia smoothed her palms across her own face. She'd come to this house, to Bardill's Ridge for Evan. The swaying pines seemed to whisper his name in a warning, or maybe they were gossiping about how foolish she'd almost been. The wooden planks froze her feet in no time, but the cold night proved more effective than a dip in one of the icy springs that gurgled somewhere up there on the dark ridge.

Maybe Zach had a point. Instead of being insulted, she should thank him. If he'd taken her up on her silent offer, they'd have to decide where to go next. This time he'd left her in no doubt. He'd wisely stated his intentions of going nowhere.

She might feel hungry and discarded, but as long as she kept her hands to herself, she'd have no regrets. Her son's bond with Zach mattered. She had no other connection with him anymore.

She tucked her hands in the loose hem of her borrowed shirt for warmth, but shuddered anyway. Glancing back at the house, she hoped Zach would pass the windows, turning out lights so he could go to bed.

"Olivia?"

Startled, she turned toward the lawn and the sound of his voice. "Where are you?"

He climbed the steps to the lower deck, into a spill of light from the kitchen window. "I'm making mistakes with you."

"I know you think so." She swallowed the rest. If he flat out said he didn't want her, she'd have to throw the grill at him.

"I meant when I ran out here." He crossed the lower deck and quickly strode up to her level. "I wanted to—" He stopped, but clenched his hands in fists in front of her. "I don't know what I wanted. Most of all I want to know if I remember you—if I can—"

"You can't." She might be confused, but no way was he going to try her out as a magic potion to cure his amnesia.

"Because of Evan?" He came closer, his tone harsh, his rigid body a challenge. "Maybe Evan's the reason we should find out how we really feel."

"I'm not saying no just because of Evan. Remember what you said that first day in your office? That you wouldn't have felt comfortable with me knowing about your personal life." Adrenaline pulsed through her body with explosive force. "Back then I didn't know you were holding back. I loved you. I cared more about you than myself."

She felt almost faint after admitting how much he'd mattered. Maybe he thought she was finished. Maybe he just wanted—needed to shut her up. Either way, he caught her arms and pulled her close. She couldn't even shake her head as he stared at her mouth.

The moment his lips covered hers, tears burned in

her eyes. He had amnesia, but she'd forgotten plenty. The firm message of need in the kindness of his kiss hadn't changed at all. She wanted to run from him, but if she moved, she'd give in to his mouth stroking hers, begging her to open to him.

She tried to turn her head away. He followed, starting over at the curve of her cheek, flexing his hands around her shoulders, as if he had to reassure himself he was holding her. He kissed her again, his mouth, his lips and breath teasing a path of desperate yearning across her skin.

She slid her arms around his waist. He was harder, leaner, tougher than he'd been. His very maleness frightened her. She'd been so long alone. She pushed her hands between them, tangling her fingers in his soft shirt.

"Olivia." That was all it took. Her name in a whisper. Cupping her face, he angled her head and took her in a kiss that brought her up hard against him and destroyed her last clear thought.

She opened her mouth because she remembered his taste and she'd once been addicted. She'd dreamed of this moment and wakened night after night, his child kicking in her belly while she cried at the certainty of knowing she'd never hold Zach again.

She wrapped her arms around his shoulders. "Please," she said, not even sure what she was pleading for.

He seemed to know. His voice, without words, rode his breath to her mouth. He kissed her again and again, sliding his hands beneath the baggy shirt to caress her back, her shoulders. She pressed against his fingertips as he brushed the curve of her breasts.

She ached for more, but her need was so intense his touch almost hurt. Tears sprang to her eyes, but suddenly he eased her away from him, and that hurt more.

"I can't." He didn't sound like Zach. Not before and not now. He was a stranger she'd loved, and she still wanted to be with him.

"What?"

"I don't have the right."

She narrowed her gaze, hollow inside, unable to believe he'd reject her when he so clearly wanted her. "I was giving you the right, Zach."

"I can't explain." He rubbed his face, guilt written on every plane and angle his hand couldn't cover.

"Is it Helene?"

"No, worse, it's Salva."

"Your friend from the crash." Olivia took a deep breath, almost choking. "At least you said she was your friend."

"She was." He caught her hand as she backed away. "She was only a friend, but she's dead. Maybe because of me. Maybe that's why I screwed up with Helene. And I can't forget I all but ruined your life."

"Hardly."

He grimaced. "I know you made your own decision. You love Evan, and he's not a problem for you, but you faced it all by yourself, and for all I know, he's the reason your dad is such a nut."

"Zach, Dad is who he is." She should stick up for him. "And Evan adds to my life every day. I honestly don't know what you're talking about, and I don't understand what you mean about your friend after all this time. You tried to save her."

"Tried and failed, but I lived. I have a life and two children. Salva didn't get to see her daughter grow up."

"You married Helene. Salva didn't keep you from her."

"I only married her because she was pregnant."

"And this is the way you want your future? You're okay with rejecting—" What? Love? She wasn't declaring any such feeling ever again. "You don't intend to let any woman need you."

"Exactly."

"I'm sorry, but that sounds like an excuse. If you don't want me, say so. Don't try to be kind."

"You know that's not the problem."

The hint of ruefulness in his tone annoyed her even more. "You can't believe you'll be able to—"

"Come inside. You're freezing out here."

"You're freezing in here." She flattened her hands across his chest. "Where it counts more."

"You never talked in clichés before."

"It might be a cliché, but it's also the truth." And a deeper truth remained. She'd better say goodnight—goodbye—to him. She'd been lucky tonight. Better to find out now than after she'd let herself believe again. "I'm going to bed."

She walked around him, half expecting he'd draw her back. He let her go. She'd never inspire more than lust in Zach Calvert. Why?

Turning back, Olivia clasped his face. One swift kiss, the goodbye he'd denied her six years ago, couldn't hurt anyone. She kissed him with the fervent farewell of a twenty-one-year-old woman who believed he wasn't coming back. Zach's hands clung as she tried to pull away.

His gaze, tortured, no doubt reflecting her own frantic need, almost propelled her back into his arms. Somehow she took a backward step, staring into his sleepy, sexy eyes. "Good night."

He searched her face, as if he was looking for a secret, but he wasn't going to find the unswerving trust she'd felt for him before. She'd never again expose a foolish love that had nearly destroyed her.

She reached for the kitchen door. In her chest beat a heart that hurt almost as much as if he'd abandoned her once more. This time, he'd made a choice.

"I JUST THOUGHT you should know about your father, Olivia." His mom's voice. In his house. Too early in the morning after a sleepless night.

Zach hauled himself up on his elbows, his head thudding at hangover strength. In the kitchen, his mom rose from the table and went to refill her coffee cup.

"Will you bring me one of those?" he asked.

She rounded on him, startled. "You're awake. Morning, son."

"G'morning."

He rolled off the lumpy sleeper sofa and restored it to its couch identity. Last night came back with a cutting edge that dropped him into one of the armchairs. He should probably change clothes before he joined his mother and Olivia, whom he couldn't see, in the kitchen. He stared at the doorway, empty of both women.

The call of caffeine proved too strong. Olivia, miraculously clothed in her own jeans and shirt again, set a cup in front of him at the big table. She didn't look at him. He wished she would. He picked up the mug and sipped without sitting.

"What are you doing here, Mom?"

"You didn't sleep well."

"No. Did something else happen with Olivia's father?"

"Something good." Beth pushed a plate of her homemade biscuits his way. "Honey? Blackberry jam?"

He loved both, but either sounded foul. "Plain is fine." He glanced at Olivia. "Are you willing to tell me?"

"He bought all the film from the incident at the feed store." She smiled at his mother in an obvious appeal for understanding. "I am grateful to him, Beth, but you need to realize it was a onetime deal."

"You think they'll come after us again?" Zach asked.

"If I didn't, I wouldn't be here." She met his gaze fully. "I work on a magazine because I don't have the cutthroat temperament to hunt down stories every day. People know I have Evan. They know he's mine, but I simply refused to talk about him and his parentage until they stopped asking. That was easy when he was a baby. It won't be now. They'll try to talk to him. Or they'll stalk you and your family. My father is honorable. Any story that appears in his media is backed up by source after source, and he's openly disdainful of people who do the job without morals. Others have been waiting to prove he's a hypocrite. I had a child out of wedlock so I'm an opportunity for them to write a story denigrating James Kendall and our family and our business.'' She shrugged.

"Then let me explain,'' Zach said.

"No.''

Her vehemence startled him. She thought he'd rejected her again. She wanted nothing from him today.

He couldn't ask her to forget about last night in front of his mother. "It's the best way, Olivia.'' He pushed his hand through his unkempt hair. "They'll leave us alone once they have the story.''

A thud on his front door was his only answer. He and his mother and Olivia shared a questioning glance.

"I'll bet they followed me up here,'' Beth said.

"It doesn't matter, Mom. I'll take care of them.'' His rumpled sweats and just-out-of-bed look wasn't going to do much for Olivia. "Stay out of sight, and keep Evan and Lily in the back of the house.''

"No,'' Olivia said.

"We can't hide behind a door all day.'' He set his cup on the table and strode across the kitchen and living room before Olivia caught him.

"What about Evan? Do you want to see his face everywhere? Imagine what the captions underneath will say.''

"We'll take care of Evan, but we can't hide from these people.''

"I said no, Zach.''

He wanted to pay attention, but someone had to do something. Snatching the door open, he was surprised—and relieved—to find James and his two bodyguards.

The silver-and-blue Kendall mobile would be hard

to miss. He looked for it on the drive, but an almost discreet black Range Rover sat beside his mother's old bug.

"You bought a car?"

James nodded as if a Range Rover in Bardill's Ridge wasn't unusual. "I needed room for my daughter and grandson. It's still a tight fit with Jock and Ian."

Olivia spoke from behind him. "Dad, Evan and I are going to stay with you for a few days."

Zach's temper rippled over him like a heat haze. "Come on, Olivia."

"No, you come on." Her gaze froze him. She raked her hair back, baring her beautiful, furious face. The face he'd kissed until he'd wanted to take her on the cold porch floor last night. He wanted her now, but lovemaking didn't seem to be part of her current plan. "I know best about this situation, and you didn't bother to listen to me. When you're ready to share, not take charge, you let me know."

CHAPTER THIRTEEN

IAN PACKED Olivia and Evan's things and brought them to the campground. They missed a few of Evan's toys and a shirt he'd tossed under his bed. On the following Wednesday, Beth and Zach's redheaded cousin, Molly, brought Evan's forgotten belongings. Molly, as awed as everyone who saw the mobile home, demanded a tour from Evan while Beth asked Olivia to walk outside with her.

Zach's mother eyed the chain link fence that surrounded the huge leaf-strewn pool in the Kendalls' temporary backyard. "They assigned you a nice space," she said, and even managed to sound as if she wasn't laughing.

Grinning, Olivia jabbed her thumb at the silver-and-blue behemoth behind her. "My dad may not be the perfect fit for Bardill's Ridge, but he's learning. He's shopping for groceries at the farmers' market on the square right now." She ground to a halt. She didn't feel like the perfect fit either. "Anyway, I'm glad he came. He calls this thing our office on the road, and it's easier to work from here."

"And easier to hide."

Beth said it so flatly, it didn't sound like an accusation, just a statement. Still, Olivia bit back a mouthful of self-defense. "I haven't kept Evan from Zach.

And the rest of your family has been dropping by to see Evan.''

''Yes, but Zach and the family don't take the constant shadows in stride as well as Evan.''

''Jock and Ian keep everyone else away. You've heard the stories that are leaking into the news. 'Media Czar's Grandson Discovers Father.' It makes me sick.'' She wrapped her arms around her waist. ''And they're using Evan's picture. My dad and I've managed to keep his face out of the news for five years.''

''If you'd let Zach explain…''

''I understand he may feel he's not being a man if he doesn't defend his son, but making as little of this mess as possible is the best thing he can do for Evan.''

''Why don't you ask my son about all this?'' Beth looked distressed. ''He won't thank me for making trouble between the two of you.''

''You aren't making trouble.'' Olivia reached for Beth's hand. ''I'm the one with the problem, and I'll handle it. Is Zach in his office?'' She patted her back pocket in search of her car keys. ''Beth, would you mind taking Evan with you? Where are you going?''

''Up to the baby farm. And I'd love for him to come. You might like to look around up there, too. Greta provides a retreat for pregnant women whose husbands are away, or who just want some time on their own. And more than that, she gives young girls a place, too.''

''Young girls,'' Olivia said. ''You mean pregnant girls?'' She'd read an article about The Mom's Place from a Knoxville paper, but it hadn't mentioned that. ''Their parents send them?''

"Most of them turn up at Greta's because their parents are ashamed of what they've done, and they don't have anywhere else to go. Greta uses profits from the paying customers to provide for those girls."

Olivia still remembered how alone she'd felt before her father had managed to reconcile himself. "I'll make you a deal. How about an hour of looking after Evan in return for a story on the baby farm?"

Beth showed no hesitation. "I'm in. Go talk to Zach, and don't worry about Evan. I'll bring him back here when we finish my class." She glanced back. "You don't mind if he learns how to crochet?"

Olivia laughed. "Not at all. As long as you can convince him, too."

"I'll manage."

Olivia didn't doubt it. She climbed the mobile home's metal steps. The Mom's Place, or the baby farm, as the family called it, would make a good story for *Relevance,* and they might be able to scare up some funding for Greta Calvert.

In front of the television, Molly sat cross-legged, sort of. One foot in the air punctuated a particularly good curve in the race she and Evan were running.

"Move, Mollllyyyyy. I can't see."

"Sorry. I have to use my feet when I drive on video."

"Huh?"

"Forget it. I'm about to pass you, buddy."

"Evan," Olivia said, "are you listening to me?" She hated those games, maybe partly because she was terrible at them.

"I hear ya, Mom."

"Grandma Beth is going to take you with her while I go out for a while."

"Okay."

Not "where are you going?" or "why can't I go with you?" Just "Okay." Because he'd be with his Grandma Beth. She'd longed for a big, loving family like the Calverts, and she was glad Evan would always be part of them. But it still felt odd to turn him over to other people.

"Evan, wear your sweater."

"Mom, you're going to make me lose. I can't hear you and—no, Molly!"

"Sorry." Olivia grabbed her keys from the counter and tossed an apology for no real reason at Beth, who patted her arm.

Olivia dropped down the mobile home's steps, laying her hand over the warm spot where Beth had touched her and feeling as if she'd entered the Calvert clan on Evan's coattails.

ZACH PARKED his squad car behind the courthouse where none of the citizenry would smell him stinking of the still he'd broken up. He left his ax in the storeroom, trying to hide his bullet-torn sleeve from the neighbors who passed him.

He reached his office door without attracting on an audience, but the second he stepped inside, Olivia rose from the chair in front of his desk.

Her eyes rounded, her skin went pale and a nerve jumped beside her mouth.

"What?" he asked.

"You're bleeding."

He glanced at his sleeve. The bullet had come

closer than he'd thought. "It can't be too bad. It took a long time before it even started to bleed."

She grabbed the chair, as if she needed help standing. His turn to drop his jaw.

"You're afraid," he said, "for me." He couldn't help marveling.

"Someone shot you?"

"Because I broke up her still." He cracked a smile. "She said she was looking to make a little extra Christmas money."

"It's not funny." She was beside him, her hands shaking as she pulled back his sleeve. The bullet had traced a neat diagonal line just above his elbow.

"She wasn't a good shot."

"Shut up, Zach. Where's your first-aid kit?"

He didn't give a damn where it was. "I like to hear you say my name." He was serious. He forgot how well she knew him until she loaded his name with emotion he neither deserved nor understood.

"The first-aid kit?" She tried to sound detached, but a thickened note in her voice made him lean down.

She turned her head just slightly, but when he caught her chin, she didn't struggle. She kissed him back, a hint of can't-help-it on her lips. Then she moved out of reach.

"The first-aid kit." She sounded firm. "I'll clean your wound while we talk."

"It's more scratch than wound, but I'm glad it bothers you." He stared at her, hungry for more. Could she help him find the memories he'd lost— memories of them together? He crossed to the gun cabinet and locked his weapons away. Then he opened his bottom desk drawer and retrieved the first-aid kit.

"What do you want to talk about?"

"What happened the other night."

"Between us?" He almost dropped the gun. She'd seemed to be content pretending nothing had happened. "I assume my mother dropped by for a chat."

"Don't be angry with her." Olivia pointed to the chair she'd been sitting in.

"I'm not angry, but I can speak for myself, and I would have once I knew you were comfortable talking about it."

"I would have called you if she hadn't visited. I was upset because you were willing to talk to the journalists, but I was also embarrassed about the kissing." She closed her mouth for a moment, as if she didn't want to say more. "Maybe I feel things you can't."

He sat. "You know I feel plenty."

"You sound cold."

"Not emotionally, though." He pulled back the edges of his shirt and tore the tattered material. "Look at my track record. I'm trying to take care of you as well as my son."

"I'm used to taking care of myself. I'm not your problem." Olivia glanced at him as she took out a bottle of hydrogen peroxide. "I don't want to hear about your marriage. And I don't have a right to know if there's been anyone else."

Who else had she been with? He didn't care about rights. He wanted to know.

She opened the bottle. "Are you ready?"

"For this, yes." He nodded at the bottle.

"You don't have to restate your position. I understood that night." She poured peroxide on a cotton wad and then slammed it on his arm.

He bit the inside of his cheek to keep from screaming like a baby boy.

"Did I hurt you?"

"Your sarcasm is pointed," he said.

"I feel foolish, and it's not a pleasant feeling."

"Maybe I should be over what happened with Salva, but I'm not. I know people can die in a rescuer's arms, seconds from safety. I seem to scatter destruction wherever I go, and you and I have Evan to consider."

"You don't have to tell me to think of my child first."

She prepared another cotton pad with peroxide, but he took it away from her. "Don't go easy on a wounded man, okay?"

"I'm not arguing that you should care for me, Zach. It was humiliating, and I don't like being rejected, but I am actually thinking of you." She wiped her hands on another piece of clean cotton. "And of Evan. How long are you going to live in a past you can't even remember?"

He finished cleaning the gash where the bullet had dug a track across his arm. "Where I'm living is my business as long as I don't hurt you with it." He looked up at her and tossed the pad in the trash can. "And I'm not going to hurt you. You can't imagine I'm holding anything back from Evan."

She crossed her arms, taking a self-protective stance. But she looked vulnerable. If he took her in his arms, she'd give in. So he had to be smart.

"Have you ever talked to the Salvas? Maybe seen your friend's daughter?"

Horror brought him to his feet. Look Kim's little girl in the eye? Face the husband whose wife he'd lost. Not a chance. "No."

"Maybe you should. Maybe they'd let you off the hook." Uncrossing her arms, she picked up her purse. "I have to get back. Your mother will be bringing Evan back to the campground."

"Mom?"

"She took him with her to teach a class at the baby farm."

She surprised him. "Mom will like that you trust her with him."

"You've all made him feel loved, part of the family. I'm grateful." Her appreciation came out in a clipped tone. She headed for the door, a sharp gait replacing her normal grace as if saying thank-you wasn't easy. It wouldn't be—thanking your child's father for accepting his son.

"Olivia, wait."

She looked back.

"You'll come to my grandparents' anniversary on Saturday? They're renewing their vows at eight-thirty in the morning, and then we're going up on the mountain for the barbecue in my grandfather's orchard."

She softened immediately, looking uncertain. "Your grandmother sent an invitation, but I'm a stranger. I can see she'd want Evan, but maybe you should take him by yourself."

"Lily and I will come for both of you." His gran might not even notice, she was so excited about her "wedding," but he wanted Olivia and Evan with his family on Saturday.

She rocked on her heels in doubt. Zach took shameless advantage. He cupped her elbow and all but ran her out of his office. "See you at 7:45 a.m. on Saturday."

Without giving her time to answer he impelled her through the door and shut it. Then he waited, his pulse hammering, for her to come back and turn him down.

She didn't.

ZACH CALLED ON Friday morning and asked if he could take Evan camping that night. Olivia half expected him to invite her along. When he didn't, she felt left out, but she packed her son's things with good grace.

Zach planned to take the children to his and Lily's hot spring. It would be Evan's, too, after tonight. Olivia tried not to think about it. She didn't like camping anyway. She shouldn't feel tempted or forgotten.

She packed clothing for the wedding, as well, since Zach had said they'd change before they came for her. And then she waved goodbye to the three of them, a huge faux smile plastered on her face, swearing she'd bury herself in her work that night.

And she had another plan. She and Evan had found a beautiful hinged platinum picture frame in an antique shop on the square. She'd already put a picture of Evan in one side, and Beth had promised her a photo of Zach for the other.

But when she drove up to Beth's house that night, Beth took the frame and asked her to wait outside.

From within came the loud laughter of the Calvert women. Waiting obediently with the closed door in her face, Olivia felt excluded again. It seemed odd coming from Zach's family.

Beth eased back through the door, holding the photo to her chest. She handed it to Olivia and swept her into a hug.

"What do you think?" She turned the picture so they could both see it.

Zach, also late in his fifth year, was the image of his son. Down to the touching light of trust in his eyes and hair that cowlicked in several directions.

"I love it. In this frame they look as if they're joined." Olivia let Beth see her tear-wet eyes. "As if they've always been together."

Beth grabbed her in another rib-shattering hug. "Greta won't let any of us touch it after it makes the rounds at the party. I wouldn't mind one myself when you can spare another picture of Evan."

"My assistant overnighted this to me, but I'll send you one as soon as we go back to Chicago," Olivia promised.

"I'll hold you to that."

Silence dropped with a reverberating thud. Olivia muttered, "Well," listening to the women inside again.

"I'll see you in the morning, Olivia." Beth held on when Olivia, her feelings hurt at being dismissed, would have pulled away. "I'm so glad you're joining us."

"Thank you." Not much in the way of a response, but wanting to be one of them tonight unnerved her. Just as she'd once pumped Zach for information, she wanted to ask Beth what made these women—and their men—cling together without a family business in common. They didn't need daily planners or limos or bodyguards. They only needed a chance to be together. "Good night," she said and moseyed to the car, not letting herself run.

Beth was already inside when Olivia started the engine. She stared at the closed door, and then turned to head down the steep drive. Against her own will, surprisingly weak these days, she glanced over her shoulder. But no one came out.

A night alone wasn't so bad. Her father had somehow persuaded an excellent cook to prepare meals for them in the mobile home. While Zach and the children were eating burned dogs and marshmallows, and Beth and her Calvert cohorts were sharing finger foods, Olivia prodded exquisite salmon and a seasonal pumpkin seed salad.

A nice, blackened marshmallow sure sounded good.

After dinner she argued with her father, neglected her work and turned in to twist like a tornado in sheets that felt too hot. Every time she thought she might be drifting off, she awoke to an overwhelming memory of the demands of Zach's lips against hers.

She finally scrambled out of bed to stare through the living room windows at the darkened tents and smaller mobile homes. The campground had filled up for the weekend, with playing children and parents who'd spent the afternoon shouting for them to come back or to stay away from the pool fence. Even the reporters seemed to have taken a break. After sundown, only the leaves roamed the narrow, wet roads. All the people had taken shelter inside.

Except her son and his father and sister. She pictured Lily and Evan clamped on each side of Zach for warmth. And she wanted to be with them. During her time in Bardill's Ridge, she'd grown to need the sound of Lily's unabashed laughter. She felt her son was safe if he shared Zach's indulgent gaze with his little sister.

"What's on your mind, Olivia?"

She'd awakened her dad after all. "Zach and the children."

"Why?"

"I miss them."

"Them." He digested the pronoun. "Not just Evan?"

"No. All three."

"You know what's going through my mind."

"I'm in big trouble. Again."

"Not pregnant, though?"

"Dad," she said, turning. "I'm not that foolish."

"I don't know. Zach was bad news for you, but you couldn't stay away from him before."

"I loved him."

"And now?"

"I'm angry." She leaned against her father's arm. "I want those years back. I want to know why he left without telling me where he was really going—what I might lose." She sighed. According to Zach's explanation about not letting her get close before, she hadn't lost half as much as she'd mourned.

"He was a Navy pilot. I don't know what he felt

about you, but you can bet he never considered he might die.''

Olivia felt the pull of truth, the way she scented honesty when she was interviewing a reluctant subject. ''Dad, that's why he can't forgive himself about the accident. He didn't think he'd crash. The impossible happened.''

''Why does it matter, Olivia?''

At least he wasn't rampaging for once. ''I don't know. Maybe it doesn't or shouldn't. But even if I felt nothing for him, I'd want him to be capable of having a relationship. He's my son's father.''

''And he obviously loves Evan. It's you he doesn't remember.'' He said it gently, obviously trying to point out the truth without hurting her.

''Me he doesn't want.''

Her dad straightened as if he'd suffered an electric shock, but she'd had to say it out loud. If she said it often enough, maybe she'd learn to accept it.

''You still can't stay away from him.''

''I have to, for Evan's sake, because Zach's broken inside. Look at the way he lives—fighting moonshiners and bank robbers—and he's just as excited, whichever turns up to shoot at him. I think he doesn't want to stop long enough to see what might pop out of the past. And what I have to believe is that when the past catches up with him, he's likely to run again.''

''He won't run out on Evan or Lily.''

Olivia smiled, turning her face against her father's sleeve. ''I know what it cost you to say that, but you don't have to worry I'll go into some tailspin because

I'm not Zach's ideal woman. I'm not about to join the broken brigade. Evan needs me to be okay.''

Her dad shifted to put his arm around her. ''I may not show love like Zach Calvert, with camping trips in the great dirty outdoors and train whistles, but I love you as much as he loves his children, and if he ever hurts you again, I'll kill the man.''

He startled a laugh out of her.

''Has it been so bad, the two of us together?'' he asked.

''No. It's been a family.'' She might long for the cozy Calvert kind of family, but she wouldn't trade the love her father had given her—even if he barged in and drove her nuts on a regular basis.

''Be careful.''

''Yeah.''

''His mother invited me to the picnic tomorrow.''

''Beth?'' Olivia found herself in her father's usual position. She inspected the anticipation in his gaze. ''What are you doing with Beth?''

''Battle with a tart-tongued woman. Keeping an eye out for my daughter's welfare. Which I'll be better able to do if I'm picking apples in the next tree. Can you tell me what kind of people pick their apples from trees when they have access to a perfectly good grocery store?''

''Calverts.'' She tugged at her T-shirt collar. ''Have you noticed how good all this fresh-off-the-farm produce tastes, Dad?''

''No, but I'm not imagining myself in love.'' He took her arm again. ''And you should think about whether you're actually looking to Evan's future or yours. His ideal family might be confusing you.''

CHAPTER FOURTEEN

TOWARD MORNING, Olivia fell asleep and then had to rush to dress for the wedding. When her father shouted from the bathroom where he was shaving that Zach and the children had come, she hopped to the door, putting on a sage-green pump that matched her dress.

She yanked down her skirt, twitched at her hair and stepped into a near-frosty morning that made her linen, three-quarter-sleeved jacket insubstantial. But Evan and Lily waving from the back seat quickly distracted her from the cold. She dashed to the front passenger seat, hardly even noticing how Zach's black suit emphasized his light hair and sharp features.

She had eyes only for Evan and Lily. "Hey, guys, you survived the night."

"There weren't no bears," Evan said solemnly.

"Bears?" She attempted to control the squeak in her voice.

"We talked about them when Evan woke up about midnight." Zach looked solemn, though his eyes—which matched her dress a lot better than her shoes did—seemed to glow with joy.

"But Dad did a no-bear dance outside the tent," Lily said. "So we weren't scared."

Olivia turned swiftly, so the children wouldn't see her laugh at their father's safety measures. "I can see you'd feel safe. Zach, maybe you could teach me that dance sometime."

He seemed to study her, and she erased her smile. She might not trust her feelings for Zach, but she had to deal with them before they showed like a neon sign.

"I'll gladly teach you," he said in a deep note for her alone.

She might have hated him for letting her see he was attracted, but she suffered the same problem— being unable to hide her feelings just because she believed she should.

"I know how to do the dance now," Evan said.

"Me, too."

Two children dancing at rogue bears presented a scary picture. "But you have to be six feet tall for it to work," Olivia said.

"See, your mom knows all about it, too," Zach said. To her, he added, "Sorry. I didn't think of that part of it."

She smiled, absently checking to see if she'd remembered to comb her hair as she turned to see Evan and Lily. "What did you eat?"

"I caught a fish," Lily said. "It was too small, so we ate the ones Dad bought from the store."

"That was smart planning."

"My grandfather would say I cursed myself with no faith." Zach turned toward the campground entrance. "But we would have had a big fight over Lily's fish."

"Nope." Lily smoothed her pink silk skirt over her white tights. "All mine."

"Hear the woman roar." Olivia offered Lily a high five, which the little girl returned with enthusiasm.

"What does that mean, Miss Livia?" she asked.

"I mean you're strong. You're making your own way."

"You woulda been hogging the fish," Evan added.

Olivia caressed his soft cheek. "Thanks for clearing that up, sweetie."

"Mom, your face looks funny."

Great. "Your grandfather was in the bathroom." She turned and flipped down the visor. She'd applied lipstick with a fine Bozo effect. Glancing at Zach, she searched for her purse and realized she'd left it behind. "You might have mentioned it when I got in."

"I thought you meant to do it." He made a sound suspiciously like a snort. "I have some baby wipes in the glove box."

"'Cause I spill stuff," Lily said from the back. "And I can't see Mommy dirty."

Olivia sobered. She'd forgotten about Helene. She must be kidding herself. Deal with her feelings? Whatever she felt, she'd end up hurting Helene and possibly Lily, and maybe even Evan. Physical attraction, however strong, wasn't worth it.

Olivia stared at her hands as Zach turned through the square. She shouldn't assume he was still interested. He seemed to be an expert at backing away.

"I think we're going to have to walk," Zach said. The parking spots closer to the church were full. He turned into the closest open slot.

"This is fine." Olivia got out and turned to the

back door. She shivered in the chilly morning as she helped Lily out of her booster seat.

Zach must have seen as he and Evan circled the car. He let go of Evan's hand, moving between their son and the road as he shrugged off his jacket. "Take this."

"I'm not cold."

"Olivia."

He held it out, but she still hesitated. "It'll look funny," she said.

"You're cold. Fashion comes second to pneumonia."

"I'm not talking fashion." She glanced toward the people filing into the church. "I mean, me climbing out of your car at this time of the morning, wearing your clothes...."

He followed her gaze. "Oh." He took Evan's hand again. "Don't worry about it. Lily, button your coat."

It was pink wool and perfectly matched her dress. "You look beautiful, Lily." Olivia pulled Zach's coat around her. His warmth seemed to reach all the way to her toes. The smell of his body in the material made her breathe in.

"Thanks, Miss Livia. You look funny in Daddy's coat." But Lily slipped her hand into Olivia's with the same trust Evan showed Zach.

They slipped into the back of the candlelit church. At the front, in dark pine pews, Beth and Eliza beckoned them forward. Calvert relatives had been spilling into town over the past few days. Young, old, in between, they'd all shown up this morning, talking and laughing, mostly focused on a tall, white-haired man at the top of the aisle.

"Zach," he called, "bring those babies up here. Join us."

The crowd made way for them. Lily leaped into the man's arms. "Grandpa." She sang his name as he hugged her.

He leaned down, offering his hand to Evan, who took it and clung.

"Hi, Grandpa."

"Morning. I'm glad you brought your mom." The lean, older man looked down at her through green eyes that seemed to be a Calvert genetic trait. "I met this fine boy a few days ago at Zach's. Been looking forward to making your acquaintance."

"Hello. Thank you for inviting me."

His smile seemed to warm the cool church. "Thank you for bringing Evan into our lives." He nodded at her, his heart in his eyes. "Family means a lot to us, and we feel more whole with Evan among us."

Olivia's throat contracted. Zach slipped his arm around her, curving his hand around her waist. She should have pulled away, but she appreciated his support as she fought her own emotions. "I wish I'd looked for you all sooner, Mr. Calvert. Evan should have known you before now."

"My name is Seth, and I guess you won't be so shy from now on."

"Ode to Joy" suddenly blared from speakers hidden in the choir gallery. Conversation ended. Olivia turned toward a pew, but Seth set Lily back on her feet and spoke to his family.

"Why are you all hanging back? You're all part of this ceremony. I like to believe you were here with us when we married, in the form of the future Greta and I were going to give each other. Stand close to us now.''

Another man burst through a door to the right of the altar, adjusting his long black robe. ''Seth, she wants to start now—says it'll be too cold to let the children bob for apples if we don't get a move on.''

Beethoven started over. Apparently Greta had used the first ode as an attention-getter. She strode down the aisle—the heck with walking in time to the music. She reached Seth, a woman claiming her husband of fifty-five years.

Lily tugged Olivia's hand and Olivia lifted her. On her other side, Evan tugged, too, frowning in his first show of sibling jealousy. Olivia hoisted him onto her other hip, but then Zach pulled their son into his arms.

The music faded to silence. Greta, smiling into her husband's eyes, lifted her hand to stop the minister. ''I have a wedding present for you, Seth Calvert. I want to tell you about it now before I'm all mushy with love and you think I'm just offering on the spur of the moment.''

Seth laughed. His amusement flowed with love that brought a lump of tears to Olivia's throat. She wanted love like that.

''It's the one thing you've asked me for—over and over, by the way.'' She glanced from face to beaming face, and then stopped at her husband again. ''I'm seventy-six years old, only the prime of life for women of my family, but I'm going to retire,'' Greta said. She turned and glared pointedly at a tall, blond woman standing beside Beth and a man old enough to be the blonde's father. ''As soon as I can find a capable replacement, I'm going to devote my time to us, Seth—until you beg me to go back to work.''

Olivia looked inquiringly over Lily's head at Zach.

''Sophie,'' he said. ''My cousin, an OB/GYN, and that's my uncle Ethan beside her. Gran considers Sophie her optimum replacement.''

She should have recognized Sophie, but the other woman had been thinner in her pictures six years ago, deep in the stress of her training. Now she was voluptuous and red in the face. Greta must have already started her campaign.

''Today is a new day,'' Seth said. ''Fire away, Reverend. We've got apples to pick, barbecue to grill and the rest of a fruitful life to live. Together.'' And with that he reversed the order of the ceremony and kissed his bride until Olivia had to look away.

ZACH MIGHT NOT HAVE any memory of the more vulnerable Olivia he'd known before, but he recognized the moment she came back, the moment his grandfather had greeted his gran with a kiss that rendered the rest of the ceremony superfluous. Olivia had sagged against him without seeming to notice she had. Fortunately, he had plenty of strength and a longing to hold her up.

After the ceremony, his clan fled to their cars with shouts about meeting at the orchard. Zach took Lily and Evan by their hands, peering over his shoulder at Olivia.

Her gaze was lost in dreams he couldn't remember, couldn't fathom. If the children weren't between them, he'd have taken her in his arms to remind her he existed in the here and now.

"I brought our clothes," he said. "We can change at the campground if you don't think James would mind."

"Dad's probably already on his way. Your mom invited him."

"Why?" His mother had to be up to something.

"I wonder if they kind of like each other," she said, "unless your grandparents' wedding is blurring my thought processes. Your mom came to tell me when he—" she glanced at the children "—handled the reporters. He enjoys baiting her."

"What's been going on behind my back?" All this time James had been warning him off. Maybe it was his turn to have a word with Olivia's father.

"You can be as single-minded as my dad with your animal feed and bank robbers."

"You're extremely annoying when you offer advice in that smug tone."

Olivia laughed, not taking him seriously.

"Feed the animals, Daddy?" Lily asked.

"Tomorrow, sweetie. We're going to play with Grandma Beth and the cousins today."

"I know all the cousins," Lily said to Evan.

"They're mine, too."

Zach leaned toward Olivia. "Power struggle."

"If we're lucky, it'll come to a draw."

"I WAS KIND OF HOPING you wouldn't bring us a gift." Rubbing the glass over Evan's photo with one hand, Greta swiped at her eyes with the other. "So I could shame you into doing a story on my resort. But I'm a selfish woman, and I love this. It's going on my desk until I leave the office."

Olivia searched among the colorful Calverts for Zach's mom. She'd disappeared in the dancing, over-loaded trees with Evan and Lily, recounting the story of the first Ethan Calvert, who'd bought this land and planted it.

Evan had known all his life that Kendall Press would come to him some day. He liked to copy things on the machines. He loved playing computer games in her office. But he'd roamed off with his grandma and his sister, eyeing the apple trees with an acquis-itiveness he'd never shown toward anything at Ken-dall.

"I think you should talk to Beth, Greta." She didn't spill her promise to do a story. Beth might have saved it for another surprise today.

"Why?"

"About a story on the baby farm. There she is." Olivia hurried after Zach's mom and the children. They'd picked up her dad along the way. "Beth, hold on."

The group turned. Where were Ian and Jock? The bodyguards rarely left more than ten feet of space between themselves and Evan these days. Maybe her dad had given them some time off since they were fairly safe up here.

"Greta just hinted about asking me to do a story." Olivia dropped her hands on the children's heads as she reached them.

Zach's mom wrinkled her forehead in dismay. "Wouldn't you know? That's my gift to her. Let's go talk."

Olivia fell in step, avoiding apples on the ground.

"Hi, Dad." As her father nodded, she smoothed Evan's hair. "Are you picking as many as you eat?"

"They're good just off the trees, Mom."

"You're 'posed to wash 'em," Lily said.

"She ate some, too." Evan claimed his sister as a partner in crime.

Olivia pretended not to worry about airborne particulates or germs on the apples. She sniffed the aroma of barbecue. "I'm looking forward to lunch, myself."

"You don't eat—"

At her sharp glance, her father bit back the news that she wasn't a meat eater. Today, she'd eat whatever the Calverts put in front of her.

He shook his head.

"You taught me manners," she said, low-voiced.

"I didn't teach you that euphoric look for something you—"

Wisely, he didn't finish. "Dad, I'm sure someone's made beans, too. Did you notice the picnic tables?"

"Notice. They could feed the whole town."

Beth reached Greta first, and after a few words, Greta flung her arms around Beth and then she threw herself at Olivia, who held on beneath the onslaught.

"You can't imagine what this will mean to our funding. Your circulation—you could keep us afloat for a year if even a fraction of your subscribers are interested enough to call us."

"I'll make sure the article is worded that way," Olivia said.

"Hey, what's up?" Zach materialized out of the trees.

Greta explained, Olivia's dad looked amused and

Olivia wanted to sink into the ground as another round of thank-yous showered her. One article about a great story didn't seem like that big a deal. "You're doing me a favor, too, letting me interview you." She rubbed her hands together. "I'm starving. I think I'll go see what's ready. Evan, Lily, want to come?" Whooping, the children ran ahead of her.

"I have to go tell Seth." Greta scanned the family members hanging off ladders in the trees. "And maybe Sophie."

"Gran, she's happy in D.C." Zach shook his head at Olivia, obviously concerned for Sophie in this recurring argument.

All-powerful and happy because she could use her job to help, and Greta and Beth were so pleased, Olivia grimaced. Being part of a dispute in this family would be painful. Beth caught her arm.

"Don't worry. Sophie won't hold it against you." She pulled Zach to her other side. "I was thinking, if you don't mind," she said, "I'd like Lily and Evan to spend the night at my house tonight."

"Mom, I don't know. I don't get to see Lily that much."

"Neither do I. Of course if you think I can't take care of her, you can come, too."

"It's not that," he said.

"Good." She didn't let him continue. "What do you say, Olivia?"

The conversation and nuances changed too swiftly around here. "I don't want to be the one who says you don't know how to care for your grandchildren." She eyed Evan and Lily already sampling from the laden tables. "Though I think my father's been teaching you spin."

"As if I need James Kendall to teach me anything." Beth laughed, drawing her son's concerned gaze.

Olivia stared at him, reading his mind without psychic abilities. He didn't want her father to use his mother to burrow deeper into their oddly amassing family.

"You can both come and pick them up at noon tomorrow." Beth waited no longer for an answer. "They'll sleep in and I'll make them a nice brunch. I do this sausage-and-egg casserole, Olivia. You're going to beg me for the recipe after you hear Evan rave about it."

She swept toward Evan and Lily with everything settled to her liking. Olivia stared after Beth and the children. Her father pushed away from a tree and trailed behind them, astoundingly like a lost puppy.

"He's not a bad guy," she said.

"But what's he up to?" Zach asked. "Maybe I'll go question him."

"He won't tell you." She spun slowly on her heels, looking for the bodyguards. "Where are Jock and Ian?"

"I saw Ian carrying a basket for Sophie a little while ago. I haven't seen Jock."

"I'm surprised they're not hanging around Dad and the children."

"Are you worried?"

"We can see anyone who drives up here?"

He nodded. "But I thought I'd take a turn around

the orchard.'' He headed toward the grassy area where they'd parked. ''You can come along.''

She went, walking closer than she needed to. ''How did the hot spring go last night?''

''It didn't.'' His smile lit her up inside, as if he'd built a fire out of cold embers. ''Evan didn't believe it would really be warm.''

''But hasn't Lily been in it before?''

''She seems to have forgotten. She sided with Evan.''

Olivia laughed, kicking through high grass. ''I love seeing them together.''

''Me, too.'' Zach headed down the rows of cars, watching the ground. ''How do you suppose two children can instinctively become brother and sister?''

''Evan's always wanted a sibling. Lily must be a gift to him.''

''As long as he's in charge.'' Zach's voice deepened with a little laughter. ''But she won't be pushed around. She taught him how to toast marshmallows.'' He glanced at her, his eyes teasing. ''Apparently, no one ever burned a marshmallow with him before.''

''Dad's doing the only kind of camping that interests me,'' she said.

''Lightweight.''

''You bet.''

As they reached the farthest car, they both turned. Zach looked down the ridge. Olivia glanced along the stand of apple trees. Movement on a branch caught her eye. She narrowed her gaze. Arms winding around each other. Blond hair sifting through an upswept hand.

''Zach?'' She pointed. ''I don't have my glasses,

and I hope you're not going to feel you have to protect Sophie's honor, but is that Jock with her?''

Zach followed her pointing finger, but he looked uncomfortable. ''Ian.''

''Unless he caught her on the verge of firing a blowgun at my dad, he seems to have forgotten his job. What does this place do to people? My dad's suddenly fine without protection, and Ian…''

''Yeah, it seems out of character.'' He looked away from the other couple. ''Olivia, how do you feel about hot springs?''

''What?'' Her heart beat a desperate path into her throat.

''Would you like to see it?''

''Sort of, but why do you want me to?'' She couldn't take much more of his push and pull.

''Nothing has to happen. We're Evan's parents getting to know each other. We have to learn to be just his parents.'' Even he didn't look as if he believed it was possible.

''That *sounds* good.'' She looked down at his hands, flexing on the wide leather belt at his hips. He'd always had beautiful hands, expressive, capable, sensual when he… ''I'm not a camper.''

''I'm not asking you to sleep in the woods. You can take my bed again.''

She must be out of her ever-loving mind. She couldn't even lie to herself about her motives. She wanted to be alone with Zach Calvert, and Evan need never know. He'd have no reason to hope one night could turn into every day.

She lifted her head and hoped he was lying to himself in the worst way. Her legs trembled. "I'll need clothes," she said.

"I'll lend you my sweats again."

His hoarse tone warned her she was going to have to decide if she was willing to take what he'd give and not one thing more.

CHAPTER FIFTEEN

ZACH'S FLASHLIGHT BOBBED on the thickly strewn pine needles and grass in front of them, but Olivia couldn't make out a path through the woods. She'd be amazed if her father didn't show up at Zach's house, once he heard her message on his answering machine. She'd declined to lie about where she was spending the night.

The trees overhead and the stream she'd never actually seen seemed to chat together, but she and Zach had both lost the ability to speak.

At last they came to the tent he and the children had shared the night before. "You just left it up?" she asked.

"I'm not supposed to tell you, but Lily woke up scared, and we went home at 2:33 exactly."

Olivia permitted herself a proud smile. "Evan kept her secret."

"He's a pretty good brother."

"We aren't staying here tonight, right?"

"I heard what you said about camping." He shone the light on her face. "Besides, we wouldn't be smart to share the same bed space."

"I don't understand you."

"I know. The spring's through here. It has a sulfuric smell, but you get used to it in a hurry." He turned sideways and twisted through some low pine branches. "Careful of the sap."

"Where?" She looked up and a long thin, armlike sapling slapped her on the shoulder.

"On the branches."

"Oh." She checked the sleeve of another coat she'd borrowed from him. "I guess it's sticky?"

"Yeah."

"All clear, then— Wow."

The pool was lovely, in a clearing just a few yards wider than the spring itself. Zach set his flashlight on the ground.

"There's a ledge about here," he said.

The smell already seemed less offensive. Olivia inched her jacket off her shoulders. Then she stopped. "You're sure no one else will have the same idea?"

"Are you kidding? It's freezing." He glanced at the steam rising into moonlight over the water. "I remember hearing my parents over here after they thought I was asleep in the tent."

Olivia twisted her mouth. "You could hear them?"

"Just laughter now and then. I didn't know what they were doing." He shrugged. "I don't suppose they always—"

"Probably not." Although the setting suggested romantic goings-on. She pulled her sweater over her head. "You don't mind a bra and panties, do you?"

He swallowed so hard, she suddenly felt naked in perfectly concealing lace. "No," he muttered. "It's fine. Most fine."

"Since I'm not going for any more of your start-and-stop, you'll have to wait your turn to come in if you're going to sound like that."

"I'd better turn around."

"You know best." She quickly shucked off her jeans and socks and shoes and stepped, shivering into the spring. "It's almost hot."

"Yeah." His tone dropped suspiciously near a groan.

She imagined herself naked in his mind's eye. She couldn't help hoping she looked good in his fantasy. She let it go, trying to ignore her racing pulse. It wasn't fair to push him unless she was willing to take another rejection.

Just act normal, natural. Her underwear covered everything discreetly. She slid into the water, lifting her feet off the rock and sand bottom.

"I call the ledge," she said and swam two strokes toward the flashlight. She bumped into rock and dirt and turned over to lean back on her elbows, resting her head against the moss-covered ground. "You can come in now."

He stripped quickly to plaid boxers. Some things hadn't changed. He still wore them. She still found them ridiculously sexy.

He dropped into the pool.

"What do you think?" he asked.

"I don't hate the idea of camping so much now. This is like being held." She lifted her legs to float. "I love to swim."

"You call this swimming?"

"I love water." She grinned. "You're in a bad mood all of a sudden."

"Lust does that to me." He splashed water across his shoulders and chest. The droplets glittered on his skin in the meager light. "What bothers me more is that you don't seem to be as bothered as I am."

She dropped to the ledge again. "Maybe I'm bothered."

"You don't show it."

"I don't usually play games with grown men, so I assume we aren't playing anymore."

He turned to her, and the water caught the ends of his hair, darkening them. "I haven't been playing. I want you, but I don't want to hurt you. How can I explain in a way you'll understand?"

She shifted, putting just a few inches of important space between them. "You can't explain because you don't understand yourself. I don't know if it's because your dad died and you don't remember your parents together very well, or if your time with Helene was really that bad, but you can forgive yourself for Salva. You can change if you want to." She gasped for air. It was a huge speech, and she'd had no right to make it.

"Tell me about change, Olivia." Irritation only strengthened the hard lines that made her want to touch his mouth. "The only change you've made in six years is moving to your own home. Otherwise, is your life different than it was the day you found out about Evan? What risks do you take?"

Far from making her angry, his argument made her smile. "I'm here right now. I know what I want from tonight." Not the truth actually. Why she wanted to make love to him when she believed implicitly that it would be a one-night-only event was beyond her. Maybe she just needed the goodbye he'd denied her by disappearing.

He turned to her and his hand drifted over hers under the water. "You talk as if you know me, Olivia."

"I'm making guesses." She held her breath as his fingers skimmed her wrist and her forearm and her elbow.

"Who was I in Chicago? Did I love you?"

"I thought so." She delivered herself to his intent gaze, hiding nothing. "But I'm not sure now."

"Who were you to me?"

She shivered as his thighs brushed her legs apart. Want grew deep in her belly, an ache that might kill her if he backed away. "Zach, I don't think—"

"Don't think. Just feel how good this is. You're the one who's willing to take a chance."

He slid his arms around her waist and pulled her against his chest. She hated him blindly for a moment. "I don't trust you." No amount of "good" could make up for the agony of losing him before.

"You shouldn't." He nudged her cheek with his chin. She had to look at him, had to meet his tortured gaze, dark as a world with no light, blank as sheer pain.

"I'm hurting you," she said.

He pressed his mouth to her shoulder. Heat and teeth scraped her. She shuddered, and he tightened his arms. He brushed his lips back and forth over her skin until he reached her jaw.

She only had to turn her head. To lift her face slightly. She looked at him, but closed her eyes as he covered her mouth.

His body against hers, his angles fitting her softness to him was "good" in an elemental way that bore no

relation to the gentle love they'd made when she'd
been twenty-one.

She cupped his face. He traced the line of her
breastbone until he found her bra clasp. Her nipples
were tight, her breasts full.

"Olivia?" he said.

She should walk away and hurt him as he'd hurt
her time and again. But she needed this, yearned to
feel one more time as if he loved her.

She reached between them for the catch on her bra,
but when her fingers shook so hard, she couldn't work
the clasp, he opened it and pushed the straps off her
shoulders. He touched her with his fingertips first, as
if he didn't dare to take more.

She wrapped her arms around him, gasping with
fierce relief as her bare skin met the crisp wet hair on
his chest.

"No," she said, but she meant, "You left me.
Don't leave me ever again." She slid her hands down
his back, tracing each rib beneath his skin.

"No?" His faint voice reached her as if she were
far away—where she didn't want to be anymore.

He breathed harshly against her throat, but Olivia
splayed her fingers on both sides of his head again.

"You left me," she said. "I needed you."

"I'm here."

As if being here now made up for six years.

She turned his face to her nipple. Immediately, he
opened his mouth and took her inside, stroking her
with hunger that fired all the wanting she'd repressed.

Her rough breathing hurt her throat. Zach lifted his
face and swept her lips in a soft kiss, but she had no
time for gentleness now.

She twisted from beneath him without breaking their kiss and began to punish him, using the passion he'd thrown away. Soon he forgot to be careful with her as he had been when she was twenty-one. He opened her mouth with his and took her as if he had to possess her.

As she wrapped her legs around his waist, Zach stroked her breasts until she feared she might scream for more. She broke the kiss and swam away from him. He stared at her, his eyes glazed, his forehead damp with sweat.

"Wait." He held on to the mud bank, speaking through clenched teeth. "I'm not giving you another baby."

"I'm taking the pill. Since Evan, I have to for— I just have to."

"Are you okay?"

She shook, growing cold without his arms around her, but still said, "I'm fine." She pushed her panties down her legs and kicked them away.

At the same time, Zach pulled off his boxers and then grabbed her ankles to pull her back. She twined her fingers with his, forcing his hands onto the bank, teasing him, rubbing her aching body against his. If he thought he could leave her again, she'd ensure he wouldn't forget her.

Freeing one hand, he caressed her nape. For a long second, cloaked in a tender haze, he kissed her. She lowered herself on him, and he tore his mouth from hers to moan against her forehead.

Free of the sweet persuasion of his mouth, she took from him. Satisfaction and pleasure and vengeance that had nothing to do with love. She wanted him to spill inside her, because she needed release. She needed to make Zach feel for her again. Maybe for the first time, she wanted to be everything that mattered to him.

As he had been to her.

He lifted himself to thrust, but she pulled away, staring into his eyes in a silent, sensual challenge. Catching his hands again, she forced him to meet her rhythm. His ragged attempt at control fed her hunger for him—her convoluted desire for retribution. Tears washed her face.

"Olivia." He arched against her, and she relented, sharing his need to join their bodies. "Olivia." His broken voice echoed all the days and nights she'd called his name in the same desperate tone.

Suddenly he gripped her hips and at the same time took her open mouth. His groan fed her as his release pulsed inside her body, and he took her with him. Colors writhed in the darkness of her closed eyes as pleasure curled her toes, numbing her hands and fingers. Locking her legs around his waist, she rocked against him to drag out the last shocking second.

He kissed her again and again, his mouth gentle, comforting her until sanity trickled back, and she struggled to be free of him, of the shame of taking him in revenge.

He refused to let her go, smoothing her hair away from her face. When he pressed his lips to the corner of her mouth, she met his kiss. At last she slumped against his chest, hearing and feeling only the still-frenzied beat of his heart.

"Do you feel better?" Concern and forgiveness threaded his voice.

She would have been furious. "I wasn't very kind."

He buried his face in her hair, but his laughter sounded as unsettled as she felt. "I'm a man. You were plenty kind, and I could have stopped you any time."

"I doubt it."

He kissed her head. "I like the way you exact reprisal," he said, "as long as you plan to make love to me now."

She wanted to raise her head, but she couldn't seem to look him in the eye. "Why aren't you angry?"

"We're adults and I hurt you. Your body speaks to mine, and I guess mine speaks to yours. You had some irate things to say. I have more loving responses I'd like to show you."

"I don't understand you, Zach."

"Turns out I don't know you either." He tipped up her chin and kissed her tender lips, his arousal already stirring. "But I plan to learn all about you."

And though she'd ravaged him, he worshiped where she'd tried to punish. He gave where she'd taken.

His care awoke new passion, a different need equally as vast. She tasted him, kissing his salty skin, caressing his body with a sweeter passion.

He turned her, lifting her onto the ledge as he slid inside her. Each stroke floated her mouth against his. She'd burned with anger and fear. She'd regretted the love that had shaped her from the age of twenty-one.

Zach touched her with compassion and desire. He offered an addictive sharing of generous pleasure.

Crying when the colors exploded again, she swam

on a sensation of wonder, on joy she'd believed un-
attainable. She'd never known anything as loving as
his protective arms around her, his voice whispering
her name like a vow when he found a second release
within her. They both held on as if some threat lay
in wait to break them apart.

When Zach finally let her go, Olivia sank against
the bank, too tired to turn her head. He dropped beside her and pulled her onto his chest.

"I knew we could be nice to each other."

She wrapped her arms around him. "I'd like to
sleep in your bed tonight."

He didn't answer at first, but she refused to assume
the worst.

"Can you walk?" he finally asked. "And if you
can, will you let me rest a few minutes?"

"We should have brought towels."

"I didn't think clearly."

"Me, neither." Morning would bring an avalanche
of clarity.

ZACH OPENED HIS EYES to the disturbing sensation of
Olivia's lips on his belly. He wrapped his hand in her
hair, uncertain whether he meant to urge her closer
or ease her away from him. The ringing telephone
took the decision out of his hands.

"It's probably Lily," he said, seduced by the regret
in Olivia's eyes. "She calls every morning, since my
work hours are so erratic."

It wasn't Lily. His deputy, Tyler, announced
there'd been a car accident before Zach could say
hello.

"How serious?" Zach asked.

"Fairly. An eighteen-wheeler ran a family van into a guardrail up on the interstate. The truck driver is unhurt. In the car, we have two children in car seats. They're fine. The dad was asleep in the front passenger seat—he's going to need stitches in his forearm for a laceration. The mom was driving. She's not so lucky. I've called for a life flight, but I could use some help."

"I'm on my way, and I'll call the state troopers. Give me your mile marker."

He took directions and turned over to find Olivia pulling one of his T-shirts over her head. In the shirt and a pair of his socks, she looked sleepy, delectable and concerned.

"I have to go," he said.

"I know." She scrunched her hands into the rumpled bedding. "Are you coming back?"

She meant to her, not to his house.

"I have to change." He went to the closet. "Come talk while I dress."

"How long does it take to admit you care about me?"

She pushed herself off the bed and departed. He stood there, with his dark blue shirt in his hands, frustration showing him pictures of himself easing Olivia back onto the bed. He could tell her everything she needed to know without words. She seemed to need the words.

Swearing, he pulled on his uniform.

He cared about her. He cared too damn much.

He took his gun from the safe in his room and was strapping it on when the shower from the guest room began to run. He went as far as the door.

What could he say? "I think I've fallen in love with you—give us a chance" would only start their most furious argument yet. He wanted to fight for her. She and Evan and the family they might make with Lily were worth fighting for. But if he made a mistake, if he couldn't stay, she wouldn't forgive him again.

On the way to the accident, he tried to put Olivia out of his head. She wouldn't go.

He did his job. He tried to comfort the father and the crying children, and he arranged for a car so that they could go to the hospital in Maryville.

He helped Tyler direct the growing crowd of on-lookers away from the scene, and they cleared a section of the interstate to give the life flight helicopter room to land. At last the chopper came down on their makeshift landing pad, and the state troopers rolled up.

Zach stood back while the paramedics took care of the woman and then waited with the family until the rental company dropped off a car. He offered the father the services of Bardill's Ridge's clinic. Unsurprisingly, the concerned husband only wanted to reach his wife.

As they stood together, each holding one of the man's crying sons, Zach watched the chopper take off. That was the kind of work he should be doing. Moonshiners and bank robbers in Bardill's Ridge, Tennessee, were serious felons, but he had the training to provide a real service to his fellow citizens.

He closed his eyes, ostensibly against prop-wash, but in his head he saw the cockpit controls. Metal flying at crazy angles, snapping, fire flashing through the air. Blood and smoke. Memories? Or facts he knew so well they felt like memories? He couldn't tell, but he gulped a breath as fear washed him in sweat.

What if he did fly for life flight and this happened to him in midair?

He couldn't risk taking everything that mattered from another human being. He couldn't risk failing Olivia as he'd failed Salva and her family and Helene—and himself.

He'd tried to save Kim's life. In losing her, he'd also lost his own right to the kind of joy she'd never know. Worst of all, he was afraid. He couldn't ever take responsibility for someone else's life again.

OLIVIA'S FIRST INSTINCT was to grab Evan and fly him home to Chicago, where she'd been safe for six years. Safe, untouched and maybe a little sterile. Nothing had hurt this much, but her good times hadn't measured up to a single second of last night either.

Not that she wasn't angry and frustrated, but Zach had been honest all along. She dressed and made coffee, worked the crossword puzzle in the paper and tried not to think. What came next? Return to Chicago and a businesslike conversation about visitation for Evan? Was she willing to retreat again without a fight?

No. Anyone could change, and she had. She cared for Zach. She'd frozen all possible feelings for anyone other than her son because she'd been scared of getting hurt again, but she was willing to help Zach even if he couldn't love her. In the end, he'd be a better father to Evan if he could face his past and find a future. Even without her.

On the margin beside the crossword puzzle, she noted everything she knew about Zach's accident. The woman who'd died was named Kimberly Salva. Olivia didn't know her rank. She noted the approximate date the accident had happened. She added Kerwin Gould's name.

She didn't have enough. She tapped her pen against her teeth. Helene would know more. But what if she found the Salvas? They might not want to talk to Zach. They might hold him responsible, too. Either way, he'd resent her interference.

She couldn't blame him, but the chance that his friend's family could ease his guilt made this a risk worth taking. She dialed Helene's number.

"Zach?" Helene's voice bit through the phone line. "Is it true you took that woman home with you last night?"

CHAPTER SIXTEEN

"IT'S ME, HELENE."

"What are you doing in my ex-husband's home when your son is with Beth?"

How did she know? And why would she ask?

"Do you know how fast rumors fly in this town, how quickly a good friend rushed to tell me where you slept last night?"

Worse than merely having sex with Zach, Olivia had fallen in love with him again. Maybe she'd never been smart enough or strong enough to fall out of love.

"Helene, I'll tell you though you have no right to ask, and I don't want to talk about it. I am in love with Zach. He doesn't feel the same way about me. I'll learn to live with that, but I'd like to try just once to help him. Do you know the Salvas?"

"That woman he was supposed to rescue? She was an intelligence officer and she got caught in an off-limits area."

"But do you know where her family lives?"

Helene hesitated. "Why? Zach won't want you to talk to them."

"Because he thinks he's responsible for what happened to her, and he doesn't want to remind them.

"They're in Maryland, somewhere near Annapolis.

He spent a couple of holidays with them while they were at the Academy together.''

''How about her maiden name?''

''She kept her name when she married.''

''Can you tell me anything else about her?''

''No, but you're wrong. You're the one he needs. He might still want to wear a hair shirt because of Salva, but I've seen you together and I know you're the one.''

Olivia ignored Helene's suspicions. She was hardly in a position to scorn them. ''Talking to the Salvas can't hurt. If they don't want to speak to Zach, I'll never tell him.'' She swallowed, staring at the newspaper. ''Helene, you won't tell him either?''

''Of course not, but listen to me. Don't get in touch with them through the Navy.''

''Why?''

''They might not want anyone to dig up the story again—especially not a journalist. Why involve them if you don't have to?''

''You're right.''

''Actually, I was wrong about one thing.'' Helene said. ''What I asked about you and Zach—I shouldn't have. I'm married. I'm not in love with Zach, and I should stop being annoyed that he didn't turn out the way I wanted.''

''I can't hear about your marriage.'' She wasn't brave or kind enough to be civil about it just now.

''I'm trying to suggest you shouldn't be a fool. You may be what's wrong with Zach Calvert. He is different now. He looks at you with tenderness he never felt for me. He wants you to be happy. If he could dump that mountain of guilt he carries around, he would for you.''

Olivia nodded, bewildered. ''Why are you saying this?'' It wasn't a good response, but what did you say when a woman offered you the redemption you'd been looking for?

''Because I didn't care if Zach suffered when I left. I tried to hurt him. You're trying to help him, and I guess that means you really love him.'' Helene sniffed as if she'd had enough. ''And one more thing.''

''Uh-huh?''

''Lily tells me you love her, too.''

''I'm glad she knows.'' Olivia smiled. ''She's a lovable girl.''

''She's the only reason Zach and I were right to marry.'' Helene swallowed hard enough for Olivia to hear it over the phone. ''Well, I still make mistakes with her, too, when I get mad at him. But overall we do all right with her. Who knew you could be so screwed up with each other and yet raise a healthy child if you both try hard enough?''

OLIVIA TOOK Helene's advice and started dialing Salvas in Annapolis. After an hour and a half, she found Kim Salva's mother, who connected her with Kim's husband, Joel Bestowe.

''I've wanted to talk to Zach since the day they told me about the crash,'' he said. ''But he was in the hospital, and then Captain Gould told us about his injuries. I got smothered in raising my daughter, and I guess I let it go. Please tell him I'd like to meet.''

Kim's mom, Linda, broke in. ''We're not talking about an interview for your magazine?''

"No." Though she'd used her name without a second's trouble to her conscience, she wasn't a monster. "But I'm interfering without Zach's permission. I had to make sure you wanted to talk to him before I brought it up. He misses Kim, and he feels responsible." She broke off, hearing a sound behind her. Naturally, when she turned, Zach stood in the doorway, his collar open, his tie dangling, death or something close to it on his face.

"What have you done?" he asked in a voice she didn't recognize.

She said goodbye and hung up the phone. Turning back to Zach, she lifted her chin, prepared to take a punch, even if it came in the form of dismissal. "She was your friend, but your guilt is more demanding than any lover. You won't be a whole man until you fix this, and Lily and Evan are eventually going to notice their father's determination to be alone. They deserve to know you when you're happy."

"And what do you deserve, Olivia?"

She looked at herself honestly. "I think deep down I wanted you back or I wanted you to suffer. I needed some sign that I mattered to you." Apparently, nothing was too childish and mortifying for her to admit. "Now I just need to be sure I've done what I would have done then. I loved you, and I would have helped you any way I could, even if helping meant I never saw you again."

ZACH GRIPPED the airplane armrest with sweat-slicked hands. This flight included a map that projected their progress across all the land they could crash on.

"You could have used the company's jet." Olivia's edgy tone at his side didn't help. "You didn't even have to ask me along."

"I thought you'd want to see how it all came out." He took refuge in sarcasm because he needed her, and he couldn't say so. If talking to Salva's family didn't help, he didn't want to harm her any more.

She leaned into the plane's bulkhead, as far from him as possible. "How it comes out is none of my business."

Nothing could be further from the truth. If he could change for anyone, he'd change for Olivia. He loved Lily and Evan, but he wanted to be right again for Olivia. She'd risked facing his rage. And he believed she was trying to help, knowing she might be freeing him so that he could love someone else eventually.

After six years of never letting Joel's name cross his mind, he should have been thinking of Salva's husband and her family. Instead, for once, he wanted the right to think of his own future, his children and the woman he loved. Olivia mattered more.

Zach had taken his seat on this plane, thanked Joel for agreeing to see him and accepted a dinner invitation from Salva's mother, all in the hope that their forgiveness would give him a glimpse of a future with Olivia.

At BWI, she hung back after he signed for the rental car. "Why don't I wait for you?"

He hunched his shoulders in his jacket. Every curve of her face had become vital to him. Her slightest glance had the ability to change his mood for good or bad.

"I want you to come with me."

Surprise widened her troubled gaze. "Oh. Okay."

They discussed only directions as they drove to Salva's childhood home. Joel had agreed to meet them there.

Olivia displayed atypical nerves, tapping her nails on the console between them. When he couldn't stand the sound any more, he covered her hand with his—surprisingly, in offering comfort, he found it.

"Next exit," he said.

A few turns after the off ramp brought them to a line of federal-style townhouses. A tall, dark-haired man waited on the steps outside the Salvas'. Zach parked, studying the man he'd hardly known, whose life he'd changed irrevocably.

"He looks anxious, too." Olivia unlocked her door. "Unless you want me to wait here?"

"No."

Together, they climbed the steps. Joel met them halfway. He held out his hand, and Zach took it to shake. To his utter amazement, the other man pulled him into a loose hug.

"Hey, man. I should have thanked you years ago." Backing up, he shook Olivia's hand. "I'm glad you called."

"Why would you want to thank me?" Zach asked.

Joel made a scoffing sound. "Because you tried so damn hard. You almost brought Kim home."

"Almost," Zach said, feeling his friend's loss more than ever. Olivia slid her fingers into his, and he pulled her closer. "It's the 'almost' I can't live with."

Joel frowned. "What do you mean? I admit I

missed her—I still do, but I have a daughter who needed a living, functioning father. I've had to go on, but I'll do that with a clearer conscience now that I've finally thanked you for trying to save my wife. I don't know if they told you, but she aborted the first rescue attempt and had to go deeper into hiding. She didn't trust the pilot, for some reason. So they chose you for the second try because you were such good friends. They knew when she saw you, she'd run for the chopper.''

The memories evaded him, but he heard her screams in his head. ''She ran, but she needed help.''

''They told us she was shot in the leg when she tried to climb aboard.''

''If I'd only yanked her by one hand, I might have gotten us out of there. But I left my seat to drag her in and she was shot again.''

''Do some time in the real world.'' Joel gripped Zach's forearm for a second, softening the blow. ''How long would your arms have to be to reach her? Your choice was help her or leave her behind. I don't know what I would have done if you'd left her.''

The meaning behind his words made Zach feel sick. Joel and Kim's daughter had a grave to visit. Her parents could say a prayer over her once a year, maybe on her birthday.

''You did everything you could.'' Joel rubbed his hand down his own throat, as if to facilitate swallowing. ''I can't ever thank you like I should. You brought my wife home.''

Zach glanced at Olivia, whose hand had to be aching. He loosened his hold. ''How can you forgive the man who failed Kim?''

"You were one of her best friends at the Academy." Joel braced his hands on his hips. "You almost gave your life to help her. How can I hold a grudge against the man who nearly died trying to save her?"

Even Zach knew from the tapes that he'd done all he could. Thanks to his training, he'd been able to fly the broken chopper out when he was hardly conscious. He'd never thought he should do more. Being unable to do enough had haunted him.

"Come meet my daughter," Joel said. "And my fiancée." He smiled, giving Zach time to absorb the shock. "Kim's mom has made her favorite meal for you. We'll toast her, and I'll know she'd think we've finally thanked you and we're all square."

Zach eyed Olivia, who nodded in a your-choice gesture. Before, he would have made for the relative safety of the flight home. But if Joel Bestowe could find someone else to love maybe it was time he let Kim rest in peace, too. "I guess we're having turkey with the fixings?"

Joel's laughter reminded Zach of attending Kim's wedding. She'd given Joel his bridegroom's gift, a model of her first ship assignment. Joel had declared himself the happiest war bride in history because he was going to meet her when she docked in Naples.

"Turkey with the fixings," Joel said, his voice reflective. "We haven't heard that around here in a long time."

"She could eat it on the Fourth of July." Zach looked down at Olivia. "Thanks."

"You're okay?"

The other man started up the sidewalk, as if he

knew they needed privacy. "Joel's still living. I haven't been in a lot of ways."

Joel must have heard. He came back, stopping in Zach's face. "Hear what I say, because I don't need any guilt for not finding you myself." He glanced at Olivia, but then fastened dark, resolute eyes on Zach. "You knew Kim almost as well as I did. She'd kick your ass if she suspected you were wasting time. To fight that hard for her, and then to give up on yourself? She'd say you've been wasting *her* time."

Her husband was right. Remembering her without agony for the first time in six years, Zach chuckled. "If anyone could come back to dispense an ass-kicking, I guess it'd be Kim."

SURROUNDED BY BOXES he hadn't opened since the Navy had packed his apartment for him, Zach tapped a knife against his hand. Which one to open first?

He'd hated leaving the Navy and the job he'd dreamed of from the day he'd first sat in a cockpit. Once the boxes arrived, he'd only unpacked clothes and papers. Everything else he'd simply shoved into the attic.

Four boxes into the pile on his first night back from Annapolis, he found pictures of Olivia. A different Olivia. Laughing, uninhibited, striking a gangly ballet pose in front of her father's front porch. In another one she sprawled in short shorts and a tank top on the hood of a car he didn't recognize.

In a third, she was beneath the branch of a weeping willow, smiling pensively with more joy than he'd ever seen on her beautiful face. He could just see his hand wrapped around her wrist. Holding her to him.

He must have taken these pictures. He brushed dusty fingers over her face. He'd robbed her of all that joy.

He rummaged through the rest of the boxes, but found nothing else that seemed to belong to Olivia. Wiping his hands on the seat of his jeans, he carried the photos downstairs to find her on the threshold of his unlocked door.

He held up the pictures. "The Navy packed these, but I never looked in the boxes."

She moved to his side. Her hair brushed his forearm, arousing him, like a slide of silk over his skin.

"They're me," she said. "I don't even remember them."

"If I'd seen these, I would have looked for you."

With a slight smile, she took the photos from him and then set them on the nearest table. Her bland gaze suggested she wasn't interested any more in how he felt about her. "I promise I won't keep dropping in, but I was worried about you."

He reached around her to shut the door. "You look as if you're freezing." He breathed in her scent. It was like oxygen to him. "Come in and stay, Olivia."

She checked the time on her watch. "For a few minutes. I left Evan with Dad, and you never know what'll happen. He may be teaching the boy to drive the camper by the time I get back."

"Are you trying to tell me your work here is done?"

Her fine black eyebrows tilted upward. "Isn't that what you want?"

He shook his head, tenderness for her flowing all

the way to his fingertips as he took her face in his hands. "You have everything I want." He touched her hungrily, needing a response she didn't offer. "You're everything I want. I thought I'd all but killed Kim Salva on my last mission, and I honestly believed I wasn't safe for you to know."

She covered his hands. "You have to be sure, Zach. I don't have one more rejection in me. If you tell me you don't want me again, I can't come back, and I can't stay in the hope you'll commit. I'm not asking for forever as of today, but I have to know you feel the possibility."

He shook his head. "It's so much more simple than that. I want you now. I love you. I'll want you the rest of my life." He kissed her forehead, enjoying the subtle scratch of her bangs against his mouth. "Safe or not, I'm exhausted with wasting time."

She pulled free, leaving him cold, empty-armed and alone. "Then we should wait until you're rested enough to know you're not settling for the woman in front of you."

He reached for her, but she caught his hand. "I must have put that badly." He twisted his hand gently from hers and pressed his thumb to the corner of her mouth. She stood her ground as he leaned toward her.

Without preliminaries, he nudged her lips open. He kissed her, offering his future, his broken past, his children, his life. A surprised, vulnerable sound from deep in her throat made him wrap her in his arms. She linked her hands behind his neck.

"I didn't want to love you," she said.

"I could tell at the spring, but I liked it." He kissed

her again, but lifted his head when the matters they needed to settle began to recede from his mind. "Do you think Chicago needs a sheriff who can chase moonshiners and bank robbers with equal skill?"

Warmth filled her laughter and seduced him. He stroked the curve of her waist. This woman belonged to him.

"I think we should live here," she said, as if everything else were decided.

Zach smiled, happiness coming back to life inside him. He pretended to take her acceptance in stride. "I really would have moved to Chicago, but I'm glad Evan will get to know his Calvert family, too."

"We'll have to build a guest house for Dad," Olivia said.

"Before or after you marry me?"

She went a little rigid in his arms. "Let's make sure of each other. We both have time, and if it happens I want bells and whistles and shooting stars, not a sense that we're finally making things right." Her kiss held a plea for understanding. He couldn't blame her for needing security. "But I have a request."

"Anything." He tightened his arms. He'd win her with time, because he wouldn't change. "But be generous. I feel like a fool for not seeing the Salvas before and I'm so angry I didn't open those boxes, I'd promise stuff I couldn't possibly give you."

"Just promise that if you ever plan to leave again, you'll say exactly why—and when you'll come home."

That last word had resonance. They were both where they belonged. Together.

"You never ask enough for yourself." He leaned

back, forcing her to meet his gaze. He wanted her to see how much she meant to him. How much he wanted her future tied to his. "I go nowhere without you."

"Never?"

It was a harebrained vow, but her hopeful, trusting smile drove him to swear.

"Not ever."

EPILOGUE

HE MADE THE SAME PROMISE every morning in the bed they shared, and then he asked her to marry him. On the six-month anniversary of the day she and Evan had moved to Tennessee for good, Olivia finally believed.

She stretched in his arms as he kissed a disturbing path down her breastbone, and the spring sun spread warmth across them, and her father's workmen drummed away on the office/guest house down the ridge, and Evan slept peacefully in his bedroom down the hall.

"Yes," she said.

"What?" Zach lifted his tousled blond head, distracted, but willing to listen.

She laughed, drowning in eyes filled with the turbulence of loving lust. "We've already been together three times as long as before. I guess you are staying."

"Let's tell everyone." But he lowered his head, and his mouth, suckling a freckle he professed to love on her ribcage, spoke of more interesting intentions.

Olivia reached for him with perfect confidence. "Let's not say anything until Lily's here for dinner Friday night." She wanted to share her happiness with their little family first, in their new home.

"Maybe we should tell Helene, so she won't hear we're getting married from the rumor mill."

"Helene understands." He kissed her temple. "From now on let's concentrate on Evan and Lily and you and me."

"We can try, but my dad's probably already tried to rent the Sistine Chapel, and Greta will find a way to turn the ceremony into a fund-raiser. Your mom's going to remind them both that simple things have made me happier here in Bardill's Ridge than I ever dreamed of being in Chicago."

"Is that true?" He kissed her until his breathing was as ragged as hers.

"What did you..." She couldn't quite remember the question.

"Are you happier here?"

He had to ask? "My father accuses me of turning *Relevance* into a 'happy rag,' because I'm so content. I'd sing my way through town every day, except I don't want to shame you in front of the neighbors." She wrapped him in her arms, giving him one of Evan's patented "big" hugs.

"Back to the family." He lifted her hand. "Mom offered us her and my father's wedding rings."

Olivia pressed her cheek to his chest. "Can we take them? I'd love to use your parents' rings."

"I'm glad because I already accepted—but let me tell you what Evan and Lily are going to say."

"They'll sing with me."

He kissed her as if he was tasting her. She couldn't have changed much since the last time he'd kissed her, but he reacquainted himself often. "They're going to ask when we'll give them another brother or sister.''

"We gave them a kitten," she said in an isn't-that-enough tone. She reached for his wallet on the nightstand. "Time for a wager. You're wrong, and you might as well ante up, because those two are still fighting for top spot with each other. Neither of them is going to ask for another contender.''

"Give me that." Laughing so that his eyes crinkled just the way she loved best, he took back his wallet. "And I'll bet whatever you want.''

"I pay for the honeymoon. I'm thinking Greece.''

"Anything except money.''

"It's not money. It's more like an itinerary. And we can take Evan and Lily.''

"No, I want you to myself. My mom will take the children.''

"Winner gets to decide." She rolled over him, and a few minutes later he agreed to anything she ever wanted.

Friday night, while Zach and Evan went for Lily, Olivia decorated the dining room with strings of shooting stars and small silver bells and whistles. She prepared hot dogs for Evan, fried chicken for Lily, and homemade macaroni for both of them.

As they trooped inside, she was uncorking a bottle of sparkling grape juice. It went down a bit too sweet, but she'd iced champagne to share with Zach in their bedroom later.

"Mom?" Evan searched the room. "Is this a birthday?"

"Pretty." Lily ran her hands through the dangling bells. "Look, Evan, more whistles."

Zach burst into laughter. Olivia felt herself blushing. "I said I wanted it all."

He kissed her with more joy than she'd ever dreamed of. Life was going to be good on Bardill's Ridge. She sank against him, turning to face their bemused children.

"We have news." Zach took Olivia's hand and then fished something out of his pocket. He slid a simple platinum engagement ring over her finger. "We're getting married."

Olivia curved her hand around his. Her throat felt too tight to speak as she stared into Zach's eyes. When he looked at her with so much unabashed desire, she tended to forget they weren't alone.

"Married?" Lily finally sang in a delighted voice.

Turning, Olivia hugged the little girl who was quickly becoming hers, too.

"Mom, can we have a brother? 'Cause I need more boys around here."

Evan—always on Zach's side.

"Did you put him up to that?" she demanded as the laughing man she'd always loved kissed her nearly senseless. As if from a distance, she thought she heard Lily speaking.

"Nuh-uh, Evan. We get to have a sister next, 'cause I'm the girl, and I say so."

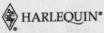

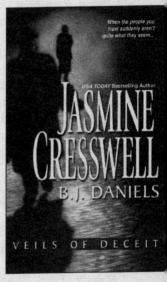

Your opinion is important to us! Please take a few moments to share your thoughts with us about your experiences with Harlequin and Silhouette books. Your comments will be very useful in ensuring that we deliver books you love to read. *Please take a few minutes to complete the questionnaire, then send it to us at the address below.*

Send your completed questionnaires to:
Harlequin/Silhouette Reader Survey, P.O. Box 9046, Buffalo, NY 14269-9046

1. As you may know, there are many different lines under the Harlequin and Silhouette brands. Each of the lines is listed below. Please check the box that most represents your reading habit for each line.

Line	Currently read this line	Do not read this line	Not sure if I read this line
Harlequin American Romance	❏	❏	❏
Harlequin Duets	❏	❏	❏
Harlequin Romance	❏	❏	❏
Harlequin Historicals	❏	❏	❏
Harlequin Superromance	❏	❏	❏
Harlequin Intrigue	❏	❏	❏
Harlequin Presents	❏	❏	❏
Harlequin Temptation	❏	❏	❏
Harlequin Blaze	❏	❏	❏
Silhouette Special Edition	❏	❏	❏
Silhouette Romance	❏	❏	❏
Silhouette Intimate Moments	❏	❏	❏
Silhouette Desire	❏	❏	❏

2. Which of the following best describes why you bought *this book*? One answer only, please.

the picture on the cover	❏	the title	❏
the author	❏	the line is one I read often	❏
part of a miniseries	❏	saw an ad in another book	❏
saw an ad in a magazine/newsletter	❏	a friend told me about it	❏
I borrowed/was given this book	❏	other: _____	❏

3. Where did you buy *this book*? One answer only, please.

at Barnes & Noble	❏	at a grocery store	❏
at Waldenbooks	❏	at a drugstore	❏
at Borders	❏	on eHarlequin.com Web site	❏
at another bookstore	❏	from another Web site	❏
at Wal-Mart	❏	Harlequin/Silhouette Reader	❏
at Target	❏	Service/through the mail	
at Kmart	❏	used books from anywhere	❏
at another department store	❏	I borrowed/was given this	❏
or mass merchandiser		book	

4. On average, how many Harlequin and Silhouette books do you buy at one time?

I buy _____ books at one time ❏
I rarely buy a book ❏

MRQ403HSR-1A

5. How many times per month do you shop for any *Harlequin and/or Silhouette* books?
One answer only, please.

1 or more times a week	❑	a few times per year	❑
1 to 3 times per month	❑	less often than once a year	❑
1 to 2 times every 3 months	❑	never	❑

6. When you think of your ideal heroine, which *one* statement describes her the best?
One answer only, please.

She's a woman who is strong-willed	❑	She's a desirable woman	❑
She's a woman who is needed by others	❑	She's a powerful woman	❑
She's a woman who is taken care of	❑	She's a passionate woman	❑
She's an adventurous woman	❑	She's a sensitive woman	❑

7. The following statements describe types or genres of books that you may be interested in reading. Pick *up to 2 types* of books that you are most interested in.

I like to read about truly romantic relationships	❑
I like to read stories that are sexy romances	❑
I like to read romantic comedies	❑
I like to read a romantic mystery/suspense	❑
I like to read about romantic adventures	❑
I like to read romance stories that involve family	❑
I like to read about a romance in times or places that I have never seen	❑
Other: _____	❑

The following questions help us to group your answers with those readers who are similar to you. Your answers will remain confidential.

8. Please record your year of birth below.

19 ____

9. What is your marital status?

single ❑   married ❑   common-law ❑   widowed ❑
divorced/separated ❑

10. Do you have children 18 years of age or younger currently living at home?

yes ❑   no ❑

11. Which of the following best describes your employment status?

employed full-time or part-time ❑   homemaker ❑   student ❑
retired ❑   unemployed ❑

12. Do you have access to the Internet from either home or work?

yes ❑   no ❑

13. Have you ever visited eHarlequin.com?

yes ❑   no ❑

14. What state do you live in?

_____

15. Are you a member of Harlequin/Silhouette Reader Service?

yes ❑   Account # _____   no ❑   MRQ403HSR-1B

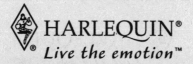

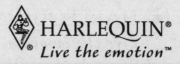